Cass Moriarty lives and writes in Brisbane. Her debut novel, *The Promise Seed*, was longlisted for the 2017 International DUBLIN Literary Award, and shortlisted for the 2016 People's Choice category and the 2013 Emerging Queensland Author category in the Queensland Literary Awards. She has a Bachelor of Business – Communication degree from Queensland University of Technology, and has worked in public relations, advertising and marketing. She and her husband have six children.

Website: www.cassmoriarty.com
Facebook: cassmoriartyauthor
Twitter: @MoriartyCass

Bookclub notes for *Parting Words* are available at www.uqp.com.au.

PRAISE FOR *THE PROMISE SEED*

'An affecting debut from talented Australian newcomer Cass Moriarty ... I'm excited to see where Moriarty goes next.' Hannah Richell, *Australian Women's Weekly*

'The most impressive aspect of Moriarty's novel is the relationship between the protagonists, which is expertly constructed and believable ... *The Promise Seed* [is] to be highly recommended.' *The Weekend Australian*

'This is a beautifully paced debut … It's a thoughtful portrait of friendship, family and loneliness, and Moriarty's finely drawn characters … bring levity and pathos to a sombre but moving story.' *Books+Publishing*

'I loved it and thoroughly recommend it – it was very hard to put down. Definitely a must-read …' Queensland Premier Annastacia Palaszczuk, Books of the Year 2016, *The Australian Financial Review*

'This is a powerful story, simply told, that delivers an emotionally satisfying reading experience. Many readers may, like me, be moved to tears in the closing chapters.' *Readings Monthly*

'Through the gentle but raw introspections of the old man, and the uneasy, fearful life of the boy, the story moves with a sprinkling of humour amid the chilling drama towards a gripping climax.' *Good Reading*

'*The Promise Seed* is the story of a burgeoning friendship between old man and boy, unfolding at an elegant pace as each finds something valuable and necessary in the presence of the other.' *Sydney Review of Books*

'Cass Moriarty has written an engaging and heart-wrenching book. It is well worth the read.' *The Big Book Club*

'*The Promise Seed* is an incredibly poignant piece of fiction that has the reader absolutely gripped from beginning to end.' *Lip Magazine*

Parting Words

CASS MORIARTY

UQP

First published 2017 by University of Queensland Press
PO Box 6042, St Lucia, Queensland 4067 Australia

www.uqp.com.au
uqp@uqp.uq.edu.au

Cover design by Kirby Armstrong
Cover images: Front cover © Maria Tomova/Trevillion Images
Back cover background © ColorMaker/Shutterstock, envelope © Cbenjasuwan/Shutterstock
Author photograph by Giulio Saggin
Typeset in 12/17 pt Bembo Std by Post Pre-press Group, Brisbane
Printed in Australia by McPherson's Printing Group

 This project is supported by the Queensland
Government through Arts Queensland.

  The University of Queensland Press is assisted by
the Australian Government through the Australia
Council, its arts funding and advisory body.

National Library of Australia
Cataloguing-in-Publication data is available at http://catalogue.nla.gov.au

ISBN
978 0 7022 5953 1 (pbk)
978 0 7022 5886 2 (ePDF)
978 0 7022 5887 9 (ePub)
978 0 7022 5888 6 (Kindle)

To my children:
each of you holds a piece of my heart in your hands.

The tragedy of life is what dies inside a man while he lives.
Albert Schweitzer

There is a strange charm in the thoughts of a good legacy,
or the hopes of an estate, which wondrously alleviates
the sorrow that men would otherwise feel for the death
of friends.
Miguel de Cervantes Saavedra

AND SO, LOOK AT THEM. His family. Gathered on the edges of the artificial grass, the dark hole yawning from its centre. Each afraid of their own mortality so rudely addressed. Frightened of stepping too close, in case of experiencing the vertiginous rush that might pull them in — up becoming down, sky becoming sea, gravity a mirage.

Three-year-old Eden steps forward to add his drawing to the others. He deliberates, staring at the polished rosewood coffin hovering as if by magic, at the wreaths and flowers of every colour that sit atop the burnished lid. He squats on the ground, folds his drawing into a rough semblance of a paper plane, and throws it triumphantly across the gap. At that very instant, his tangle of limbs — soft and pliable and clumsy — wobbles in a precarious dance at the edge of the grave … and Richard reaches out to pull his nephew back. The laughter. Relief. Black suits and black dresses flapping, the mourners released from their frozen aspects of grief.

The deep, haunting tones of 'Danny Boy' startle everyone into silence. A woman behind Richard begins to weep; small, hiccupping sobs.

'I should never have let you choose the music,' he mutters.

Kelly glares, her eyes red-rimmed behind her sunglasses. 'For your information, Dad loved this song.' She shifts her weight from one foot to the other. She complained earlier of a blister on her left heel. New shoes. Black. Not her style. Conservative court shoes, purchased reluctantly for the occasion as she will probably never wear them again.

'Where is Grandma?' Violetta, her enunciation perfect, the clipped tones of her pre-pubescent voice carrying across the sea of black.

'She's in there. Underneath Grandpa.' Victoria, her twin, all-knowing.

Richard shushes his daughters as a murmured aside passes between their cousins Kara and Ben, the words *missionary position*. He silences their levity with a glare that would halt a train.

The sky a sweeping dome of china blue; wisps of white floating. A winter sky, clear and sharp, in the midst of high summer. The air dry and crisp. The drought has withered the buds before they can ripen, stopped the leaves from unfurling. Thin leafless boughs, skeletal, echoing what lies under the earth in this place.

As the strains of music fall away, Reverend Peterson resumes speaking in his rumbling, gravelly voice. 'Friends, we are gathered to commit Daniel Jeremiah Whittaker to his final place of rest …' The timbre of his voice rises and falls in a background hum, the tone more comforting than the words of peace and love and everlasting life, heard at a dozen other funerals. The shrill caw of a crow cuts through like an insult.

A breath of wind brings the smell of freshly turned soil, the fragrance of the many bouquets; it ruffles the drawings on the coffin. Inside, his body lies in repose, his hands clasped across his chest, resting on his medals. His children had discovered them by chance in the days before the funeral, had never seen them before – as if their father had never wanted the medals to be found.

His son and daughters huddle with their partners and children: the inner sanctum of the chief mourners. They are flanked by their close friends and even a few of his own acquaintances (those still standing; not a great number. More lost each passing year. Lost. Is that what he is now? Here, in this place so familiar? Is he lost now too?) Then on the fringes – like the dregs of a receding tide – the friends of friends, the work colleagues from so long ago, the hangers-on, the nosy; the people for whom a funeral is an occasion to dress up, to come forth with just the right amount of propriety and respect. To be swept up in the hymns and the ceremony, to show their faces, their presence duly noted. To join the throng of mourners and to consider life, not only the life of the one now gone, but also their own.

To look into the void.

...

Reverend Peterson stops talking. A respectful calm ensues, broken only by the caw of the crow and the sigh of the wind, and a ringtone (Bach?), quickly muted.

The gauzy clouds do little to dispel the sun's expanding warmth, the promise of another still, hot day ahead. Those unfortunate enough to remain standing crowd nearer under the shelter, the closeness of other bodies preferable to the rising heat overhead. Men run their fingers around their collars. Women lift the hair from the backs of their necks. Those seated lift their thighs from the sticky plastic chairs with small, sucking noises.

The Reverend lifts his head from his silent prayer, signals

sanction with a glance. Amidst muffled murmurings and stifled coughs, they rise as one.

They shuffle forward now, towards the basket of rose petals and the pail of earth. Dust to dust. All eyes are on Richard as first-born: his movements stiff and formal, a full head of grey hair, his face a chiselled mask, his imported three-piece suit. His body betrays the encroachment of his sixth decade, yet his stance − one foot slightly behind the other, a fight-or-flight posture − is a remainder from childhood.

Does being here, burying his father, make him feel like a child again?

He scatters the blossoms and a handful of soil. Reaches into his pocket for a crisply ironed handkerchief to wipe his hands. Dabs at the corner of his eye, a subtle movement, noticed by no-one.

Evonne next, looking every day of her fifty-eight years. Dry-eyed, but her sadness written in hieroglyphic wrinkles. Loss inscribed in plain view. Those years of IVF took their toll, and with nothing to show at the end. Children have always flocked to her: her nieces and nephews, the children of friends. Attracted to the persona they sense, as children sense these things − her forgiving nature, her capacity for fun, her appreciation of the ridiculous. And yet, on occasions such as these, it seems the absence within her expands.

Finally, the baby of the three, Kelly, with her red-rimmed eyes and her once-only shoes. She alone bows her head, with its helmet of ash-blonde hair, and takes a moment. Perhaps she is conjuring up the good times, memories to sustain her through the whirl of relatives and finger food and cheap wine that is the wake to come.

Serendipitous that she farewells him at the age he fathered her. Their late-in-life surprise. Her siblings already teenagers, Richard angling to leave home, and Evonne – at fourteen – amidst the quagmire of her burgeoning personality. Into that mix a sunny baby with a thatch of blonde hair and a ready smile. Perhaps Kelly kept everyone sane for a few years. Perhaps she had kept her parents together.

The ceremony dwindles to the last few stragglers. No rose petals left. The mass of black has transformed into a river of mourners making their way towards the teahouse. Richard strides ahead to see to arrangements, pausing at the top of the rise to watch those dawdling over the graves of others: friends or family, or strangers with interesting headstones. Gravel crunches underfoot. Mynah birds swoop and play. The sound of heavy machinery signals the preparation of another grave for another somebody who is now a nobody.

Adjoining the green baize, the three rows of plastic chairs sit empty under the white marquee. The unsecured corners of the tarpaulin flap against the upright poles with a regular, dull thump. A few discarded orders of service lift in the gentle breeze.

Two men in blue uniforms remove the bands that lowered Daniel Whittaker into the ground, and begin to shovel from the pile of soil. One whistles.

So, that's that, then.

Eighty-eight years. It's a long time to keep secrets.

EVONNE SAT FORWARD IN THE deep leather armchair, her arms folded across the bulge of her generous stomach. She regretted that second helping of pasta. If Libby were here, she would be running her fingers over the matching tooled leather desktop, making witty comments about the heavy law tomes on the shelves, opening a window – making herself at home. Making Evonne feel comfortable. But the solicitor had been very clear: Daniel's children only. No partners, no grandchildren, just the three of them, for the reading of the will.

Her sister sat on the sofa, tracing the burgundy patterns with her forefinger. Kelly's large silver earrings jangled when she moved her head. She looked thin, thought Evonne, thinner even than when Mum had passed. Her clothes hung from her frame; her blouse dipped too low. Evonne had hugged her when she'd arrived, embraced her with an urgent need to reconnect with that child-like sense of sisterhood, now that both their parents were gone. Kelly had felt frail, as though she might snap if Evonne gripped too hard. She felt tears prickling beneath her lids and blinked them away before they could emerge.

The heavy drapes and soft furnishings cocooned the room in a muffled silence. Even the traffic noise was muted. There was only the insistent ticking of an old-fashioned carriage clock, marking the seconds as they passed.

The door opened and John Hardcastle entered his office, accompanied by Richard. The solicitor apologised for keeping them waiting, even though it had been Richard they were all waiting on. Her brother went first to Kelly, who stood and opened her arms; the two held each other for a moment. It was Richard who let go first. He moved to Evonne and gave her a one-armed hug where she sat, his cologne too strong, his intimacy forced. He squeezed her shoulder and sat in the other armchair. The three siblings looked at John Hardcastle, expectant. He had settled his bulk behind the solidity of his desk. He straightened the blotter and placed a pen next to it. He cleared his throat; the signal, Evonne realised, that he was ready to begin.

'Thank you all for coming today, and may I say again how sorry I am for your loss. Your father was a client when I first met him but over the years he became a friend. I'm honoured that he appointed me as executor of his estate and I hope to carry out my responsibilities in accordance with his wishes.'

Richard shifted in his chair. 'Steady on, John. I feel like I'm in an Agatha Christie novel.' He turned to Kelly. 'You be Mrs Peacock. I'll be Colonel Mustard.' He let out a gruff laugh, which sounded more like a snort of exasperation.

'I think you'll find that's Cluedo,' said Kelly. 'And if it was meant to be funny, I hardly think it's appropriate.'

Richard raised his hands in a gesture of surrender. 'Not being funny. Not at all. I do think it's a bit strange that Dad didn't appoint me – or the three of us, for that matter,' he corrected, '– as executors, but …' He gave the solicitor a wan smile. 'But I have every confidence in you, John.'

'Thank you, Richard, and I apologise for the formality,' John responded. 'But Daniel has attached very specific instructions and – if I might say so – some rather unusual conditions to his last will and testament.' He paused, and Evonne sensed the solicitor marshalling his thoughts and gauging the atmosphere. 'What I am about to tell you will no doubt come as a surprise. But I want to assure you before we begin that Daniel was entirely clear in his instructions to me. As you know, he has been my client for over fifty years, since I first started with the firm, and he remained lucid until the last. In fact, he updated his will only a couple of years ago, after your mother died. And no matter how unconventional you may find his last requests, I assure you that, from a legal standpoint, the will is sound.'

'You make it sound as if he's left everything to a home for orphaned cats or something,' said Richard.

'No, no, nothing like that. Daniel has provided for all of you more than adequately. I'm merely forewarning you that there are some conditions attached and that, much as we might debate the moral grounds of Daniel's decisions, the document is legally watertight.'

'Why on earth would we contest Dad's will?' said Kelly.

'Now hold on,' said Richard. 'No-one's talking about contesting anything. I think you'd better back up and explain exactly what you mean, John.' Evonne heard an unfamiliar waver of apprehension or anxiety in his voice.

'Certainly. Perhaps we should begin with the contents of your father's estate.'

John Hardcastle handed a photocopied page to Evonne and one each to Richard and Kelly. Evonne rummaged in her tote bag for her reading glasses. The sheet listed her father's assets and investments. He had always been wealthy, even while they were growing up. Evonne could not remember ever wanting. Quite the opposite – she had come through her adolescence with a particular embarrassment at the sheer number of dresses and skirts her mother brought home, both for herself and for her daughters, the quality of food on the table, the sporting equipment provided to Richard at the first mention of interest, the exotic holiday locations she admitted to her friends in a cautious way, unsure of their reactions. She had felt the humiliation of wealth unearned, the sharp barbs of jealousy.

She had never been privy to the details of her parents' income. That was 'a private matter'. All three children had been encouraged to become independent from their first jobs delivering newspapers, washing cars or mowing lawns; Evonne had followed her own path, as had her siblings, and she had been incurious as to her father's position.

A movement at the window caught her eye: two pigeons squabbling over the shadiest spot. Her father had hated pigeons – rats of the skies, he called them. He was forever installing complicated spikes to deter them from perching outside his office and, later, on the roof of his house. A vivid picture emerged in her mind – her father in his shirtsleeves, high on a ladder, trying to attach the ugly pointed plastic to his guttering. She remembered the flutter in her stomach, her fear that he would fall. The precariousness of the ladder.

But he had descended without incident, and Evonne had expelled her held breath.

She returned to the sheet of paper that so neatly delineated her father's financial position. He had been a real estate agent for most of his adult working life, employed for several years by one of the major firms before opening his own office – a hole-in-the-wall in Ashgrove, tucked behind the supermarket, with a dripping enamel sink and a back door that led onto a filthy lane. He had hired a sign writer to stencil *Whittaker Real Estate* above the shopfront, and furnished the room with a couple of desks, although it would be another year before he could afford a secretary.

His business flourished and he sold it over three decades later to the same firm where he had worked all those years earlier. By that stage, he had five Brisbane offices and over forty employees. Upon retirement, he took his wife on a three-month cruise to celebrate his seventieth birthday.

Evonne cast her eye over her father's investment portfolio: a list of shares, stocks and bonds from fields as diverse as mining, banking, the IT industry, childcare and theatre companies; both Australian and foreign interests. She had heard him mention these a few years ago, at a family dinner. Richard – pale and wan, his job precarious as the top dogs of the banking fraternity tumbled like so many dominoes – had made a throwaway comment, something about their father being lucky he was in property. Daniel had barely glanced up from his roast lamb.

'Most of my money's in shares,' he said.

'What?' sputtered Richard.

'I said, most of my money, about ninety per cent, is invested in the share market.' He had taken another mouthful of meat.

Richard was apoplectic. 'What? You can't be serious. You'd know better than anyone not to over-commit to the share market.' He glared at their father. 'Why haven't you mentioned this before? How much of our money's gone down the great GFC black hole?'

He had realised his mistake as soon as it came out of his mouth and at least, Evonne recalled, had the decency to look shame-faced.

Their father had finished chewing his lamb, swallowed, sat back in his chair and wiped at his mouth with a napkin.

'On paper, "our" money is mostly disappearing,' he said. 'More every day.' He had fixed Richard with a steely gaze. 'But as it's actually "my" money, I don't suppose you have anything to worry about.'

'But … your future … all you've worked so hard for … I don't understand why you aren't more upset. We've been talking about the crisis for months now and you've never said a word.'

Their father had sighed and held his glass of wine to the light. After a deep draught, he had said in a low voice: 'If it's my money, and I'm not worried, then I don't think you should be worried, either.' And with that, the conversation was ended, and the state of his financial affairs was not discussed again.

Evonne now saw the properties he had owned: the four-bedroom family home in which he had resided until their mother's death; the two-bedroom apartment in New Farm where he had moved afterwards; a block of shops up north in a Bargara development; and several units on the Gold Coast. She didn't have much of a head for figures, but even to her untrained eye the totals tallied at the bottom of the page amounted to some very large numbers. She looked up. Kelly had already put her sheet aside, but Richard was studying his. His face gave nothing away.

The long-ago boy was still visible in his ageing features, in the curve of his sagging cheek, in the blue of his eyes behind his expensive bifocals. Evonne tried to put her finger on what it was about her brother that seemed unsettled, not only since their father had passed, but for months prior to that. It was Richard who had been dealing with the solicitor, pushing this meeting forward and making arrangements. Yet he seemed uneasy, uncertain in a way Evonne did not recognise. The pointy end of middle age, perhaps.

Richard folded his sheet neatly in two. 'Well, this all looks in order. I had no idea the old man had so much squirrelled away in mining. Had some good advice from somebody there. And all those blue chips have done all right, haven't they? Weathered the storm. Now, the properties. Can we arrange that through your office? Probably best to deal with Dad's old firm. Only bastards I'd trust.' He looked at Evonne and Kelly. 'I take it we're agreed to sell everything? The properties, I mean. Not worth the hassle … maintenance, body corporates. Neither of you want to tackle any of that, I bet?'

'Well,' said Kelly, 'it might be nice to keep the house we grew up in. Happy memories and all that … something solid for the kids …'

Richard stopped mid-guffaw as he realised Kelly was serious.

'Oh, right. I suppose we could consider keeping the house. Good little renter. And Ashgrove's only going to get closer to the CBD as the city grows.'

'It was just a thought, Richard,' Kelly replied, with a flutter of her hand. 'It's not that important. Whatever you think is best.'

'In point of fact, you may have some time to consider your options regarding the properties and indeed the shareholdings as well,' said John. 'I've been authorised to keep the status quo with the properties regarding tenants and leases, et cetera, and the same with the shares – no buying or selling, at least until the conditions of the will have been met. Your father has made provision for our office to continue to handle his affairs through power of attorney for at least twelve months.'

'Right,' said Richard, drawing out the word. 'He was certainly organised, wasn't he? I can't imagine it'll take anything like twelve months, but glad you've got it all under control, John. All of us are very busy, as I'm sure you appreciate. Good to know the family fortune's safe in your hands until we get everything sorted out. Now, have you got documents ready for us to sign? Or do we need to come back for that?'

John Hardcastle leant back in his swivel chair, took off his glasses and polished the lenses with a tissue. He returned them to the bridge of his nose and regarded the three of them, peering in particular at Richard across the solid wooden desk. Evonne knew that John had always considered her brother a bit too arrogant. *He's enjoying himself*, she thought.

'Actually, Richard,' he said, 'I'm afraid it isn't quite as simple as that.'

Evonne noticed Richard stiffening as the solicitor continued.

'There's a reason he requested that only his three children attend today.'

...

Richard felt the strangeness of he, Evonne and Kelly being referred to, collectively, as 'children', when each was greying and sun-spotted and thick around the middle. He and Kelly had children of their own now; grandchildren, in Richard's case. He had come together with his sisters so infrequently over recent years. He knew the two of them kept in close contact: in the last months of their father's life, they had phoned each other almost every day, reporting on Daniel's condition and making arrangements. But it went beyond that. Kelly had always relied on Evonne and Libby for childcare.

His wife, too, made sure their twins visited their aunts and cousins: Jemima was always taking the girls to Kelly's or Evonne's. Even his older children – and his first wife – were drawn together by some magnetic pull, emailing and phoning often, despite living in different countries these days. He had never seen the need for such intimacies. Christmases and birthdays had been enough for him.

There was one Christmas in particular, when Kelly had been a toddler, that stood out in his mind. As usual, they had feasted on succulent roast pork with salty crackling, crunchy golden potatoes, and beans and silverbeet from the garden. The mouth-watering aroma still permeated the house as they opened presents around the tree, with Evonne collecting all the wrapping paper for their mother, who always smoothed the creases and folded it into neat squares for the next year. Kelly was crawling amongst the discarded boxes, putting everything into her mouth: ribbon, half a dropped mince pie – she would chew on the chair legs when she was a tot, his sister. But then she got hold of a marble and chaos ensued – Kelly going blue in the face, Mum screeching, Evonne fallen silent, Dad with his fingers in Kelly's mouth, prodding about uselessly. Richard had grabbed Kelly, turned her upside down and pounded on her small back, hoping he looked more confident than he felt. And it worked. Out popped the marble. Kelly's cries rang in Richard's ears as his parents bundled her up and took her into the next room, checking that she was all right.

Kelly was crying now, in John Hardcastle's rooms. Richard blinked. He felt a tug on the cord that joined him to his younger siblings. He was the patriarch of the family now. Richard looked at his thin, pale sister and wondered how she would cope. Forty-four was far too young to see both parents in the ground. And with her lot still a handful.

He had been jealous of her when they were younger, of her bond with their father. But he knew she had needed their father, especially with Mum becoming so withdrawn after Kelly's birth. For many months, it was their dad who had soaked the nappies and hung them out to dry in flapping lines that flew around violently with the wind. Dad who had cobbled together dinners of lamb chops and lumpy mashed potatoes; Dad who had hacked great chunks of bread and spread them thickly with jam for Evonne's lunches.

But after that incident with the marble, their mother had returned to herself. Perhaps that had been the turning point for her – watching Kelly silently turning blue, then the relief of hearing her throaty cries. She had taken Richard aside after lunch, while everyone was resting and listening to carols. She had cupped his chin in her hand and looked at him, really looked at him, as if she hadn't actually seen him for the longest time.

'Thank you,' she had said. 'Thank you, Richard.'

And he had turned away, embarrassed, and pleased, and proud of what he'd done. Proud of that small act of protection.

He wasn't sure how – or when, or even why – he had lost that connection. It struck him with a pang that his jealousy towards Kelly and her relationship with their father had returned in recent years, especially since their mother died three summers ago. This time, it had been Kelly who made time for their father and his growing needs as he aged: she had popped over early in the morning with fresh bread and coffee, driven Daniel to watch the kids' sport on the weekends, regularly changed and washed his linen. And all this despite the stress of being a single parent after her marriage had fallen apart. Evonne, too, had done her bit – kept his lawn mown and his garden tidy, and she and Libby often arrived unannounced with Thai takeaway and a movie. Richard knew all this because his father would tell him, during their (he was ashamed to admit it) occasional phone calls. Mostly he justified his sisters' ministrations as a singularly female trait, but in darker moments he knew he had deliberately kept his father at a distance.

And now that Daniel was gone, it would be them against him, with whatever surprises their father had left behind. Evonne would probably accept it as one more strangeness in a lifetime of unexplained oddities, undeserved joys and unjustified wrongs. Imperturbable. Kelly, young enough to feel cheated by the death of their parents, would still be too caught up in her grief. Richard, however, would rail. He knew his sisters thought of him as ponderous and imperious. But at least he wouldn't be putting up with any nonsense.

...

Evonne watched Kelly and thought again how fragile she seemed. The antithesis of Richard, stiff and unmoving. Remarkable, she pondered, how three siblings with the same parents could turn out so differently.

John Hardcastle's words returned her to the matter at hand.

'Before he died, your father left in my possession a number of envelopes – letters, I believe, although I have not witnessed their contents. My instructions were to furnish the three of you with these envelopes at his passing. His further instructions are that each envelope is to be hand-delivered by one or more of his children to the addressee.'

John withdrew from a desk drawer a sepia-toned folder with an old-fashioned string binding. He unwound the string from the circular tabs and fanned a handful of envelopes for the trio to see.

A couple were standard-issue DL envelopes. One or two were yellowed with age. One was A5-sized and thick, clearly containing more than a letter. Three bore the logo of their father's old real estate firm.

For a moment, no-one said anything. Richard was very still. Evonne expected John to continue and, when he didn't, she said: 'I don't understand. Who are these letters to? Are they part of Dad's will? Has he left things to other people?'

'Of course he hasn't. That would be completely out of order,' interjected Richard, finally recovering his speech. He reached across and grabbed a letter. 'Margaret Sonnet,' he read. He threw the envelope back onto the desk. 'Never heard of her. The idea's absurd. Clearly the old man wasn't as with it as we thought.'

'I can assure you that your father was of sound mind each and every time he presented me with another letter.'

'What do you mean, each time?' asked Evonne.

'Your father gave me the first letter over thirty years ago. I can check my notes for the exact date.'

'Thirty years?' spluttered Richard.

'Approximately, yes. Thereafter, there was one every few years or so. Sometimes nothing for five or six years, and then he'd bring another to add to the folder.'

Her brother was on his feet now. His eyes blazed. 'Now see here, John. I have no idea what you're playing at, or what my addled father was up to, but what you're suggesting is outlandish, and I won't have it.'

'I'm afraid you have no choice, Richard. On the whole, the estate is to be bequeathed to Daniel's family, but the dispersion of your father's assets depends on the specific instructions of his will being carried out in a thorough and timely manner.'

'But I don't even know a ...' he glanced at the desk, 'an Irene White. Haven't got the foggiest. Or that one. Or that one.' He pointed in turn to the correspondence spread across the desk. Evonne noticed that Kelly had blanched. Was it the mention of that particular name? Or the whole peculiar situation?

'Then I suggest you make some effort to find them. Each of them. My client's instructions were very clear. Each letter is to be delivered, in person. By one of the three of you.'

'And if they're not?'

'I'm afraid,' said John Hardcastle, peering at them again over his glasses, 'that should the conditions of the will fail to be met, your father's entire estate is to be bequeathed to the Red Cross, specifically to fund its work in the' – he consulted his notes – 'ah yes, "to fund Red Cross and Red Crescent emergency medical teams in war-torn or disaster zones",' he quoted.

Would that be a bad thing? wondered Evonne, and realised by the look on her brother's face that she must have spoken aloud.

'*A bad thing* ... good grief, Evonne. Have you taken leave of your senses? This is our inheritance we're talking about. Dad always meant it to come to us. He didn't even like the Red Cross. Used to send all those doorknockers packing.'

'Perhaps he changed his mind,' said Kelly. 'Decided to do something good at the last.'

'We'll contest it,' announced Richard. 'The whole thing's absurd.'

Kelly stared at him. 'I thought you said no-one was talking about contesting the will.'

'Well, that was before I bloody well knew what was in it.'

'Of course, you are free to contest any aspect of your father's will,' said John, 'but I must reiterate to you my view that your father was of sound mind when he made his testament, and each time he amended it, and that – legally – I believe it is watertight.' He gathered the envelopes into a tidy pile. 'And of course, contesting his will could become a time-consuming and rather expensive exercise.'

Richard paced back and forth before the solicitor's desk. 'What if we *can't* find these people?'

'In the event that Daniel's heirs are unable – or unwilling – to locate the addressees, I am under instruction to engage a private investigator to carry out his final instructions.'

'A PI? Oh, this just gets better and better. Who's going to pay for that, then?'

'Should it be necessary, Richard, the fees charged by the investigating firm will be deducted from the net value of the estate.' John matched Richard's stare. 'I have taken the liberty of looking into the fee structure for such a firm, and at approximately four hundred and fifty dollars per hour, minimum, I would suggest that it might be worth your while, financially, to at least attempt to locate these people yourselves.'

Richard glared for a moment longer, then threw up his hands in exasperation. 'What if they're dead? Moved? What if they don't want to be found and given a letter from some … some deceased crackpot?'

Kelly gave a little hiccupping sob.

John Hardcastle passed her a box of tissues. 'In the event that the addressee has predeceased your father, the correspondence is to be passed to that person's next of kin.'

'This is absurd,' Richard said again, and dropped into his chair, his head in his hands.

The pigeons fluttered against the window. The ticking of the clock sounded overloud.

Evonne addressed the solicitor. 'These are Dad's wishes?' she clarified.

'Yes, unequivocally. I do of course have Daniel's last will and testament here for your perusal, now or at your leisure, but I can assure you that your father was quite firm on the matter.'

'Dad never did anything without a reason, Richard, you know that,' said Evonne. 'And no matter what you think about this … this unusual situation … it's not something he would've contemplated lightly.'

'And he's not … he was not … a crackpot,' added Kelly. 'You know as well as I do that he was in his right mind until the last, and it's unfair of you to suggest otherwise.'

Evonne found in herself the voice of reason. 'You don't know what's in these letters, John?'

'No. I'm not privy to the contents of any of them.'

'They could say anything,' Richard whispered. 'Anything. We haven't a clue. God knows what skeletons he's decided to take out of the cupboards. And we're to deliver them personally? It could be embarrassing. Humiliating.'

'Look,' said Evonne. 'Obviously this is something Dad felt strongly about. He's been writing these letters or whatever they are, and giving them to John for safe-keeping, for … how long did you say, John? Over thirty years? This is not some whim, a fancy of an old man who knew he was dying. He's planned this, Richard. Planned for those people – whoever they are – to receive those letters, and planned for us to deliver them.' She glared at her brother. 'He's never asked us to do much.'

'What about all those medical bills? Who do you think paid for that treatment? If I'd known—'

'What, Richard?' asked Evonne, her voice now as steely as his.

'You wouldn't have paid? Are you seriously telling me you resented paying a few hospital bills?'

'You'll get it all back now, a hundred times over,' said Kelly. 'What a horrible thing to say. Anyway, you might have paid the bills but it was me over there every Sunday, trimming his toenails and changing the sheets on the bed.'

'Stop it, both of you,' said Evonne. 'This is hardly the time or the place for this discussion.' She turned to the solicitor. 'I'm sorry, John. Dad could be a bit difficult, especially after Mum died, but we all did our bit. I wouldn't want you to think any of us resented caring for him as he got older.' She glared at Richard as if willing him to defy her. 'Anyway, it sounds to me like it isn't such a lot for him to ask. Deliver what, a dozen or so letters? How hard can it be?'

'I agree,' said Kelly. 'And even if it is an old man's foible as you seem to think, Richard, it can't do any harm. It's Dad's money. He can do whatever he likes with it. Who are we to question his last wishes?'

'We're his family, his children, that's who. And while it's lovely that you think no harm can come of this, knowing Dad I would have to disagree. God knows what's in there.'

'You can't abide uncertainty, Richard, that's your problem,' said Evonne. 'Never done a spontaneous thing in your life.'

Kelly reached out and took their brother's hand. Her tears had gone; a hint of a smile played around her eyes. 'Come on, Richard, it could be an adventure. Maybe we'll learn something about Dad.'

'Or maybe we'll just deliver the letters and learn nothing,' said Evonne. 'Doesn't matter. Point is, Dad's asked us to do it. And I, for one, am not going to let him down.'

Kelly interlaced her fingers with Richard's and moved to sit on the arm of Evonne's chair. 'We'll be doing it together,' she said.

'Unless you want to leave it all to John here, with his PI poking about for thousands of dollars?'

Richard closed his eyes and leant his head back. He disentangled his hand from Kelly's and rubbed his eyelids. 'Bloody migraine starting up, I'm sure of it.'

Evonne smiled. It wasn't much of an agreement, but she knew that for Richard it was capitulation.

'Right then,' she said to John. 'You'd better give us all the details.'

'Bloody Dad,' said Richard. 'Unbelievable. He's managed to keep control from the bloody grave.'

. . .

Kelly thought Richard was wrong. Whatever the puzzling nature of their father's request, she refused to believe it stemmed from an issue of control. But Richard's brain seemed to be wired differently. Always suspicious of motives and behaviours, particularly where their father was concerned.

She supposed their father had always related to Richard differently than he had to her and Evonne. After all, he was a boy, and the first-born. Years ago, that had meant something. Richard had been expected to walk a certain path. She wasn't sure whether her brother had felt he had to prove himself to their father, or whether his determination was driven by Daniel's own ambition. By the time she was old enough to recall, Richard had been a young man, already studying at university and training at the bank, mature and responsible. Kelly had felt as if she'd grown up with four parents rather than two parents and two siblings.

Her mind lingered on her father's last days. She saw him reclining in his easy chair, the remote control on one arm, a packet of liquorice allsorts on the other. The crocheted antimacassar behind his head, a remnant from the days when her mother had been alive to care about such things. She searched the memory of his face for some clue as to the conundrum with which he had left them. She tried to imagine the story behind his actions.

His story.

Her father had been old even when she was young. He had been in his mid-forties when Kelly was born, and she had always pictured him with grey hair, stooped shoulders and a face full of wrinkles. It wasn't until she herself reached the age of forty, and realised that she felt no different, that she understood how skewed her perception had been. Surely her father had once been physically stronger and more resilient, his memory sharper, but her dominant image of her father was that of his last years, when he had been stubborn and difficult, forgetful. Frail. Frustrated. Her siblings, who could remember their father as a younger man, had found his descent into infirmity even more startling.

He had doted on Kelly when she was small – taken her for ice-cream, or into the city to see the lights, or shelled out for horse-riding lessons. Sometimes she had felt like an only child, showered with privileges not bestowed on Evonne, or even Richard. It was not related to money – it was his precious time, doled out exclusively to her, that made her feel distinct. Evonne had told her how it had begun when Kelly was a baby, when their mother had been unwell. Kelly had been thrust into their father's arms and he had been forced to confront the challenge, and she was grateful for that bond.

One of her strongest memories was of her father pushing her on the tyre swing that hung off the massive fig tree in their backyard. She would've been eight, maybe nine, her legs outstretched, her hands gripping tight to the nylon rope that chafed and rubbed. Her father behind her, mouth open, shouting encouragement, strong arms ready to push again, ready to catch her should she fall.

In recent years, of course, their roles had been reversed. Caring for her father had been at times heart-breaking. Watching him struggle to recall a name, or even a familiar household word, his voice desperate. His habit of wiping at his constantly weeping eye. The way his signature had deteriorated – once a strong flourish, it had become weak and insubstantial, his hand shakier each time he wrote. She had cringed at the marks on his underwear that he tried to hide and, somehow worse, the food stains on his shirts that he didn't even notice. Every time she visited, she saw a new nick or scratch, never anything he noticed himself. *What have you done now?* she would say, and he would reply, *It's nothing. I don't even feel it.*

In the end, he had slipped away quietly. One morning she was replenishing his bread and milk and massaging a cramp from his calf; a few days later she and Evonne were poking about in his bathroom cabinet, sweeping whole shelves of out-of-date medications and skin care products into black garbage bags, sorting out the paperwork in his filing cabinet, divvying up the houseplants and pantry items. They had found dusty ornaments and piles of newspapers, faded photographs of ancestors they couldn't identify, childish handcrafted knick-knacks from his grandchildren, and even dresses of their mother's that they hadn't realised he'd kept. The detritus of a lifetime, disposed of in no more than a week. With each bag of rubbish that went out for the tip, or each box of salvageables that was earmarked for the charity bin, a little more of her father left the dwelling, until barely a trace of him remained – the scent of his aftershave clinging to the walls, the sounds of his silences lingering in the empty rooms.

Silences: yes, their father had gathered his silences about him like a heavy coat. Richard and Evonne had both been with Kelly the day they found the medals in a small, velvet-lined case, packed in a larger cardboard box that had been shoved under the stairs between a broken vacuum cleaner and a suitcase of old shoes. Kelly had opened the small case and held up the medals by their striped ribbons, the metal discs reflecting the light as they swung from her hand. Richard had been silent, as if he hadn't wanted to admit that the discovery was a surprise to him too. Their father had never talked about the war much, or his experiences.

'What are they for?' she had asked.

'I don't know,' Evonne had answered. 'We could look them up, I suppose.'

But somehow it was never done; none of them had found the time. When Kelly had chosen a suit in which to bury their father, and polished his shoes, and approved of the way the funeral director had parted his hair and knotted his tie, she had pinned the medals to their father's chest herself. Richard and Evonne had come to view his body, and none of them mentioned the medals again, as if she and her siblings tacitly agreed that this would remain a silent subject, closed for discussion, the medals and all they represented buried with their father.

And now, these letters, scattered across the desk. Innocuous and yet vaguely discomfiting. She stared, willing something – some meaning or witticism or posthumous remark – to fly out and make itself known. But of course that didn't happen. They were merely letters, ink scribbled on paper. What other secrets did their father have?

. . .

Richard watched as the solicitor straightened himself in his chair and tapped his fingers on the pile of envelopes. He wished John would just get on with it. He had no desire to jump through whatever hoops were about to appear, but he wanted the ordeal to be over, and quickly. He couldn't keep lying to Jemima. Although he didn't think of it as lying, exactly; more as sidestepping the truth. And once his father's inheritance came through, it wouldn't matter anyway. His problems would be solved and he could be honest with Jemima and know that she wouldn't have to worry. For that was what he was doing, he reasoned – preventing her from a whole lot of unnecessary worry. Yet now his father was impeding things, with whatever nonsense John Hardcastle was on about.

'Right. As I explained, your father left a number of envelopes with me to be distributed. I have a total of twelve letters and they must all be delivered in person by the three of you,' said John. 'Perhaps if you all have a look at them and then we can work out how to proceed.'

Richard and his sisters crowded towards the desk. Kelly clutched a handful of letters and began to look through them, passing some to Evonne, and soon all of the flimsy envelopes were circulating between the three of them.

'I don't know any of these people …'

'I don't think we're meant to …'

'How on earth are we going to find them?'

'What if they're not in Brisbane, do we have to travel?'

Evonne dropped back into her chair. 'Where do we start? How do we decide who's delivering what?'

'May I suggest,' said John, 'that we approach this in an orderly fashion.' He collected the envelopes back into a pile.

Richard pointed at the letter on top. 'Irene White,' he read.

'Never heard of her. Do you have any information about her, John, or are we supposed to use our powers of extra-sensory perception to figure it out? Huh. I don't have the first clue.'

'Actually,' murmured Kelly, 'I know that name. That's ... that was ...'

Evonne and Richard both turned to her expectantly.

She sighed. 'I think Irene White was Dad's first wife.'

Richard opened his mouth in disbelief, but no sound came out. Evonne looked as though her stomach had lurched.

'First wife?' Richard spluttered. 'Dad never had a first wife. He was married to Mum for sixty-one years! When did he get time for a first wife?'

'He married her during the war,' said Kelly. 'He told me about it one night when he'd been drinking. It was just after Simon and I broke up. Think he wanted to make me feel better.'

'Oh, for the love of God. You're serious?' Richard could feel himself turning an unpleasant shade of puce. 'And you didn't think to share this with any of us?'

'Don't know if I really believed it myself,' Kelly said in a small voice.

'What, you think Dad made up having a first wife to make you feel better about the collapse of your marriage? Why didn't you say something?'

'And what would have been the point, Richard? Mum was still alive. I didn't want to hurt her. Can't even recall if she knew. Besides, Dad was drunk. He could have said anything. I didn't know if there was any truth in it.'

He glowered at his younger sister. 'I cannot believe, I simply *cannot* believe, what I'm hearing. Dad was not married to anyone but Mum. Whatever he told you was bullshit.'

'Maybe it was,' said Kelly. 'Like I told you, he'd been drinking.'

John Hardcastle held the envelope between the two with a questioning look. Richard shrank back. 'Give it to her. I don't want anything to do with it.'

Kelly took it, not with reluctance, thought Richard, but with reverence.

His hands were sweating. Kelly was turning the envelope over in her hands, as if staring at it hard enough would cause some information to magically appear.

Evonne spoke up. 'John, just give me a couple of random ones. I don't care who they are.'

The solicitor handed over three envelopes. 'That should be your share.'

Evonne read out the names. 'Michael Adamson, Nigel Lawless, Audrey Blackson. Sound innocuous enough.'

'Lawless. I know that name. Didn't Dad work with a fellow called Lawless for a while?' asked Richard.

'Guess I'll find out,' said Evonne.

'Give me two more too, then,' said Kelly. 'Jennifer Ibsen,' she read. 'And Monteray Max.'

'What kind of a name is Monteray Max,' muttered Richard. 'All right, all right. Hand the rest this way,' he said in resignation. 'Leanne Young, Margaret Sonnet, Jeffrey Upton.' This last was more a packet than an envelope; it bulged with unseen material. 'Three names that mean nothing at all to me.' He counted in his head. 'John,' he said, 'that's only nine. I thought you said there were twelve letters.'

'Yes,' said John. 'I was just getting to that. There are three more, one to be delivered specifically by you Richard, one by Evonne and one by Kelly—'

'Well, hand them over then,' interrupted Richard.

'—but they are not to be given to you until all the others have been delivered. I don't even have the envelopes here with me; they're in the safe.'

'Are they for us then?' asked Kelly, a glimmer of hope in her voice. Richard knew what she was probably thinking. A last message for each of them from their father. Some last great words of wisdom, some sign of his love.

'No,' said John, 'not *for* you, but to be delivered *by* you. I'm sorry, I don't know any more than that.'

Don't know, thought Richard, *or can't say?*

Into the silence of the room drifted the unasked questions, like petals shaken free from the boughs of a tree by a gust of wind. Richard wanted to sweep them all up – the questions, the envelopes, everything – and dump the whole mess into the bin. But his father's last requests hung heavy in his hands, the envelopes weighed down with uncertainty, his mind reeling with doubt. Who, when, where, why and how. The most basic of questions, unanswered.

EVONNE BACKED HER AGEING TOYOTA into the carport and turned off the ignition. She sat listening to the engine tick as it cooled. The door opened with a creak and she heaved herself out. God but she was tired. She heard her doctor repeating that she must make an effort, to walk more, to eat less. But right at this moment all she wanted was to put her feet up and have Libby pour her a glass of shiraz.

The stinging heat of the day had dissipated into a fug that hung around the house like a warm shawl. Their home was a worker's cottage skirted on two sides by state forest; from its depths came the trills and carols of songbirds that heralded the arrival of dusk. The air felt gritty with dust and she could smell the smoke of a distant fire up the mountain.

She went down the unevenly paved path and across the porch, the decking boards cracked and shrunken so that popped nails created a hazard for the barefoot. When she pulled open the screen door, the cat sped out between her legs and disappeared into the thick foliage.

The house was cool inside, the hundred-year-old stumps still doing their job. She hung her tote bag on the hook and slipped off her shoes, wriggling her toes with relief. In the kitchen, the cluttered bench held two chopping boards of diced vegetables and an old ice-cream container full of peelings. She sank into a chair, crossed her arms on the tabletop and rested her head on them, allowing her heavy lids to drift closed.

'Vonnie? Is that you?'

She heard the toilet flush and Libby emerged.

'Good, you're home. I'm making a vegie lasagne. How did it go?'

At Libby's touch, Evonne opened her eyes to discover they had filled with hot tears that began cascading down her cheeks, wetting her arms and her hair.

'Oh, Vonnie,' sighed Libby. She stretched her arms around Evonne and held her, rocking slightly on the balls of her feet. 'Vonnie, I'm so sorry. Was it terrible? It was terrible, of course it was, what am I saying. Oh, my dear, let me make you a cup of tea.' But Evonne didn't respond and Libby made no move to the kettle. The two women remained entwined, Libby's chin on Evonne's head, Evonne's sobs shuddering through her body. Libby tightened her hold and rubbed her fingers up and down Evonne's arm in a soothing gesture.

'Oh, Vonnie,' she said again. There was nothing to add, nothing that would make any difference.

...

An hour later, Evonne was stretched out on the sofa, her feet resting in Libby's lap. The rich aroma of the lasagne wafted from the oven. Dusk had properly fallen now – the brightness leached from the

31

sky, replaced by the softer colours of evening, salmon pink, pale orange. Outside the open windows, the native trees stood in stark silhouette against the horizon. The bush was coming alive with the noises of the night – wallabies searching for tender grass; scrub turkeys scrabbling through the leaf litter; a kookaburra warbling from a high branch, calling its companions. Once, they had spotted a koala at the top of the spotted gum nearest their house. The tree was at least thirty metres high – big gums and eucalypts grew well in the reserve. They had sighted blue gum, grey gum and tallowwood, red stringybark and ironbark. All spreading their canopy towards the sky, sheltering the lesser flora below, as well as the native animals that rested beneath the safety of their green armour.

Evonne felt safe here too, cocooned in their little house, surrounded by bushland. With Libby by her side, her apprehension was abating; she felt far away from Richard, and the will, and the task that was to come.

'It was just awful, Lib,' she said. 'Richard was so … so pompous and difficult. He started saying something about the money he's paid for medical bills. God, it was dreadful. And Kelly … she was so thin and fragile-looking. And inscrutable. It was strange. It's like she's a different person. I don't think she's properly taken the whole thing in yet, to be honest. She seems to be in denial. I mean, she's treating this letter thing like some sort of adventure. In fact, I think she used that very word, *adventure*. And then Richard started talking about Dad managing to control us from the grave and …' She put her cup on the side table, closed her eyes and massaged her temples.

Libby took a sip of tea. 'It seems incredible that none of you had any inkling of what he had in mind.'

'Well, I certainly knew nothing about it. And it was clearly a complete surprise to Richard.'

'What about Kelly? She was over there more than you two.'

'No, she didn't know either, I'm sure of it. It's baffling.'

'So where did Hardcastle leave it? What happens next?'

'Well, we start looking for these people, I suppose. Here.' She pushed her three envelopes across the table. Libby held each one to the light, trying to see inside. A mischievous grin crossed her face.

'Don't even suggest it,' said Evonne. 'They are only to be opened by the person to whom they're addressed. John was very clear.'

'Yeah, but it's tempting, isn't it? You know, I used to be able to steam open envelopes when I was a kid. You could seal it back up without—'

'Libby! I can't believe you'd consider such a thing. This is a proper legal requirement.'

'I'll bet the thought's crossed Richard's mind.'

'Well, he'd be in serious trouble if he did anything about it. We all would. Besides,' she added, 'these are Dad's final wishes. I wouldn't want to go against them, however odd they seem.'

Libby handed back the letters and squeezed Evonne's shoulder. 'Of course you wouldn't, darling. I'm only teasing. You'll do the right thing. You all will. Even Richard.'

'He seemed to think it would all happen very quickly. I don't know why, when we don't know these people from Adam.'

'What's his hurry? It's not like he needs the money.'

'God knows. Although I suppose keeping Catherine in the manner to which she'd become accustomed doesn't come cheap.'

'They've been divorced for over twenty years!'

'I know, I know. The twins turn forty this year, if you can believe it.'

'I still can't believe he found another woman to marry him, let alone that he produced a second set of twins,' said Libby, deadpan.

Evonne laughed. 'I think I'm about ready for that glass of red.' She shifted her feet off Libby's lap.

'I'll get it. You stay there.'

Evonne watched as her partner collected the teacups and moved into the kitchen. She could hear her opening the oven door and adjusting the temperature. There was the tinkle of wine glasses. For a moment, she saw Libby's outline in the doorway, her frizzy hair a golden halo framing her face, her body compact and lithe and stocky all at once. Evonne imagined an angel might look this way, ethereal but present, specific features lost in a general bearing of virtue and kindness. *I am so lucky*, she thought, *to have her in my life*.

'You look really tired,' Libby said as she handed her a glass.

'I feel tired. Drained.'

'Losing someone's bad enough, but I have to say this whole business does sound a bit like a circus. He's making you work for your money, isn't he?'

'I don't know, Lib. I'm not sure it's about the money. Dad's been planning this for some time. He must have had his reasons. I suppose we might find out when we see what's in those envelopes. *If* we see what's in them. There's no guarantee people will share, I suppose.'

'You must be curious. I know I would be.'

'Richard's worried the skeletons will reflect badly on him.'

Libby snorted. 'Yeah, I can just imagine. Wouldn't want anything upsetting his applecart.'

'He doesn't deal well with surprises,' surmised Evonne, 'especially of the nasty kind.'

'You can say that again.'

The two women shared a conspiratorial grin.

'*You're* not worried, though, are you, Vonnie? About what might be in the letters?'

'God, no. Whatever it is, it's probably just Dad tying up a few loose ends. I mean, it's not like he's been an absent father. Eighty-eight years on the earth, and I've been around for fifty-eight of them. There's not much we don't know. How bad could it be?'

Libby's face was a mask, and Evonne thought again, *how bad could it be?* And anticipated (not foolishly, she hoped) that she was right in thinking the answer to that question was *not very*.

Perhaps it was her father's wish only to see his children working together. Blood of his blood. Flesh of his flesh. The proof that life goes on through those you leave behind.

But what would his legacy be? That remained to be seen.

…

Evonne went to bed that night spooned around Libby's sleeping form, the names going around and around in her head … Michael Adamson, Nigel Lawless, Audrey Blackson. Michael, Nigel, Audrey. She would begin with Nigel Lawless, she decided, since Richard had mentioned that Dad might have worked with a Lawless.

It was past nine when she awoke the next morning. She could hear Libby singing in the kitchen. The smell of something baking wafted in on the warm morning air. Evonne fumbled on the bedside table for her reading glasses and picked up the three envelopes. They were nondescript, but when she looked closely at Michael Adamson's, she saw a number on the back of the envelope – 1935. A year, perhaps. And Audrey's envelope was addressed to Audrey Blackson, BSHS. Brisbane State High? Evonne wondered if she had been a teacher there.

But then she remembered her resolve to tackle Nigel Lawless first. She reached for her mobile and searched for Rochester, the company where her father had been employed before he went out on his own. She cleared her throat and dialled the number.

'Good morning, Rochester Real Estate. You're speaking with Sherrie. How may I help you?'

'Sherrie, my name's Evonne Whittaker. This may sound a little strange, but I'm trying to locate someone who may have worked for you quite a few years ago. Nigel Lawless?'

'Okay, we have no-one here by that name. How long ago did you say he worked here?'

'I don't really know. Maybe … maybe fifty years ago?'

There was a silence at the other end of the line.

'Sorry? Did you say fifteen years?'

'No, fifty. Five-zero. Maybe, during the sixties?'

Evonne thought she heard a twitter.

'The sixties? I'm sorry, that's a bit before my time. I wasn't born until '92.'

'No. No, of course not. Um … perhaps I could have a word with someone a bit more senior? Someone who's been there a while?'

'You could try talking to Dave Blackburn. He's our most senior consultant. Can I have your name again, and your number, and I'll ask him to call you back.'

Evonne was looking at Michael Adamson's letter when Libby came into the room, carrying two mugs of tea.

'What do you think of this, Lib?' She pointed to the number on the back of the envelope.

'Hmm. It's a clue.' Libby raised her eyebrows. 'What was your dad doing in 1935?'

'Well, umm. He was born in '25, so he would have been ten years old. At primary school, I suppose. Grade four or five?'

'There you go. Where did he attend school? I'd begin there, if I were you.'

'Milton State School. I know that much. And speaking of schools, see what's written on this one? Audrey Blackson, BSHS. Could be State High, I thought. But 1935, we're talking, what, almost eighty years ago. Whoever this Michael Adamson is, or Audrey Blackson for that matter, they're likely long dead. And how are we supposed to find them, anyway. The words needle and haystack come to mind.'

Libby blew on the surface of her tea and sipped the scalding liquid. She slipped her free hand behind Evonne's head and began to massage her neck. 'Think of it as a challenge.'

Evonne put her mug down and closed her eyes, surrendering herself to Libby's rhythmic movements. 'Mmm. That's nice.' She looked up. 'Will you come with me?'

'Of course I will, Von. I'll help however you want me to. Do you think these two are connected, then? Blackson and Adamson? Seeing as they're the only two with extra details?'

'I haven't got the foggiest, Lib. Not the foggiest.'

. . .

Evonne wished that her father had been nicer to Libby. Libby had taken such good care of her. Always had. Surely that should have counted for something? They'd been together over thirty-five years, and Evonne had never been so content as since she'd met Libby. Yes, she thought, he should've been nicer. More tolerant. After all, he must've suspected for a long time, and her mother too, even before Evonne met Libby. But she was sure her parents never discussed it. Her mother had pushed her to go to all the dances and mixed tennis days. Dressed her up like a doll. All they ended up doing was making Evonne confused, while they became frustrated and cross at her lack of interest in boys. And then even when they finally did meet Libby, this 'special friend', they still didn't cotton on, even though it was staring them straight in the face.

Her mother had nearly had a stroke when Evonne told her. *You can't be serious,* she kept shouting. *It's a phase, you'll grow out of it.* But Evonne was in her mid-twenties by then; she was already grown. Knew her own mind. She had shouted and raged, slammed doors and sobbed angry tears; she had called her mother and her father intolerant, judgemental bigots.

Before that, Libby had been a regular visitor, even staying weekends, the girls sharing a room like they were ten-year-olds having a sleepover. But after their relationship was all out in the open, her mother wouldn't have Libby back in the house. *It's disgusting,* she would hear her mother mutter to her father. And she would hear his quiet agreement.

Evonne knew that it was old Nana Holliday dying that made them come round. Shirley's mum had suffered from dementia, and lived in a care facility up on the Sunshine Coast. One of the staff let slip to Evonne's parents that Libby used to visit Nana Holliday every week, sometimes alone. She would take her out in the garden. Brush her hair. Libby's own father had died when she was young, her mother only a few years after she and Evonne had begun their relationship, and her grandparents had been long gone by that point. So Libby had sort of adopted Nana Holliday. Evonne's mother only made it up there herself every month or so; she was always so busy. But the staff couldn't speak highly enough of Libby, said she treated Nana like her own flesh and blood. And when she died, Libby came to the funeral with Evonne – that was so brave, thought Evonne, Libby knew she wasn't invited and wouldn't be welcome. But she came anyway, and sat up the back – Evonne wished that she herself had been braver; that she had insisted Libby sit at the front, as part of the family. Still, Libby's genuine emotion towards Nana Holliday was apparent, and that's what had finally done it for Shirley. They hugged that day, at the funeral, and afterwards Shirley asked Libby to help serve the cake. That was a sign. Then she gradually started coming to the house again.

Evonne knew her parents had still found it hard. Thinking about all that Evonne was giving up by choosing to be with Libby. Kids and family, they assumed, for a start. A 'normal' life. She knew they struggled to accept it even in their own minds, let alone explain their daughter's situation to others. Their friends and workmates. All producing grandchildren at a great rate of knots. Even their other children – Richard and Kelly – reproducing with reckless abandon.

Not that she and Libby hadn't tried. Those endless rounds of IVF, year after year, each cycle reducing their sense of hope further and further until it was merely an echo of yearning. No result. Not for Libby, who had had frequent bouts of endometriosis when she was younger. And not for Evonne, for no reason that anybody seemed able to provide. Nothing wrong on the male side of things, apparently. All fine sperm from fine men, eager to reproduce – even anonymously – little replicas of their own fineness. No, the fault lay with her. And although her mother never said as much, there were many times Evonne felt her pointing a figurative finger as if to say, *See? You didn't want children the natural way and so God is punishing you by not giving you any at all. You should've thought of that before you decided which way you wanted to jump.* Her mother would never have stooped so low as to utter the actual words, but she managed to twist the knife nonetheless. She was matter-of-fact about their IVF attempts. Cold.

At least she and Libby were able to surround themselves with children at work. Libby worked at the special-care nursery at the hospital, taking care of those tiny babies clinging to life, while Evonne managed the large multicultural childcare centre where she had been for over twenty years. She was a natural; she found caring for the youngest kids invigorating and satisfying. She used her artistic skills to engage with children with all sorts of behavioural and family problems. She was proud of the fact that for the eighth year in a row, foreign countries outnumbered Australia as places of birth for her enrolled children. But her mother had found her passion difficult to embrace.

'I don't understand why you can't get a nice job teaching at a private school somewhere in the western suburbs. Surely you've earned that. You've paid your dues to the lower socio-economic groups.'

'It's not a matter of "paying my dues", Mum. I *want* to work with these kids. I love that they come from different faiths and backgrounds. We have so much fun learning about each other's special celebrations and cultures.'

'I would've thought that some of those parents wouldn't appreciate having other cultures being shoved down their necks. Particularly the Muslims. They're not very tolerant, or so I've heard.'

'Oh, Mum. To be perfectly honest, the few times we've had complaints from parents it's always been from middle-class white parents, wanting to know why we can't stick to the curriculum. And even they've been rare. People are mostly very inclusive. They want their kids to grow up to be tolerant and compassionate.'

'But what about all those terrorist countries?' her mother had continued. 'Surely you don't want the other kids being polluted with all that nonsense.'

Evonne had given a patient sigh. 'Terrorists don't have their own country, Mum. That's the point …' She was always tempted to be drawn into a political discussion, but usually managed to avoid it. 'Most of our refugee kids are fleeing from terrorists. Or from regimes in their own countries that persecute them because of their religion or their ethnicity.'

'Well then,' her mother had sniffed. 'When they come here, they should assimilate, shouldn't they. Learn our ways. Dress like us. Speak English.'

It was often at that point that Evonne threw up her hands. 'I give up. Honestly, Mum, you go around spouting these comments without any idea of the damage you're doing.'

'Damage? It's not me causing riots and stabbings and those, what do you call them, those honour killings. If you ask me,' she said, not that Evonne had, 'some of our politicians have got their heads screwed on the right way. Read the riot act, I say. You choose to come to our country, you follow our laws and abide by our customs. End of story.'

'And the Indigenous people, Mum? What rights did they have when white people arrived and colonised the country?'

'That was years ago. It's hardly relevant today. They should have assimilated too. It's a pity they can't pull themselves together and act like real Australians.'

'Oh my God, Mum. No wonder Richard goes off the way he does. It's a miracle Kelly and I have managed to emerge unscathed. If you could only listen to yourself.'

'I think you're being rather unfair, Evonne. You know perfectly well that we provide financial support – quite a lot, I'll have you know – to third world countries, through the church and clubs and goodness knows what else. Poverty, water contamination, schooling for youngsters – you can't say we don't do our bit.'

'Yes, but that's all overseas. You're quite happy to help as long as it's at an arm's length away. But you refuse to look in your own backyard.'

'My backyard is quite tidy, thank you, Evonne.'

And Evonne would rake her fingers through her hair, and glare at her mother with her impenetrable arguments, and despair that nothing she ever did – in her personal or her professional life – would ever meet her mother's strict requirements, and that she would never be able to persuade her mother from her narrow-minded views.

...

Dave Blackburn telephoned Evonne the following Monday and they arranged to meet near his office in Wynnum; she planned to go for a walk on the beachfront afterwards. Kelly had rented in the area many years earlier, before all the new freeways and tunnels and toll roads, but there was little that Evonne recognised now. She found a parking spot that didn't even have a meter – unheard of in the inner suburbs. The day was hot; sunshine streamed from a cloudless sky. She could smell the salt air and the fried tang of fish and chips. She strolled past a Salvos store, a boutique dress shop and a gift store, searching for the 'authentic Greek place on the corner' that Dave had described to her.

She shaded her eyes and peered around the tables at the cafe, looking for a man sitting on his own. She caught Dave's eye and he waved her over. They shook hands.

'So you're Daniel Whittaker's daughter, hey. Well, I'll be blowed. Daniel and I used to work together back in the day, when you were this high.' Dave gestured to his waist, then pulled out a chair for Evonne and called for the waitress.

He gave their order – a skinny flat white for her; a mixed grill for him, comprising kebab, kofta, homemade hummus and tzatziki, pita bread and olives. Evonne appraised him – stocky, sparse grey hair. He looked younger than her father's era, in his seventies, she thought. His belly suggested the cafe might be his regular local lunch spot.

'He was a legend, your old man. Sharp as a whip. Didn't suffer fools. After he left to start up his own firm, our sales dropped through the floor. Still worked with him occasionally, you know, on joint sales. He drove a hard bargain, that's for sure. Sorry to hear about his passing.' He rested his hand on Evonne's arm. 'They broke the mould when they made Daniel.'

Evonne reached into her bag to extricate her arm from Dave Blackburn's heavy fingers. She pulled out the envelope with Nigel Lawless written on it, fanned herself with it – the air was still and hot – and passed it across for the man to read.

'I'm actually looking for information about this man, Nigel Lawless. It's in connection with Dad's will. Do you know him?'

Dave wiped his greasy fingers on a paper napkin and picked up the envelope. 'Lawless, Lawless. Let me think now. Yes, I do remember a Lawless. Big man, overweight, you know, almost obese. Used to work for Rochester years ago, but I thought that was after your father left. No, hang on a minute, maybe they were there at the same time.'

He rubbed one hand on the side of his sandpapery cheek. 'Yes, I think they might have been. I remember something … some unpleasantness … huh, it's on the tip of my tongue … nope. Nothing. Memory like a sieve these days, I'm afraid.'

'That's okay,' said Evonne. 'I do need to get in touch with him if I can, though. Do you know where he might be now?'

'Well, if he's not six feet under he'd be in a retirement home or something for sure. He was at least as old as your father, maybe older. I'd be surprised if he was still alive.'

'Oh.' Evonne sighed. 'Well, thanks for your—'

'Hang on a minute, he did have a son in the game. Real estate, I mean. He's a big boy too, or was the last time I laid eyes on him.'

Size is relative, thought Evonne.

He chewed thoughtfully and squinted into the sunlight. 'Name of Evan or Ethan or something like that. Ivan, that's it. Ivan Lawless. Think he worked for Ganter Property, but that was going back a few years. Not sure if he'd still be there now.'

The proprietor, a short Greek man in his fifties, hovered with a plate containing two sticky pieces of baklava. 'On the house,' he said.

'Lovely,' said Dave Blackburn as he offered the plate to Evonne. When she shook her head, he shovelled both pieces into his mouth in quick succession.

After she left the cafe, Evonne wandered down to the beachfront. She slipped off her shoes and walked along the shoreline. The sand was cool and grainy on the soles of her feet. The waves rolled in and out, a restless tide, forever moving but never going forward. By the time the white caps crashed onto the sand, they were tiny replicas of their ocean selves, impotent and weak.

Was that how her father had felt towards the end? Mellowed by age, lacking the power and strength of his younger years? The waves broke in a regular rhythm, the white froth dissolving into the sand, leaving webs of gossamer lace stencilled across the shore. The shrill cries of gulls carried on the gusts of wind that blew Evonne's hair across her face and threw smatterings of grit against her body. The sun was relentless; only the breeze made it bearable.

Dave Blackburn's words echoed in her mind. She wondered about the details of the 'unpleasantness' he half-remembered, and whether she was stepping closer to solving the riddle.

The shore was strewn with detritus: broken shells, a plastic bottlecap, stringy lines of pungent seaweed, the occasional swollen jellyfish. Evonne spotted an unusual shell, curled into a comma, swirled with pink and palest brown, broken-off tips touched with a faded orange. She tucked it into her pocket to give to Libby.

...

Evonne made an appointment to see Ivan Lawless at his office a few days later. This time she took Libby along for moral support. The day was stifling and Evonne squirmed in her itchy clothes. The heat beat down onto the concrete of the car park, reflecting from windshields and plate-glass shopfronts.

'God, I hate summer. Can't wait for it to get cooler.'

Libby smiled. 'Yes, and then you'll be complaining about the cold. Can't you take off that jacket?'

'No. This top's sleeveless.'

'Oh,' said Libby, 'right.'

'My arms?' Evonne elaborated, as if that explained her predicament.

Ivan Lawless was indeed a big man, much heavier than Dave Blackburn, his short-sleeved shirt straining at the seams and around the buttons, his gut hanging over his belt, his short arms covered in a thick matting of black hair and ending in callused hands with bitten-down nails. His body odour was unpleasant, only thinly masked by a cheap cologne. The real estate office had the uncomfortable, lukewarm temperature of air-conditioning struggling to cope. Ivan Lawless was brusque, no-nonsense. He sprawled his bulk across most of the visitors' couch, while Evonne and Libby perched on separate chairs.

'Now then, ladies, a drink? Tea? Coffee? Water?'

'No, thank you,' said Evonne. Libby shook her head.

'What can I do for you then? Alana said it had something to do with my father?'

'Yes.' Evonne hesitated, unsure how to broach the subject. 'Is your father … is he still …' Her words petered out and Libby finished for her.

'Is your father still with us?' she asked.

'Yes, yes of course, Dad's still hanging in there. Not doing so well, though. He's in a nursing home over at Albany Creek. One of those three-stage places. He's in the last stage. Full-care, round-the-clock nursing. Very good place. He's been there for, what, must be eight years now. Started off in a unit, but then he had a fall and you know what that's like, you break a hip that's a death sentence when you're his age. Never really walked after that. We get over as often as we can. He likes to see the littlies, though they tear around there like nobody's business. Staff are always yelling at them to quieten down. Sorry, how do you know him again?'

'Oh, we don't. Well, I think my father might have. Some time ago.'

'Of course. What did you say your name was?'

'Whittaker. Evonne Whittaker. My father was Daniel Whittaker. He just passed away recently …' Evonne stopped speaking as Ivan Lawless paled. He started coughing, first into his hand and then into a handkerchief that he pulled from his trouser pocket. He gasped for breath, reached for a glass of water on the side table and took a gulp. Finally, he spoke.

'Daniel bloody Whittaker. You're kidding me.' He marched over to his desk and sat heavily on his office chair. 'Alana!' he yelled. 'Bloody useless girl. Get their last name. I'm always telling her.' He pushed his chair forward with a scrape. The people nearby were staring, and a young woman – Alana, Evonne presumed – was cowering behind the reception desk. 'We're done here. I have nothing to say to you. And you're certainly not getting anywhere near my father.'

Evonne started to babble and Libby shushed her with a hand on her arm.

'I gather your father and Evonne's father didn't get along,' she said gently. 'We know nothing about that. I'm sorry. This is obviously upsetting for you. But it's taken us a while to track you down. Won't you at least listen to what we've got to say?'

Ivan Lawless swallowed some more water.

'Please,' Evonne added. She took a tissue from her bag and blew her nose. 'I know Dad could be difficult. I don't know what went on between him and your father but ...' She placed an envelope on the table. 'I know it sounds odd, but according to Dad's will, we've got to deliver these letters, to about a dozen different people, and your father's name is on this one, and, well ...'

Ivan Lawless swung his chair from side to side as he appraised the two women. He scowled at the envelope.

'Dad's not in any shape to be receiving letters from anyone, let alone your bloody father. I've got power of attorney; I look after all his affairs. Whatever it is, he probably wouldn't understand it anyway. And I've got absolutely no intention of upsetting him.'

Evonne and Libby exchanged a glance.

'Well,' said Evonne, 'in that case, I think we're authorised to give the letter to you, on your father's behalf. That's what our lawyer told us. If you'll accept it, of course.'

People had returned to their phones and computers. Alana had disappeared into a back room.

The man sighed. 'All right then. Hand it over.' He reached across the desk and Evonne passed him the envelope. 'Am I supposed to open it now or what?'

'That's up to you,' said Evonne. 'You can do it after we've gone, of course, in private. It's entirely up to you.'

He tapped the corner of the envelope on the desk and gave them a hard stare. 'But you're both curious about what's in here, aren't you.'

'Well …' said Evonne.

'Yes,' said Libby firmly. 'Yes, we are.'

'Oh, what the hell.' He ripped open the envelope and removed a single handwritten sheet, with a smaller piece of paper stapled to the back. He read in silence, his lips moving. He stared at the documents for quite a long while before placing them on the desk.

'Well, that's some turn-up for the bloody books, I must say.'

Evonne waited for him to continue.

'Let me explain something to you. Fifty years ago, give or take, your father cheated my old man out of some money. A lot of money. Something to the tune of twenty-five thousand dollars. Whittaker took advantage of the fact that they had fought together in the tropics, made out they were mates. Got Dad caught up in a fraudulent investment scheme, buying and selling postage stamps and foreign currency. They were both returned servicemen – Dad trusted him. Your father had it all figured out. How to turn a few dollars of his own money into mega bucks with the help of a poor sap like my dad who fell for his claptrap. Something about the Axis states having to create new postal and financial systems, and blokes over here being able to make a fortune if they could get their hands on the old stuff. All bullshit, of course. It was worthless, all of it. Took him for everything he had. All he'd saved towards a house, everything Mum had inherited from her folks. Gone. All gone. They never saw a penny.'

Evonne dropped her gaze to the desk under his withering glare. 'I'm … I don't know what to say. I had no idea. I'm … I'm sorry.'

'Yeah, well, sorry doesn't really cut it. My father was a broken man for quite some years. He had to start again from scratch. Built himself back up, but. Did it honestly, too. No help from anyone.'

Evonne felt stunned. 'I'm so sorry,' she repeated.

'Huh,' Ivan Lawless muttered. 'Well, looks like Whittaker might've had a change of heart in his old age.' He picked up the papers and waved them at Evonne. 'He's written a letter of apology, of sorts. Not that Dad is compos mentis enough to comprehend it. Still.' He ripped off the small piece of paper, and Evonne now saw it was a cheque. 'And he's had a bit of a laugh, too.' He slapped the cheque down on the desk and said in a mocking tone: 'This should help with the nursing-home costs.'

Evonne couldn't make out the figure, and fumbled for her reading glasses.

'Says here it's for two hundred and fifty thousand,' said Ivan Lawless, stabbing a stubby finger at the cheque. 'If this is some sort of joke, it's in very poor taste.'

She reached for the cheque. 'May I?'

Ivan Lawless pushed it towards her. She examined it, both sides. It was from her father's bank. It was her father's signature. It was indeed made out to Nigel Lawless for the amount of two hundred and fifty thousand dollars. She handed it back, the sounds of the room echoing in her ears.

'It's no joke,' she said. 'I believe it's genuine. If Dad made out a cheque to your father for that amount, then that's what he must have felt he owed him for whatever ... whatever wrongs he did back then.'

'Plus inflation,' added Libby helpfully.

Ivan Lawless stared at them again then whistled through his teeth. 'Son of a bitch,' he said. 'Son. Of. A. Bitch.'

...

Evonne and Libby made it back to their car before their nervous energy dissipated into a fit of undignified giggles.

'Oh. My. God.'

'Did you see his face when he realised?'

'He didn't know whether to throw us out or hug us.'

Evonne sighed. 'I can't believe I knew nothing about any of that. Never heard a whiff. I wonder if Richard knows anything about it?'

'I doubt it. He would've said. Probably would've tried to deliver that envelope himself, if he'd known.'

'Yeah, taken the cheque out and just handed over the apology.'

An unaccountable sense of relief washed over Evonne. 'It was a pretty good feeling, wasn't it, giving that amount of money to someone. I mean, I know Dad took it in the first place, but they obviously never thought they were getting it back. And now, today, to be able to ... oh, it's like winning the lottery or something, on behalf of someone else.'

'Your dad was a dark horse, hey. Wonder how long that cheque's been sitting in that envelope, waiting to see the light of day. It'll make a bit of a hole in your inheritance, won't it?'

'Actually, Dad had a lot more than I would've imagined. Those thousands he fleeced from Nigel Lawless must have gone on to fund the wealth he finished up with. Money makes more money, right? Maybe without that dodgy deal, he wouldn't have made it so far.'

'Hmm, maybe. Hard to know.'

'Still. Good that he felt he had to put it right. Though why he couldn't have done it while he was alive, I don't know.' She turned the key in the ignition and reached across to lay her hand on Libby's thigh. They looked out into the marshalling dusk of the evening. People hurried to and fro; a group of kids on skateboards shouted to each other over the thrum of the engine.

Libby opened the window a crack and swatted at a buzzing mosquito until it slipped out into the twilight.

'Maybe he couldn't face the guy himself. Didn't want to have to do any explaining. Jeez, I wonder what else is going to be in those envelopes. If he's handing out hundreds of thousands of dollars in cheques to all twelve of them, there really won't be anything left for you three.'

Evonne smiled. The air-conditioning kicked in, and she shrugged off her jacket. 'You know what? I don't think I'd really care. After all the stress of going to see that fellow, and then the high that came from watching him realise it was true, I think it was worth every cent.'

...

Evonne could have scripted Richard's reaction, right down to his blustering and posturing and ranting at John Hardcastle. Her brother had called an emergency meeting when she had told him about the result of her first envelope.

'This can't be legal, can it, John? I mean, that cheque was dated over ten years ago.'

They were gathered in the solicitor's office once more. The carriage clock still ticked repetitively; the pigeons still squabbled and hustled on the window ledge.

'I think you'll find the banks will still accept it, given that it was dated after 1998. Especially as it's accompanied by that explanatory letter. And besides,' John added, 'Daniel did prepare me for the fact that there might be some as yet unclaimed payments to be deducted from the estate.'

'This is … preposterous.' Richard sank to his chair. 'What if there're cheques like this in the other letters? Making up for Dad's "mistakes"? Where does that leave us?'

'For goodness sake, Richard,' said Kelly. 'Dad left us more than enough. You should be more outraged that he was involved in that scheme – sounds like a criminal act, or negligent, at the very least.'

'So Lawless says.'

'And so Dad says himself. He admits it in the letter. There's no pretending it didn't happen.' Kelly was glaring at Richard, clutching the silver pendant that nestled at the base of her throat and running it back and forth along its chain. 'All that business with Japanese currency and whatever. God. Dad *hated* the Japanese. Couldn't stand to hear about them buying land over here. He didn't even have any patience with the tourists.'

'Is it any wonder, when he was in the war? How would you feel, watching people who'd tortured your mates, killed them? Swanning over to Australia for their honeymoons?'

Evonne had had enough: she didn't want talk of the war or their father's part in it to threaten or overshadow their purpose.

'Listen to me, Richard. I saw the look on that poor man's face,

Ivan Lawless, when he spoke about how this had affected his father. He's lived with that his whole life. And when he realised what we had brought him – not just the cheque but the apology too – he was … he was restored. That's the only word that comes to mind. It was like Libby and I had given him a great gift.'

'Yes, a quarter-of-a-million-dollar gift. Why wouldn't he look happy.'

'It's his money. He had a right to it. And if what Dad said is true – and there's no reason to disbelieve it, especially when Ivan Lawless is telling us the same story – then I for one think Dad did the right thing paying it back to him. And I'll tell you another thing.' She paused. 'Giving him that money, knowing I'd in some small way acknowledged what had happened to his father, that gave me more pleasure than I've had in a long time.' She gave her brother a tight smile.

'Maybe that's why Dad wanted one of us to do it, and not him,' said Kelly. 'Perhaps he wants us to experience something through this process, something … good.'

'What rubbish,' snapped Richard. 'Dad was just too cowardly to own up to this when he was alive and now he's left it to us to sort out his messes for him. I can't wait to see what's in store next.' He grabbed his briefcase and strode out the door, slamming it so hard that the window rattled, and the pigeons scattered in a flurry of feathers.

...

That night Evonne woke in darkness to the rumble of thunder, deep vibrations that shook her from sleep as if a giant hand had taken hold of the house. Flashes of lightning strobed across the window panes. The rain began as a pattering on the tin roof of the shed next door, gaining in intensity until it was an orchestra of sound, resonating in her ears. She inhaled the earthy aroma of the rain, the trapped humidity released from the soil, the tang of the eucalypts, the rich musk of nature washed clean.

She stretched out her arm against the bare sheet on the other side of the bed. Inhaled again, searching, until a whiff of smoke reached her.

On the deck, Libby was a dark shape against the darker background of night. The tip of her cigarette glowed red in the shadowy light. The lightning flashed again, although the rain had abruptly slowed to a steady drip, the clouds shifting and moving across the sky. Libby turned to see Evonne watching her from the doorway.

'Scoot over.' Evonne shuffled forward and sat next to Libby on the bench, wrinkling her nose against the smoke. 'You know that's going to kill you.'

'Yeah, I know. This or something else.'

Evonne rested her head on Libby's shoulder. They stared out together into the gloom. The bush surrounds were dense and opaque. Above the canopy, though, the dim receded, giving way to the maw of the open sky, pinioned by a swathe of glittering stars, made only more impressive when backlit by the explosions of white light that burst at random intervals, illuminating all around them – the deck, the back of the house, the neighbour's Hills hoist – with an abrupt image like a photographic negative, the trees suddenly pale and ghostly. Another roll of thunder reverberated, echoing through the reserve. The rain became heavier again, thrumming on the boards, rivulets sluicing down the rails.

'Just thinking about when Mum died,' said Libby. She exhaled a plume of smoke that disappeared into the rainy gusts. 'Clearing out the house. Remember?'

'Oh God, how could I forget,' said Evonne. 'That's a few weekends of my life I'll never get back.'

Libby gave her a playful punch on the arm. 'It wasn't that bad.'

Evonne laughed. 'The wonders of selective memory. You know I loved your mum, but you can't pretend you've forgotten what a tip that place was.'

They sat in silence for a few seconds.

'She did have quite a lot of stuff,' said Libby, in a deadpan voice.

Evonne laughed again. 'Oh. My. God. Libby. How many skips did we fill? The local Vinnies was all ready to make her their patron saint.'

'Yeah, I know. She had a bit of trouble throwing things away.'

'And don't forget she was stocking up for Armageddon. Remember the paper towels? The toilet paper? The soap?'

'Mm-hmm. The detergent. The candles.'

'The *sanitary products*,' they croaked in unison, laughing.

Libby stubbed out her cigarette. 'Ah well. Mum liked to be prepared. For herself, and on behalf of everyone else. Heaven forbid we should run out of tinned beans. Anyway, it wasn't that stuff I was thinking about so much, it was the personal things.'

'Like what?'

'Oh, I don't know. Little things. The bits and pieces she had hidden away. Like all that old jewellery. Remember we found that cupboard with all those jewellery cases?'

'That's right. I'd forgotten that. Well, you've got that rose-gold locket, haven't you.'

'Yeah. And Linda took some nice silver. But do you remember how the good stuff was mixed up with all those tacky costume trinkets? Fake pearls and glass beads. Side by side with the gold and silver. And her sapphire engagement ring, remember? Everything packed away with the same amount of care.'

'Well, I suppose each piece was special when she got it.'

'Exactly. That's what I was sitting here thinking about. How every single necklace and bracelet and ring would have been a gift from someone, or left to her by someone special to her, someone older, someone I wouldn't even have known.'

'Or perhaps bought herself with her own hard-earned cash.'

'Right. A memory attached to every stone, every pair of earrings. And then she dies, and we all go in there and rifle through her most personal possessions, and we just … divvy it up. We don't know any of the stories, do we, we just sort through according to what appeals to our taste at the time, and the rest, we just chucked it, didn't we? Gave it to Vinnies.'

'You can't keep everything,' said Evonne, with a wry smile.

'I know. I just … it seems such a shame that when she was still alive, she didn't share with us what it all meant for her, where each piece had come from, the history behind it, why it was special. It would've been nice to know which things Mum treasured. Which meant the most to her. And not just her jewellery. Everything she owned – vases, paintings, books – it would have all come with a story.' She sighed. 'Stories I'll never know now.'

Evonne squeezed her arm. 'It was thirty years ago, love,' she said gently.

Libby sniffed and wiped her eyes. 'I know. I know. It was all a long time ago.'

RICHARD AND JEMIMA'S HOME WAS a magnificent renovated Queenslander snuggled into a curve of the Brisbane River. The gardens were only just recovering after being inundated in the 2011 floods. All the landscaper's careful work – rockeries, hedged beds filled with colourful blooms, perfect white stones surrounding a stand of black bamboo – everything had gone under. When the waters receded, the damage was done. Havoc wreaked. An angry brown snake in the spa. Clothing and disposable nappies and tools and a suitcase, all kinds of rubbish. Richard had been livid. He simply could not believe that the forces of nature had conspired against him in so cruel a manner, invading his personal space, drowning his gardens, damaging his stonework, dirtying his carefully manicured lawns.

'Mind you, could have been worse,' Evonne had said. She'd reminded him that his neighbour had found a cow sprawled on the snooker table in the downstairs rumpus room, one leg stuck fast in a ball pocket, the poor animal's bloated belly split open, insides glistening. Took three men to move her. 'I'm not sure you would have coped well with that,' she'd added, and Richard hadn't liked the snide tone to her voice.

This year, after an early summer in which nothing flourished, the rains had returned and revived the landscape. Richard had been preoccupied reading about the unease that the storms caused for some, their memories of floodwaters close to the surface and lightly bidden. He felt the same anxiety. He'd just spent a small fortune restoring his garden to its former glory.

From his study, he could hear Violetta and Victoria out in the yard, playing hide and seek. His father had always forced the grandchildren outdoors. 'Outside!' he would shout. 'Go!' How the world had changed since his father had been a boy, roaming around the neighbourhood in bare feet, collecting bugs and chasing dogs, playing with his brother and sister, Geoff and Mary. Poor old Aunty Mary would be eighty-two now. She had been an artist, but these days her hands were twisted with arthritis, her knuckles like the gnarled stumps of an ageing tree. Unable to hold a pencil. Too shaky to draw a straight line. Her mind twisted, too, with the dementia that claimed her senses.

At the funeral, she had not seemed to know what was happening. Her grandchildren and her nephews and nieces had gathered around her in a huddle, distracting her, distancing her from the purpose of the day. Richard had only discerned one lucid moment. She had found her way to him at the wake, after her cup of tea and before she was whisked back to her nursing home.

'Daniel,' she had breathed, clutching at his hand with her lumpen fingers.

'Richard,' he had replied. 'It's Richard, Aunty Mary.' He had placed his own hand over hers.

Her eyes had filled with tears. 'Richard. Of course. Daniel's eldest.' She passed him her teacup with a shaking hand and felt for a handkerchief, hidden in her bra. 'Dear boy. How you'll miss him. Your father.' She wiped at her eyes. 'He was a good brother,' she said simply. 'A good man. It's a pity so much went wrong for him.'

At that moment, one of her grandchildren appeared to help her out to a waiting car, and Richard was left holding her half-empty teacup, contemplating what had gone wrong for his father, and why, particularly, his sister had thought he was a good man.

...

Jemima opened the door to Richard's study and gave a start of surprise.

'Oh, you're still here. I thought you'd gone into work.'

'Decided to stay home today.'

'Good.' She wrapped her arms around him. 'You work too hard during the week. No need to be in there on weekends as well.' She glanced at his tidy desk, devoid of bank papers or, he realised, any work-related material. She lifted the half-full tumbler of clear liquid and brought it to her nose. 'Isn't it a bit early for this?'

He took it from her hand. 'That's from yesterday.' He turned his back so she wouldn't see his expression. 'Just gathering my thoughts,' he stuttered. 'About this whole business with Dad's estate.' He slammed the glass on his desk, harder than he meant to.

'You're really not taking this well, are you?' Jemima remarked drily.

'I think I'm taking it as well as could be expected.'

'I know you, Richard. You like to be in control.'

'I like to know what's happening, if that's what you mean.'

59

Jemima turned her back, stepped towards the wall and straightened a picture frame. 'I ran into Virginia Braithwaite yesterday. Is it true you've consulted with Donald?'

'What I discuss with Donald Braithwaite is none of his wife's business,' Richard snapped. Jemima raised her eyebrows. 'Sorry,' he said. 'I'd rather Evonne and Kelly didn't know.' He exhaled. 'Nothing came of it, anyway. Braithwaite backed up Hardcastle. Said it's all sound.'

'I didn't know you were questioning its legitimacy,' said Jemima. 'Anyway, there's no use putting up a fuss about it. Just get on with it.'

'Easy for you to say.'

Jemima moved forward and pecked him on the cheek. Richard inhaled the cinnamon scent from her hair, the faint trace of Dior on her neck. Their relationship had caused a small scandal in the family at first, Jemima being two years younger than his daughters from his first marriage. But his older twins had embraced her like a sister: Richard never sensed a shred of jealousy or resentment. And when the second lot of twins arrived – his and Jemima's girls – it seemed to cement everyone's feelings for each other as family.

'Now, what did I come in here for? Oh yes, have you seen any credit card statements? I had a call from them. Something about a late payment.'

Richard waved her question away. 'Don't worry about it. Probably a mix-up with the accounts. I'll deal with it. Give them my number. I don't want them calling and hassling you.'

'Oh. Okay. If you say so. I'll just grab these samples.' She hefted a large multi-coloured swatch book of fabric. 'I'm seeing a client at two.' Jemima was an interior decorator of some renown, although Richard could never understand people handing over such huge sums of money to allow a stranger to personalise their homes.

She hesitated at the door. 'Richard, is everything all right? At work?'

'What? Of course. I told you, I'm distracted by this will business.'

'I know this is disconcerting for you.'

'That's one way of putting it.'

Jemima gave him a tight smile and left the room.

Victoria and Violetta appeared in the garden on the other side of the French doors. They stood facing each other, their hands outstretched as they enacted a vigorous clapping and rhyming game, their sing-song voices barely audible. Richard stared at his girls and wondered, not for the first time, what life must be like as a twin. One half of a whole, always to be echoed, never to stand alone.

He knew they spoilt the girls, but he took a certain pride in it. Much better than how Kelly had managed with her lot: Ben and Kara had always looked hastily put together, their uniforms stained and un-ironed, Kara's hair a tangled mess, Ben with a perpetually torn shirt and frayed shoelaces. And Eden. Good grief, the child was feral. Ran around without shoes most of the time, wore some hippie beads around his neck. Kelly had only stopped breastfeeding him before Christmas, and he'd be four this year.

In Richard's charitable moments, he recognised the difficulty of being a single parent. His sister always seemed to be scraping together to make ends meet: hand-me-downs from friends, a new pair of shoes once each year if the kids were lucky, the cheapest exercise books and pens from the supermarket. The inheritance – when all this ridiculous business was over, and the money finally came through – would mean a lot to her.

To him, too. He wasn't sure how long he could keep up the pretext. Jemima was bound to work it out sooner or later. He just hoped the estate could be settled before she realised.

Richard knew he would have to begin work on the letters today; he couldn't put it off any longer. That business with Lawless had thrown him. Somehow, although he knew it wasn't fair, he blamed Evonne for how that had turned out.

He turned one of the envelopes over and over in his hands. He hoped there wasn't another cheque hiding inside it.

Perhaps I should just check how the shares are going, he thought, but stopped himself. 'Coward,' he muttered.

Instead he typed the name Margaret Sonnet into a search engine and waited. Thousands of references appeared, mostly in relation to Shakespeare.

Blast it all, he thought, and only just resisted the temptation to rip open the flimsy paper. But no. If Evonne could do it, he could do it. How hard could it be to find someone? Especially in this day and age when you left your digital footprint everywhere you went.

He poured another whisky and added ice from the mini-bar built in under the sideboard. The warm liquid slipped down his throat and heated his belly. His father had not liked whisky, never developed a taste for it. Another thing about which they disagreed.

Maybe Sonnet wasn't a last name but a clue. Perhaps this Margaret had something to do with poetry? He went through the search results and finally came across an old entry, dated several years earlier.

Known as Margaret Sonnet, eighty-three-year-old Margaret Bergman was a fixture on the corner of Edward and Queen streets …

Bingo! he thought.

He clicked on the expanded version.

A Brisbane woman known for her musical and poetic talent – despite being homeless for many years – has passed away peacefully at the Salvation Army Care Home in Windsor.

Known as Margaret Sonnet, eighty-three-year-old Margaret Bergman was a fixture on the corner of Edward and Queen streets for over thirty years, reciting poetry and playing Jewish doina violin music. Born in a small Romanian town north of Bucharest, she came to Australia to escape the Holocaust, which took the lives of fourteen members of her extended family.

Salvation Army Chaplain Major Clarke Brown said that Ms Bergman's loss would be felt deeply by all those whose lives she had touched.

'Margaret was homeless for many years before she came to reside with us, but even in that dark time in her life she brought joy to many through her music and her poetry,' he said. 'She always said that music made her feel closer to those she had lost.'

Ms Bergman is survived by a niece.

Richard rested his head in his hands. *Great*, he thought. *A Jewish Holocaust survivor. Just great.*

...

Later that evening, Richard lay on the white leather lounge while Jemima mixed him a scotch and soda.

'But what's the connection?' he asked for the third time. 'I mean, what could Dad have possibly had in common with this Sonnet person?'

'Don't get het up, darling.'

'Don't tell me not to get het up. I'm already het up. I've got a migraine coming. I can feel it.'

Jemima picked up her pencil and continued to shade her sketch. 'You've got to calm down. Getting yourself all worked up isn't going to make things any easier.'

'Easy for you to say. You don't have your mad dead father asking you to complete impossible tasks.'

'Evonne managed all right.'

'Oh yes, Evonne managed to give away a huge portion of our inheritance without any trouble at all.'

'Now, be fair, Richard. That was your father's decision, not hers.'

He rubbed his temples. 'I don't understand what's required of me. What am I supposed to do, approach this woman's niece? And say what? Bugger this. Bugger, bugger. It's just like my father to keep all these nasty surprises until after he's gone and then leave us to sort out his messes for him.'

'That's not how Evonne saw it.'

'What do you mean?'

'Well, you heard her describe the feeling she got from the whole thing with Ivan Lawless. She felt good to be able to do something about it. She told me it was like being given permission to right a wrong. To do something worthwhile.'

'Huh. She might feel okay about giving away a quarter of a million, but I know I won't.'

'You don't know that this is anything to do with money. Maybe your father just liked her music.'

'Unlikely. Oh, my head. Grab me some painkillers, Jem, this migraine's really kicking off now.'

As Jemima left the room, Richard remembered again with a pang that it had been she – not he – who had last seen his father alive. She had dropped around a bouquet of flowers from the markets the day before he died, had made him a cup of tea.

Richard had asked her what they had spoken of, as they sat together.

'This and that,' she'd replied. 'The election results. The girls' ballet. What to do about that strange fungus that was creeping over his bottlebrush and tea-trees. I said I thought it was myrtle rust.'

'He didn't say anything … you know … significant?'

'No, darling, he didn't. If I'd known what was to come … well, I suppose we might have discussed rather different topics. But you never know, do you. Every conversation could be your last.'

Her words had not been of any comfort to Richard.

'If it's any consolation,' she had continued, 'he seemed … content. And that's all any of us can hope for, isn't it? In the end, that's all that matters.'

He pondered whether his father – or he himself – had ever been truly content. If either of them even knew what that meant.

Here, in his study, looking out over his carefully shaped garden and beyond to the river, Richard had always felt safe, secure. For years, this beautiful view – a living, moving artwork framed by his French doors – had seemed to be the culmination of his destiny as the first-born, the only son, the eventual heir. Although his father had once tried to tell him it was all a matter of genetic roulette – of chance and luck and the hand of an arbitrary, unseen God – his mother had treated him specially, and even more so after that Christmas when Kelly had choked on the marble. For some reason, Kelly was always a source of frustration to his mother, while Evonne was distant and withdrawn. Richard had known he was her favourite, and he had exploited it.

He recalled a day, like so many others, when Evonne was busy completing a long list of chores their mother had written down for her, all to be done before she was allowed to retreat to her room to read. He could see her, heaving washing from the laundry, mopping the floor, dusting the ornaments in the living room.

'What are you looking at?' Evonne had snapped.

'You,' he had replied smugly. 'Working.'

'Well, you could get off your fat backside and help, instead of lounging around doing nothing.'

'I'm not doing nothing. I'm contemplating what I should wear tonight to impress my new lady friend.'

Evonne had snorted in exasperation. 'You're so bloody spoilt, Richard,' she had said. But he had seen it as his birthright, being the oldest, and a boy.

And now, so many years later, it wasn't as though he hadn't worked hard to have everything he owned. His banking career had taken him to the top, with an executive assistant, two secretaries and a team of more than two hundred staff. He had earned the respect and admiration of every one of those employees through long hours, difficult deals brokered, and sheer determination. He had found his place in the world.

Until recent events.

Now he was practically begging for any bit of contract work to be thrown his way. Hiding from Jemima the fact that he had been retrenched more than six months ago. Pretending to go into work when he was only managing his stocks and shares, and trying to retain his dignity. He had enough secrets of his own, enough ugly truths to hide, without having to deal with his father's as well.

...

Margaret Bergman's niece lived in a cottage on acreage halfway between the tiny communities of Dayboro and Samford. Richard had managed to track her down through the Salvos. He drove his

Audi through the dust along the dirt road, cursing every time a shower of gravel peppered the car.

The landscape was dry, wide open and empty. Nothing but trees and hillocks, fences, bent road signs and cattle. The continuous white line disappeared under the bonnet of his vehicle, the sometimes-crumpled guard rails warning him against the nearness of the drop. When Richard rolled down the car window, the air was cooler here, and smelt fresher, more piquant: eucalypts and honey, cow dung and hay.

Katherine Mosely was a thin, bird-like woman in her late fifties. She ushered Richard into her cramped living room and served him hot scones with homemade jam and thick dollops of cream.

'Sorry 'bout the mess,' she explained, waving one twig-like arm at the drop sheets over some of the furniture, the opened paint tins on the floor, the pile of stacked lumber. 'Doing a bit of renovating. Can't seem to stay with the one job, though. I get started on one thing and then I get side-tracked. You know how it is.'

Richard didn't know how it was but he chose to nod sympathetically. He was perched on the edge of a worn sofa covered in what looked like dog hair.

'Hard being on my own, you know. But I'm getting there. Soon have the water on again.' She gave him a proud smile.

'Anyway, you don't want to hear me natter on. You've come about Aunty Margaret, you said?'

'Yes,' said Richard, through a mouthful of scone, which he had to admit was delicious. 'As I explained on the phone, my father passed away recently and ...' He was interrupted by Katherine Mosely jumping to her feet.

'Hold on, stop right there. Before you go on, I've got something for you.'

She dashed from the room and returned with a small black gemstone.

'Here. This is for you.'

Richard took the stone. It seemed to be the deepest black, but when he held it to the light it was transparent. 'Um, thank you. Uh … what is it?'

'Black obsidian. The grieving stone. It'll be just what you need, what with your father passing. Carry it around with you. Tell it your sadnesses, let it absorb all those negative emotions. It may even get cloudy, depending on how blocked up you are. But it'll go clear again once your grieving's done.'

'Right,' said Richard. 'Right. Well, thank you. I've never seen one before. It's quite … unusual.'

'You're welcome. It's my pleasure. I've kept mine on me every day since Aunty Margaret died. Done me the world of good.'

Good grief, thought Richard. *Crystal healing. What next.*

'Anyway,' he continued, 'as I was saying, my father left a letter addressed to a Margaret Sonnet and I believe it may be your aunt. Under the terms of the will, I am instructed to deliver it to her. Or, in the case of her death, to her surviving relatives.'

'That would be me.'

'It seems so, yes.'

Katherine Mosely's eyes began to shine and she looked past Richard's shoulder to an unseen point, with a countenance that suggested she was far away.

'Fourteen, we lost.'

Richard didn't know what to say.

'Fourteen. Fifteen if you count my mum, and I blame her death on the war as surely as if she'd stepped into the gas chambers herself. Malnourished she was; never had a strong constitution. Plus the grief. Losing her parents. She only lasted a couple of years after she immigrated here before it got the best of her. Then there was only me and Aunty Margaret left. 'Course, she suffered more than me. She lost her husband and both her husband's parents, too. "A blessing I never had children," she used to say. I couldn't understand that at first, but I do now. And all her brothers – all taken away on trains and she never saw them again. Just her and my mother left. Uncles, aunts, all gone.'

She pulled a lace handkerchief from her sleeve and wiped at her eyes. Richard could hear the lowing of cattle. A tractor starting up.

'She and Mum were both in their early twenties when they arrived in Australia. When Mum got pregnant with me she was already losing her mind to grief, and when she passed, Aunty Margaret looked after me like her own. I owe my life to her, really.'

Richard shifted in the uncomfortable silence. What did he know of grief and loss on this scale? He had a holiday house on the Sunshine Coast and daughters in private school, and two more adult daughters who came to him when they needed money. What did he know of the sufferings of a generation? A whole class of people decimated? How could he possibly comprehend the bleakness, the utter sorrow?

'I'm so sorry,' he muttered, aware of the inadequacy of his remark.

Katherine Mosely managed a smile. 'It's all right. People never know what to say. You're not alone there. There's nothing you *can* say that will help. The Holocaust was an enormous act of inhumanity, pure and simple. Man's inhumanity to man … who said that? That was perfected during the war. Evil on a grand scale.'

Richard clawed around desperately for a way to move the conversation away from the Holocaust. He could sense the envelope burning a hole in his jacket pocket, and he fervently wished that he did not have to deliver whatever news it carried.

'So, I heard your aunt was homeless for a while. Why didn't she live here, with you?'

Katherine stilled and looked down at her hands, her fingers twisting a heavy silver ring around her thumb.

'Margaret could be … difficult.'

Aha, thought Richard, satisfied that he had found a hole in her sob story. He had been feeling decidedly sorry for this Mosely woman, but now he sat a little straighter in his chair. What did he have to feel bad about? He hadn't led this woman's relatives into the gas chambers. He hadn't massacred her family. His own father had fought in the war, even if he had never talked about it.

Kelly's daughter, Kara, regularly locked horns with him about this issue – what she called the 'collective guilt' of past generations, their failure to properly atone. For the world wars, climate change, capitalism, the treatment of Aboriginal people by the colonists. Richard felt he could hold his own in any argument about his rights, but she did get under his skin. Nonetheless, he certainly bore no responsibility for the mistakes of his ancestors, or the state of Aboriginal affairs, or – for that matter – the horror of the Holocaust, and he'd be damned if Katherine Mosely could pull a Kara on him and make him squirm as if he did. No: this woman had left her own aunt homeless, for God's sake.

'Difficult?' he echoed. 'So difficult that she couldn't live here with you, but ended up on the streets?'

She returned his even gaze. 'My aunt was mentally unbalanced, Mr Whittaker. There were times in her life when she felt unable to live in a conventional house, unable to enjoy a normal family life. She felt enormous guilt, you see. She couldn't understand why she

70

had lived when so many around her had fallen. Why she could still breathe and sing and write poetry and play music when her whole family … She felt she should suffer, as those she loved had suffered.'

'Right,' said Richard, somewhat chastened. 'I see.'

The tractor sounded closer now, revving in great grumbles as it strained against some unseen burden.

'It was not for want of trying, you understand. Those years when she refused to live with me, when she wouldn't allow me to help her, the months that went by when I couldn't even communicate with her, those times were extremely difficult for me. Very frustrating. But I think I reminded her of my mother. I reminded her of all she'd lost. She found that very hard.'

Once again, Richard found he had no words. Extraordinary, really, the stories of some people's lives. For a moment he felt abashed for misjudging her. He heard again Kara's voice ringing in his ears, and he felt unexpectedly humbled by his own good fortune, and even a little ashamed.

It was only a moment, however, and it soon passed. He reminded himself he had absolutely no reason to feel guilty. He just wanted to hand over the damn letter and get out of there. He pulled it out of his pocket and placed it on the coffee table.

Katherine Mosely cleared away the tea things and came back with a silver letter opener. She sliced open the envelope, extracted the single sheet of paper within and began to read in silence.

Richard said a secret word of thanks that there didn't appear to be a cheque attached.

She refolded the letter and held it loosely in her lap. Richard could not read her expression but she didn't appear to be angry, which was something.

After a decent interval, he stuttered: 'May I see it?'

At the sound of his voice, Katherine seemed to return from wherever it was her mind had gone. 'Of course. Of course. I was just thinking about Aunty Margaret's music. It was so melancholy, but utterly beautiful.'

She handed the paper to Richard and he read his father's sloping script:

Dear Ms Bergman (Sonnet) –

You don't know me. My name is Daniel Whittaker and the fact that you are reading this means that I have passed away, gone from this world to the next.

For more years than I care to remember, I walked past you on the street corner in the city as you played your sad and moving music. I knew from looking at you that you were in straitened circumstances but, to my great regret, not once did I stop to place coins in your violin case. To my even greater humiliation, not once did I take the time to stop and tell you how much your music meant to me; and not just to me but to all those who passed you each day. You carried the souls of the lost in your lament, and through your music you released them to be free once again. It was due to my own embarrassment and human failing that I felt unable to speak to you because of who you are and what you represent. But now, as my life draws to a close, I am mindful of those I have wronged, and I count you amongst their number.

Like you, I witnessed some terrible things during the war. Oh, I am not comparing my fate to yours, nothing of the sort. Your suffering is incomparable. But I did see the misery war brings: injuries that changed lives, and emotional scars that were forever a burden.

Though we didn't know each other, our stories were joined in some small way by that great act of horror, our souls both touched by the fear of evil.

Your exquisite music captivated me every day I heard it. Through your music, I was given a glimpse of those absent. You gave meaning and remembrance to those gone.

I do not think that those who have not experienced war can ever fully comprehend the tragedy. But your music speaks across boundaries and languages, it bridges the gap between the young and the old, it sings a song of another time.

I am not a poet — that is yet another of your extraordinary abilities — but I hope I have managed to convey my sincere and heartfelt appreciation of your talents.

Yours sincerely,
Daniel Whittaker

Richard continued to stare at the letter in his hand. Hard to believe it had come from his father, the man he knew as aloof and somewhat cold. He checked the back but it was blank. It seemed Jemima was right. His father had merely wanted to tell Margaret Sonnet that he had appreciated her music. Richard felt relieved – hugely relieved – that the letter was so innocuous. And yet … it had stirred him; these words had engulfed him and left him wanting, although he could not say how or why.

He handed the sheet to Katherine Mosely and was surprised to find sharp barbs prickling his eyelids. He blinked rapidly and turned away. She put her hand on his arm.

'It's all right, Mr Whittaker. Everything's going to be okay.'

Richard slipped his hand into his pocket and rubbed the smooth stone between his fingers; he dared to hope that she might be right.

. . .

73

Later, he sat in his motionless car, the keys dangling from his hand. He could see the cows now, a herd of six or seven, ambling leisurely across a brown paddock, tails swishing, ears flicking against flies.

He couldn't recall the last time he had cried. Not at the births of the twins, neither the first set nor the second set. Not when his mother died. He was not normally given to emotions. He vaguely recalled wiping his eyes at his father's graveside, but he would hardly call that tearing up. Took after his father, he supposed, although if that letter was anything to go by, his father had been a bit of a dark horse in the emotions department. Who would've thought.

Richard conjured again his father's words. Margaret Sonnet's music certainly had an effect on him, all those years ago. He described her violin as if it spoke in a language all its own.

His father should have told her before, when he was alive, thought Richard. Should have told her how much her music meant to him.

But if Richard had passed Margaret Sonnet on the street corner and heard her sorrowful lament? Borne witness to her suffering and loss? Would he have opened his mouth to express any words of appreciation? Of admiration and enjoyment? Would he have breached the gap of human experience with a bridge of gratitude?

On balance, he thought not.

He wondered if it was too late.

KELLY SAT CROSS-LEGGED ON THE sagging daybed and blew across the surface of her tea. The scorching heat seemed, thankfully, to be over. Although the days were still hot and sticky, the early mornings and late afternoons were cool. This morning there had even been dew on a spider's web spun neatly between two rafters.

Eden lay on his stomach on the floorboards, colouring in with crayons, his teeth crushing his bottom lip in concentration. Kelly looked at her son – his mop of unruly, dark curls, his perfect compact little body. She thought back to one of the last conversations she had ever had with her father, just days before he died.

'I don't understand why you won't tell me,' he had said.

'There's no need for you to know, Dad,' she'd replied. 'No need for anyone to know.'

'Anyone? What about young Eden? What, you're not going to tell even him?'

And she had explained to him, yet again, that Eden's father had been a short-lived romance, a fling, nothing of note. She often marvelled that her bright and precious child had come from such a brief affair.

'Eden and I are fine without him. Better off, in fact.'

'But surely the fellow would want to know his own son.'

'He's not interested, Dad. I've told you. And I'm not interested in him being involved.'

'What about child support? Shouldn't he be paying that, at least? You know I don't feel able – *morally* – to give you a handout when the responsibility falls fairly and squarely on this fellow. Whoever he is,' he had added pointedly.

Kelly had sighed. She had made it clear that she didn't expect her father's financial support, but that didn't seem to make any difference. No matter how many times they had this discussion, he always brought up the matter of money – just as he always pressed her about Eden's father, when she had explained that it was her decision to go ahead with the pregnancy on her own.

The reality was somewhat more convoluted: she had never told Billy of her pregnancy. It was true that they had only seen each other a handful of times. And then he had travelled overseas with his dance company, an eight-week tour of Europe, and by the time he returned, Kelly had confirmed with her doctor that she was pregnant. He had tried to see her when he got back to Australia – he had phoned and texted and called around to the house. But Kelly was experiencing a whirlwind of confusing emotions, and didn't know what to do. Why hadn't she contacted him as soon as she suspected? How could she explain why she had waited to tell him? Billy was ten years younger than her – how could she expect him to give up his career, his travelling, his ambition, to be tied down to a forty-year-old mother of two he'd only just met? And what if she told him, and then he wanted nothing more to do with her? If she allowed herself to hope, she wouldn't be able to cope with the crushing disappointment of his rejection.

Part of her had known she was overthinking it. That she was failing Billy – and possibly doing a disservice to her unborn child – by not giving him the chance to make a choice. Or to help her make a choice. But in her heart, she knew there was only one option open to her. She was going to have the baby. With or without Billy. And as the weeks and months passed, and she continued to refuse to answer his calls, somehow the decision seemed to be made for her: that he would never know.

Often she worried whether she was doing the right thing. Whether in ten years' time, with school fees and sports excursions to worry about, she would regret making such a clean break.

She had been forty-one when Eden was born. Ben and Kara had nearly finished high school, and she had been divorced for six years. How she had railed against it when Simon had left her. She couldn't comprehend what he was doing to her, to their family. Just could not get her head around the changed facts of her life. It took her years to feel courageous enough to date again. For courage it took – she hated the thought of first dates, the nervousness and anxiety around what she looked like without make-up, without clothes. She had been reticent at first, tiptoeing through the minefield, browsing through online profiles and leaving messages unanswered. And when she had finally given in, four years ago, abandoned her shyness and thrown caution to the wind, this is what had resulted. Eden. Her gift. Her whole life changed – again – in an instant.

She had suspected she was pregnant the same month her mother became ill. By the time she was showing, her mother was having trouble recognising her, let alone noticing the small person she was growing in her belly. And Shirley had been gone before Eden took his first breath.

Like Eden, Kelly had been born when her siblings were teenagers. Maybe she had sensed some sort of synchronicity, taken some comfort in the parallels. But she liked to believe that she, Ben and Kara had managed the arrival of Eden into their lives quite differently than she herself had been welcomed into her mother's arms. Kelly wondered if her mother had suffered from postnatal depression. In 1969 – who knew? The baby books were probably quiet on the subject. Her father had told her that the doctor said Shirley was physically drained, exhausted by the birth so late in life, forty-one when Kelly was born. Yet that was the same age Kelly gave birth to Eden, with no partner there to support her, and she had found those early months exhilarating and joyous.

On occasion she suspected her mother had suffered from resentment, pure and simple. Grief for the carefree life she had carved for herself with the help of her husband's money. Guilt that Daniel had carried the burden of caring for Kelly in those early years. Not that she would ever have mentioned this to her mother when she had been alive: her mother would have ejected a stream of vitriol, just as Kelly recalled her doing so often with her father. She had asked her mother once what had kept them together for so long.

'Why don't you leave him if you're so unhappy?'

'Yes, that's typical of people your age. Give up when things get difficult. Trial separations. Trial marriages. The problem isn't that the marriage has stopped working; it's that you people lack the self-discipline to continue on regardless.'

'But if both of you aren't happy, why stay together?'

'No-one ever said marriage was about happiness, young lady. Marriage is about commitment, and children, and fulfilling your vows. Happiness doesn't necessarily come into it.'

'Well, don't complain then, if you're not willing to change things.'

And her mother would sigh and shake her head. 'I should have done something years ago, I suppose. But it's too late now.'

Back then, Kelly would never have predicted that she herself would have a failed marriage. Yet, somehow, she had survived it. She had managed to manoeuvre Ben and Kara through the mire of their school years, she had shepherded them through rental houses and a messy separation and an amicable divorce, and now they were both in university, embarking on lives of their own. And though they were grown, she was happy they still lived at home. Happy for Eden to have two more adults around who loved and adored him.

Oh, Eden. Only three. She had such a long way to go with him. Sometimes she felt so tired. Weary from her work at the medical centre; emotionally drained by the energy of Ben's and Kara's social lives; exhausted by Eden's sheer physicality, his boundless curiosity, his mind wandering with a thousand questions and his little body finding ever more bizarre ways to be scraped and injured. When she thought of the fifteen or twenty years ahead, it sometimes seemed more than she could bear; but if she tried to imagine her life without him, it was unbearably devoid and barren.

He was still scrawling across his sketch book now, as Kara came out from her room. She ruffled her brother's hair. 'What you drawing, buddy?'

'Dinosaur. Roar!'

'Roar yourself. Hey, I didn't know dinosaurs breathed fire.'

'This one does. Look, Kar, he got wings too.'

'I think what you've got yourself there is a dragon, little man.' She sat beside her mother. 'Dad just rang. He's picking me up around six tonight. We're going to a movie.'

'Oh, okay. That'll be nice.'

Kara tickled the sole of Eden's bare foot. 'I don't suppose you've done anything about Grandpa's letters yet?'

'I'll have you know I've started my research already. On first-names basis with the woman at Births, Deaths and Marriages.'

'Huh. What've you found out? Got the gossip on Grandpa's secret first wife? God, I wish I'd been there to see Uncle Richard's face when he heard.'

'I know. He's already given me the talk about what I should and shouldn't say to this Irene woman. If she's even alive, which I don't think we can count on.'

'You wouldn't do what Uncle Richard told you anyway, would you?'

''Course not. But doesn't do any harm to let him prattle on and let him think I'm listening. Mind you, I think that Jewish woman softened him up a bit. Your Aunty Jem mentioned he's been carrying around some kind of grieving stone.'

'A grieving stone? So not like Uncle Richard. I wonder if Grandpa knew the things he'd be stirring up with all these secret letters.'

'Hmm. I wonder.'

. . .

After weeks of poring over the online white pages and comparing notes with official government departments, Kelly finally had the details before her for Ms Irene White of Tewantin, who was for a brief period Mrs Irene Whittaker. The records indicated that eighteen-year-old Irene had married nineteen-year-old Daniel Whittaker on the twenty-first of August, 1944. The marriage had lasted less than a year. Irene White had reverted to using her maiden name and had not married again.

Kelly tried to think back to the night her father had told her about his first wife. It was just after she and Simon had separated, and he had taken Ben and Kara for the night. Kelly had dropped around to see her father while her mother was out with friends. He'd been halfway through a decent bottle of shiraz, and before long they had finished the bottle and started on another.

It hadn't taken much for Kelly to open up, and once she'd done that, it didn't take much more for her to fall apart. She recalled going on about Simon, about how she couldn't understand why he had left, couldn't fathom how her life had gone to pieces.

'He says he's unhappy,' she cried. 'But he won't say why. Just says he's been feeling like this for a long time. Says he loves the kids. Even says he still loves me but can't stay married to me anymore.'

'You're not the first woman to have her husband leave her,' her father had helpfully noted. 'Plenty of other fish in the sea.'

But Kelly didn't want any other fish. She wanted Simon.

'You don't understand,' she'd said. 'You've been married to Mum for fifty years.'

And that was when he'd mentioned it.

'Your mum wasn't my first love, you know. I was married before.'

'Yeah, right.'

'I was. Irene, her name was. Irene White. We got hitched during the war. Was the done thing, then, you see, tie the knot quick smart in case something happened when you were off in battle. We were just kids; I was nineteen.'

'Are you serious? How come you've never said anything? Does Richard know? Evonne? Does *Mum* even know?'

'Of course your mum knows. But I don't ever want you mentioning it to her. It'll upset her.' He paused to take another drink. 'The others don't know. Never had a reason to tell them.'

'So why are you telling me now, then?'

'Because. Because Simon's left and … and I want you to know that you can start over.'

'But I don't want to start over! I want my husband back. I want my marriage back. I want my *life* back!'

She had dissolved into tears again and she vaguely recalled her father patting her on the shoulder.

'Anyway,' she mumbled, 'why did you split up? From this Irene woman.'

'Told you, we were just kids. Middle of the war. I'd been off fighting for three years already.'

Kelly stared at her father. 'But you were nineteen.'

'Yep.'

'How on earth did you get—'

Her father interrupted her. 'I lied about my age. Lots of young lads did it. Wanted to see some action before it was all over. Biggest mistake of my life. Saw things I shouldn't have seen, that no-one should ever have to see. Things I'll take to my grave.'

Kelly softened and placed her hand on her father's cool, shaking fingers. 'You never talk about it much. The war, I mean.'

'Not a lot to say that'd make any difference. Besides, I don't like remembering. Too painful.'

When she was growing up, the war had never been mentioned. Her father never drank down at the RSL club or played Two-Up on Anzac Day. Made it a point *not* to commemorate the day at all, actually. He would spend the morning out in his garden, and the afternoon napping. He clammed up whenever the spectre of war was raised.

She had been intrigued, of course. When her history teacher had given their class an assignment on Gallipoli, she had approached her father for assistance, but even though that had not even been 'his war', he had been unhelpful.

'Go to the library,' he had said. 'Read about it in a book.'

He had nurtured a deep and abiding hatred for the Japanese. Kelly could remember the one time her mother brought home takeaway sushi for dinner – such a novelty back then. Her father had taken one look and stormed out of the house without a word. When Kelly had finished school and was debating whether to travel overseas before university began, she had toyed with the idea of Japan.

'Over my dead body,' her father had said. 'We were forced to go and fight the buggers; why on earth would you want to go there for a bloody holiday?'

In his twenties, Richard had briefly considered a career in the armed forces. Kelly had been young, still in primary school, but she could still recall her father's furious response.

'Why would you want to do that, after all the education I've provided for you? All the opportunities?'

'I wouldn't be a grunt,' Richard had replied. 'I'd do some officer training. Get into admin.'

'You'd still be a fool,' Daniel had replied. 'That was why I made the sacrifices I did, so that no child of mine would have to make the same mistakes.'

'And what mistakes would those be?'

But their father had not taken the bait. He had merely shaken his head, as if his children could never understand. So on the occasion that her father opened up about Irene White, Kelly was surprised not only by his frankness about his first wife, but also by his willingness to talk about his experience as a soldier at all.

'So ... so you and ... Irene ... weren't together long?'

'Nope. We met at a dance when I was home on leave. Got married that weekend. Stayed married for just under a year, give or take. Mind you, I was only home once in that time for leave again, so we probably only had three weeks total together.'

'That's so ... sad.'

'She was a nice girl, Irene. I don't blame her.'

'Blame her ... for what?'

'For leaving me. Oh yes,' he added, at Kelly's questioning look, '*she* left *me*. Took up with some American sailor while I was watching his friends' backs in Guinea. Told me in a letter. What they used to call a "Dear John" letter.'

'Oh, Dad, that's terrible.'

'Was over before it had begun, really. I was angry, though. Boy, was I angry. But life goes on. The only reason I'm even telling you is because I want you to realise that it's not the end of the world. You'll get over Simon leaving. You'll get over it and one day you'll wake up and realise you don't even miss him anymore.'

Kelly had doubted him at the time, but now, years later, and with Eden in her life, she supposed her father had been right.

...

Irene White lived in a retirement village on the Sunshine Coast, far enough off the highway to escape the noise of traffic. Masses of scarlet bougainvillea covered her unit's fence and walls, the spiky thorns reaching out to grab the unwary, and the ocean breeze carried the scent of salt. Worried about what reaction she might receive, Kelly hadn't called ahead of time, deciding instead to drive up for the day and take her chances.

She rang the bell and waited. A shadow moved behind the front door's glass panel and someone called out: 'Just a moment.'

The door opened a crack, stopped by a chain. 'Yes?' said the elderly woman. Her clouded eyes appeared to be peering intently, but Kelly could tell that the woman wasn't seeing her at all.

'Miss White? Miss Irene White?'

'Yes, that's me. If you're selling anything, I don't want any today.'

'No, I'm not selling anything, Miss White. I've come about … I wonder if I might come in for a moment. I've come about my father. Daniel Whittaker.'

It took all her powers of persuasion to convince the elderly lady that she was who she said she was, and Kelly cursed herself for not calling first to explain. Irene White was legally blind and not in the habit of unlatching the door to anyone she didn't know.

At last, twenty minutes later, Kelly found herself seated on a comfortable chintz sofa, sipping a cup of instant coffee and nibbling on an arrowroot biscuit. Irene's room was airy and furnished sparsely. A bright yellow canary, trilling a sweet song, hopped about in a cage hung from a stand.

'All right, Petal, we can hear you.' Irene pushed a lettuce leaf through the bars of the cage, then felt her way towards her chair. 'Goodness. Daniel Whittaker. There's a name I haven't heard for many a year. I seem to remember he married a Holliday girl. Sandra? Or was it Shirley?'

'Shirley,' replied Kelly, surprised that Irene knew of her mother.

'Brisbane was a small town back then, dear,' Irene said, as if reading her thoughts. 'Everyone knew everybody else's business. How is Daniel?'

Kelly grimaced. She had assumed Irene would know. But how could she?

'Actually, Dad passed away a few months ago.'

The older woman reached her hand across in the direction of Kelly's lap. Kelly took it in her own. 'Oh dear, I'm so sorry. My condolences for your loss.'

'Thank you. He died peacefully. He was eighty-eight.'

'I know, dear. A year older than me, and I had my eighty-eighth birthday not three weeks ago. Doesn't matter though, does it. We mourn them whether they're eight or ninety-eight. Death still comes as an unexpected shock.'

Kelly felt her eyes brimming.

'And your mother? Is she still with us?'

'No. Mum passed away just over three years ago now.'

Irene White tut-tutted and patted Kelly's hand again. 'Oh, my dear child. To be orphaned at any age is never a good thing. I hope you have other family support?'

'Yes, my older brother and sister, and I have three children myself.'

'Lovely.' Irene waited for her to elaborate, but Kelly thought of how she would have to explain about Eden being so much younger, and his dad, and Simon, so she said nothing. Instead she rifled through her bag and retrieved the envelope.

'Um, when Dad died, he left some letters for us to deliver to people. There's one here addressed to you.'

'A letter from your father? Goodness. Whatever could that be about.'

'Would you like me to … to open it? To read it for you?'

'Yes, that would be lovely. Please, go ahead. Being without sight means I've had to get used to people doing things for me, you know, even strangers. But you're hardly a stranger, now, are you, and I'm sure anything Daniel has to say will be fine for your ears too.'

Kelly slit open the envelope, and something dropped onto the floor. 'There's a key in here,' she said, and placed it in Irene's hand. 'And a letter.' She began to read.

My dearest Irene,

I am reaching the end of my life, as you are reaching the end of yours. I hope that this letter finds you still in good health. I hope you have been as blessed as I have with people in your life who love you and care for you.

I am sorry that things didn't work out between us, so many years ago. We were only children ourselves, with the shadow of war at our shoulders; is it any wonder that things did not go to plan.

I was very angry with you for some time, as you know. My anger blotted out all good thoughts towards you and served only to fuel my fear and frustration.

I do hope that you found happiness with your American soldier, or if not, then with someone else. I could never bring myself to tell you so at the time, and that has been one of the biggest regrets of my life: that I wasn't able to leave our marriage – such as it was – on better terms. I hope you may forgive me and see my actions as those of an immature and selfish man disturbed by war. I am not trying to make excuses. I merely want you to understand why I acted the way I did.

I have enclosed a key to a storage locker. My solicitor, John Hardcastle, has all the particulars. In it you will find some items that belong to you. Please accept my apologies; I took them as an act of spite, wanting to hurt you by their absence. Despite the many years that have passed, I hope that my actions now in restoring them to you may at least bring you some little happiness.

Yours sincerely,
Daniel

'Good heavens,' said Irene. 'Shall we call this John Hardcastle, then, and find out what's what?'

Petal the canary warbled her approval in her cage, and Kelly reached for her phone.

...

Two weeks later, Kelly collected Irene from her snug home and they drove to a storage shed in Kenmore. John Hardcastle had indeed had all the details, along with instructions that whoever had possession of the key was welcome to everything inside the locker.

The facility hummed with the air-conditioning. Their shoes squeaked on the shiny floor, and Irene's white-tipped cane tap-tapped a steady rhythm. They were given directions to the correct locker.

'Shall I do it?' asked Kelly. 'Why don't you sit here on this chair and I'll see what's inside.'

'Yes please, dear.' Irene grunted as Kelly helped her to lower herself down. 'I'm so stiff from sitting in the car.'

Kelly fitted the key into the lock and turned it, and the door swung open. Inside she found a few small boxes. She carried them over to Irene one by one and placed them on the floor. She opened each in turn and emptied the contents, describing every item for Irene before placing it in the old woman's hands.

'There's some ... looks like silver. A silver tea service. A teapot and a coffee pot and ... a milk jug and a sugar bowl. They're very tarnished, though. Almost black.'

'Oh my,' Irene said. 'Oh my Lord.' She ran her hands over the teapot, stroking the decorative engraving, feeling the opening of the spout, the delicate carved handle. 'Oh my,' she said again. 'This set belonged to my mother. She gave it to Daniel and me when we were married. It went missing after we separated. I thought it was lost. I'd quite forgotten about it.'

'How would Dad have gotten hold of it?'

'Well, I left for a while. Went off with that American serviceman. Mind you, it didn't last. Young and silly, I was then. But while I was away, in Sydney briefly, my mother said that Daniel turned up at the house on a short leave to collect some of his belongings. It never occurred to me that he might take anything else. By the time I'd realised my mistake with the fellow in Sydney, and come home to lick my wounds, Mother had packed all my things into boxes and put them in the spare room. She wasn't at all impressed with my behaviour. She used the word "trollop": I'll never forget that. Sounded so strange, coming from my mother's demure mouth. As close to a swear word as she ever came.' Irene handed the teapot back and reached for Kelly's fingers. 'When I'd finally straightened myself out and unpacked my boxes, I couldn't be sure what was what. I mean, I knew there were items missing, but I suppose I assumed my mother had taken them. It was only later that it occurred to me that Daniel might have them.' She patted Kelly's hand. 'I'm sorry you're hearing all this, dear. It's all rather embarrassing, at my age, to be confessing to such poor behaviour.'

'Not at all,' said Kelly. 'I can't believe your things have been sitting in storage for all these years.'

Next was a photograph album.

'I'm sorry you can't see the photos, Irene. Shall I describe them to you?'

'No need, my dear. I can feel the shape of it. I know exactly which album this is. Are there a lot of family photos at the front? Two little girls? A farm? Some cows?'

'Yes.'

'This is my old family album. I knew this was gone. I rather thought your father had destroyed it.' Her sightless eyes filled with tears; one ran down her powdery cheek. Her fingers touched each photograph, held in place with black triangular pockets, each page separated by a thin gossamer sheet.

Kelly was speechless for a moment. 'I wish you could see them,' she said simply.

'I can remember them, dear, and that's enough for me. To know they still exist, that they didn't get thrown out.' Irene turned the pages, tracing the shapes of the photographs. 'There should be some in the middle here of our wedding. Can you see them?'

Kelly lifted another page and there, in a glorious black-and-white shot, was her father, much younger, and in uniform, his arm around a woman in a simple tailored suit, his hand on top of hers as they sliced into a round marzipan cake.

'Yes, I see it,' she said. 'You're cutting your wedding cake.'

'Ah, that's the one. And there should be more. Keep looking.'

Her father stared out at her again from the next page. A more casual shot, perhaps taken by a friend. He was seated on a high-backed chair next to a fireplace. Three plaster ducks were fixed to the wall behind his head. Irene was perched on his lap, her eyes almost closed in mirth, her mouth wide and open.

'You both look so happy,' said Kelly.

'We were, for a time. Completely happy. Too happy, perhaps. You must have the one of us on the chair.'

'Yes.'

'Ridiculous man. He'd said something quite indecent. I could never repeat it.' Her eyes closed and a smile tightened her lips. 'But there should be one more. With my sister? Is that one still there, too?'

Kelly flipped the page and there, just as Irene described, was a photograph of two young women, Irene in her suit, with her pill-box hat and delicate veil, and an older woman with the same gentle eyes and rounded face.

'Yes,' said Kelly. 'It's here.' She lifted Irene's hand and placed it on the photograph.

'Iris,' she said. 'My older sister, Iris. She didn't approve, you know. Thought it was all too rushed. She died in '57. A ruptured ovarian cyst. Dreadful business. I still miss her all these years later. An older sister can never be replaced.'

Kelly thought of Evonne, and swallowed the lump that had formed in her throat. 'You're right,' she said. 'There's something special about an older sister.'

Irene closed the album and held it close to her chest. She sighed. Kelly sat with her in the silence, each consumed by their own thoughts of family.

The final box contained a bundle of letters tied with string, a few pieces of costume jewellery and the powdered remains of what could have been long-dead flowers. Irene touched each item, held it, clasped it to her nose and inhaled.

'No, I'm afraid I don't remember any of these bits of jewellery,' she said. 'Such a long time ago, now. Who are the letters to, dear?'

'Um.' Kelly lifted the corner of one to see pale, spidery writing. 'Looks like they might be from Dad to you? Some from you to Dad, maybe?'

Irene put out her hand. 'Give them to me, dear. Perhaps it's better after all if you don't read those. All water under the bridge now. A lot of things said back then that shouldn't have been said. No need to burden your ears with it all. I'll ask my neighbour to take a look at them for me later.'

Kelly handed them over reluctantly. 'I don't understand. Why would Dad have hidden all these things away like this? For so long?'

'Your father was very angry with me, dear. And probably with good reason. In the midst of the war, we all thought we could be here one minute and gone the next and so we did things … *I* did things … thoughtless things. Heart-breaking things. I was a silly fool,' she muttered. 'These photographs, this tea service … they were special to me. Your father knew that. Obviously when I hurt him as badly as I did, he wanted to hurt me right back. I thought he'd sold them, or gotten rid of them, burnt them, I don't know.'

'You never asked him? He never said anything?'

'I was too embarrassed. I thought, if he had disposed of my most treasured belongings, it probably served me right. I accepted it as my due.' She hugged the album to her chest again. 'It never occurred to me that he would have kept them. Never.'

Kelly asked the timid question that was quivering on the end of her tongue. 'How old were you when you lost your sight, Irene?'

'Oh, it'll be four years ago now. Four years.'

Kelly was grief-stricken. If only her father had returned these belongings a few years earlier, Irene would have been able to see the photographs instead of merely touching dusty old paper.

How it pained her to see poor Irene clutching on to these grimy mementos, locked up and forgotten for nigh on sixty years. They were special to Irene, and her father had taken them away. She tried to imagine the circumstances, tried to wriggle inside her father's mind. Did he not feel petty, taking what was precious to her? Kelly was glad she could return them, glad they might bring an old woman some pleasure.

It surely gave her father no pleasure in keeping them; she wondered again why he had done it.

EVONNE AND LIBBY HAD TAKEN a holiday rental right on the water. Peregian Beach was quieter than Noosa, less crowded and with fewer tourists, especially at this time of year. The rental was no more than a fibro beach shack, but it had wide sliding doors that allowed the sunlight to flood in, and a rickety verandah where they could sit in the evenings. Three wooden steps led down to the nature strip dividing the house from the beach proper. Each morning they would traverse the bushland, following the beaten path through the creepers and straggly plants. Across a low bridge and walkway of rough planks, and to the edge of the cliff, with a one-metre drop to the sand below.

It had taken Evonne three months to track down an Audrey Blackson on the Sunshine Coast. And even now she wasn't sure she had the right woman. While it was true that Ms Blackson and her father had both attended Brisbane State High School, this was the only connection she could find. She had spoken to Audrey twice by phone and neither woman could come up with any other commonality. But Audrey had said she was quite happy to meet with Evonne and see if they could put their heads together and talk it through.

Libby had suggested it was the perfect excuse for a few days at the coast.

They walked hand in hand along the tideline, their footprints quickly filled by the lapping waves, as if they had never been. Delicate orange flowers tipped the vines reaching down from the cliff edge. Jellyfish dotted the shore, one as large as a car tyre, alongside the hard balls of sand thrown up by industrious crabs. The breeze held a biting chill, and Evonne clutched her thin cardigan closed across her chest.

They headed back to the rental house as the sun rose above the horizon, dipping its skirts into the sea, bright orange taffeta. The day would be warm. Libby climbed the steep bank of earth in two strides then held out her hand for Evonne. Unseen creatures scuttled away into the undergrowth. The scrub gave way to a manicured strip of grass as their cottage hove into view. It looked warm and welcoming.

Evonne had a shower and dressed with care. They were to meet Audrey Blackson at eleven o'clock at the patisserie tucked into an alcove off the main street.

'What do you think, Lib? The floral scarf or the red one?'

'The red, definitely.' Libby watched as Evonne fussed with the scarf, knotting it first one way and then another. 'Here, let me,' she said. She draped it around Evonne's neck and tucked the ends into a casual cowl. 'There. Perfect. I'm not sure why you're so nervous, Vonnie. You're worse than when you met Ivan Lawless.'

'I didn't know what it would be like then, did I. And I knew Dad had worked with him. This time I've really got no clue as to what the connection is.' She held the envelope up to the light and peered at the shadow outline. 'Could be anything.'

'Could be another few hundred thousand dollars,' smirked Libby. 'You might be about to make some other old acquaintance of your dad's very happy.'

'That's what Richard's afraid of. Although I think it's unlikely Dad swindled two families out of their life savings. Maybe it'll be an anticlimax, like Richard's Jewish lady.'

'I don't know if I'd call that one an anticlimax. She seems to have struck a chord with him.' Libby reached out and took Evonne's hand. 'Anyway, whatever it is, we're in this together. I'll be right there next to you.'

...

Evonne spotted Audrey Blackson at once. She was sitting in the shade of an awning, stripes of light across her body. There was a certain elegance in her posture, in the turn of her head, in the angle of her long, pale neck. She wore a spotted sundress and a straw hat, and sipped from a glass of water. Waiting.

As she and Libby threaded their way through the crowded tables, Evonne wondered whether this woman would remember her father. Their phone conversations had not jogged her memory so far. If they had known each other, was he that inconsequential to her? This woman would have lived a whole lifetime since last she had seen her father, if indeed she ever had. Was it vain of her father to consider that she might recall a spectre from her past? And yet – he clearly remembered her.

'Miss Blackson?'

'Yes,' the woman replied. 'Although I should have explained on the telephone – it's Windsor now. Audrey Windsor. Please, have a seat. The coffee's very good here and they do a fabulous almond croissant.'

With coffees ordered, they settled in the autumn sunshine, Audrey Windsor chatting about the weather, the house they were staying in (she knew the previous owners), the advantages and disadvantages of being a local in a tourist area. She was warm and pleasant. Her reddish-brown hair, tangled by the wind, suited her despite her age, and she moved with the confidence and ease of a much younger person.

'I've been trying to think, Evonne. Racking my brain, as they say, but I'm afraid I can't bring your father to mind. His name escapes me, assuming we knew each other at all.'

'I know you both attended State High at around the same time. In the early forties?'

'Yes, that's right. I completed Grade Ten in '42. Went on to secretarial school. So many of us girls did then, you know. It wasn't thought necessary for us to do any higher learning. All changed now, thank God.'

'That fits. Dad left school in 1941. He was sixteen. Joined up. Lied about his age, apparently, although we've only just realised that recently. He went to New Guinea.'

'Oh dear. He was one of those lads, was he. There were a few at that time. Boys masquerading as men. And those recruiters at the war office turning a blind eye when they knew very well that they were just that – only boys.' Audrey Windsor shook her head and took another sip of her coffee. 'Terrible business, war. Thought up by men; made for men. Kills some men and makes heroes of others. And the women left at home to carry on with the business of living. Now we have Afghanistan, Iraq, Pakistan, Syria … It seems that all those lives given so many years ago made not a jot of difference.'

Evonne and Libby nodded and mumbled noises of assent.

'Anyway,' said Audrey decisively. 'You didn't meet me to get a lecture about the atrocities of war, did you. Back to your father.'

Evonne held out a photograph of her father posing in his uniform.

'This is Dad around the time he signed up. He must've been sixteen or seventeen.' She watched Audrey Windsor's face. The older woman took the photo in her manicured hand and peered at it intently.

'I wonder …' she began. 'There does seem something a little familiar about the face, the eyes … But it was so long ago. I'm sorry, I really couldn't say for sure.'

Evonne sighed. 'Well,' she said, 'on balance, I think we have to assume you might have known him. I mean, you both attended State High at around the same time.' She took out the envelope and pointed to the letters BSHS written after Audrey Blackson's name. 'I'd say we've probably got the right person. Dad left this for you. Or for someone with the same name as you.'

'Goodness. As I said, I hardly know if I remember him at all. Are you sure you want to give it to me?'

Evonne nodded. 'Absolutely. He left letters for several people, not just you. We've been trying to track everyone down. It's been … interesting.'

'I suppose I could open it and see what it says, and then if it's clearly not intended for me, I could give it back to you?'

'Yes,' said Evonne, 'I think that would be perfectly proper.'

Audrey slit the letter open with a plum-coloured manicured nail. She withdrew a single sheet of blue paper and read it silently, her lips moving. At one point, she raised a hand to her mouth in surprise. Evonne and Libby watched as she read the letter once, then again. Her eyes filled with tears.

'Heavens,' she said. 'Heavens. It's … well, it's a love letter, I suppose. Oh, it takes me back. Reminds me of the girl I was once, long ago. My goodness.'

Libby took Evonne's hand. 'So it is for you, then?'

'Gracious, yes. Your father … Daniel … it's clear that we did know each other, although I only have the haziest memory … I seem to recall a tall boy, the year above me perhaps. There was some talk at the time, but we were all very proper young ladies then. No impropriety. My goodness,' she said again, wiping at her eyes with a paper napkin. 'I'm sorry, what must you think of me, getting all emotional over this. It's like being presented with a piece of your past, a piece you had thought long forgotten. That girl seems like another person, someone I once knew. Not someone I once was. And to be reminded of my youth in such a lovely and thoughtful way. It's quite moving.'

Evonne gestured to the letter. 'May I?'

'Yes of course, of course. Here.'

And so Evonne – with Libby peering over her shoulder – read the tender words her father had penned to the woman seated before them, words that transcended the years. Her father described the flush of young love he had felt for this woman so many years ago; a love that he could not express at the time, and yet feelings that he nurtured and kept for many years afterwards.

I carried you in my heart, her father had written. *I carried you in my heart during those first years of war, even though you didn't know it. My love for you – though unrequited – sustained me, gave me the strength to carry on. It is one of my life's regrets that I did not have the courage to pursue you when we were young and innocent, or to try to find you subsequently, though my excuse is that my mind was weakened by the horrors I'd seen, the things I had done. My romantic thoughts of you*

remained pure and unsullied, and I admit that part of me wanted to keep
them that way – as something perfect that could not be spoiled.

Audrey Windsor tied up her wind-whipped hair and again wiped at her eyes. She took a deep breath and then took Evonne's hand on one side and Libby's on the other. Evonne clutched Libby's free hand with her own, and the three of them sat in a circle, smiling at each other.

'Lord have mercy,' said Audrey. 'Young love. What a marvellous thing.' She began to laugh, and Evonne and Libby could not help but join in. Evonne found herself caught up in the joy of the moment, in the discovery of her father's tenderness.

But underneath her laughter swelled an undercurrent of uncertainty, a qualm of misgiving.

...

Sunset over the water was breathtaking. Even after the molten red and orange had dissolved into the sea, the watercolour sky cast streaks of light onto the tops of the waves, glinting and winking in the approaching dark.

A cockatoo flew overhead, calling its mate. Evonne watched as it hovered, hardly moving. She could hear the slow flap of its wings. With a screech, it was off.

She was massaging Libby's bare feet, pulling at her toes, pummelling the soles, squeezing the heels.

'Ow. Steady on. You'll dislocate a toe.'

'Sorry.' Evonne put her head in her hands. 'It's no good. I'm not in the mood.' She pushed back her chair and walked to the edge of the deck. Stood with her hands clenched tight to the railing, staring out over scrubby bush, over the sand and the sea.

And then Libby was behind her, hands on her waist, chin on

her shoulder. Evonne felt herself relax into her embrace. Felt herself soften and give in to Libby's familiar hold.

'What is it, Von? I thought you'd be happy it went so well. Audrey seemed like such a nice woman. And that letter your dad wrote … well, it was amazing. Surprising.'

'I know, I know. I just …'

'Just what?' Libby asked, her voice warm with concern.

Evonne turned to face her. 'That's just it. That letter was so loving. That's not the father I knew. I mean, was that the Daniel you knew?'

'Well, no, I guess not. Like I said, the letter was surprising.'

'Exactly.' She drew her fingers through her hair. 'Describe Dad. Go on, in a few words, describe my father the way you saw him.'

'Honestly? Well … he was ambitious. Demanding. No nonsense. Didn't suffer fools and all that. He was generous. Proud. Intolerant, judgemental; want me to go on?'

'But that's it. Don't you see? Can you see that man you just described writing that letter?'

'What, you think he didn't write it?'

'No, no,' Evonne said. 'I don't think that. I have no doubt Dad wrote it.' She stared out again at the tangled mat of vegetation, hidden pockets of shadow deepening with the onset of night. 'I just can't get my head around him doing it, that's all. I can't seem to reconcile those words with the man I remember. I mean, Dad wasn't an ogre or anything, don't get me wrong. But it's like I've asked two artists to paint a picture of the same person, and the finished portraits are nothing alike.'

'He wrote that letter some years ago, I'd say. Maybe he changed.'

'But I don't remember him ever being like that. So … emotional. So open.' She took Libby's hands and looked searchingly at her.

'You know what I'm really asking, don't you? How many years did it take Dad to accept you? To accept the fact of us, as a couple? How many years did I have to deny what I was, what I am, to shield him and Mum?'

'Oh, Evonne, you know your parents were from a different generation. They didn't understand. Besides, we've been together years now, and your dad accepted us in the end.'

'Did he? I just don't know, Lib. He made it so bloody difficult. Him and Mum both. I could never talk to them. What was I, twenty-five before I came out to them? Over twenty years of living a lie. Trying to please my bloody parents. And then it was at least another five before they accepted it. Don't pretend you've forgotten how awful they were to you at the start.'

'I haven't forgotten. They wanted someone to blame, and I was an easy target,' said Libby. 'No, I haven't forgotten, but I've forgiven. I thought you had, as well.' She rubbed Evonne's hands and wrists, smoothing out the lines and wrinkles with her strong fingers.

'I thought I had, too. Turns out it's all just repressed. Something about seeing that letter – seeing the kindness, there in black and white – just does my head in. Why couldn't he have directed some of that kindness my way? Why was he always so damn self-righteous? I *wasted* all those years trying to appease him, and Mum, when I could have been true to myself.'

Libby brushed Evonne's hair off her forehead and planted a gentle kiss there. 'Think of it this way, Von. If your parents had accepted it and been no obstacle, you might have met somebody else, someone besides me, when you were younger, and by the time we crossed paths, you'd have been already taken. We might never have happened.' She grinned, her face open and honest.

But Evonne could only manage a grim smile in return. 'Yeah, maybe. Or maybe I would have met you even sooner. And maybe if my parents hadn't so spectacularly fucked up my self-image, we wouldn't be working with kids only because that's the closest we'll ever come to having our own. Through our bloody jobs.' A loud, racking sob escaped her lips and she fled into the gathering dark of the cottage.

THE STORM BLEW IN SUDDENLY just as Kelly arrived at Richard's place for a meeting at his request, for a 'summary of progress to date', as he put it. Steel-grey clouds covered the sun and lashing rain inundated the earth. She stayed in her car, waiting for a break in the torrential water that fell as if from a huge overhead bucket. A cold wind gusted; she saw a couple shuffling along the sidewalk, fighting their umbrellas. Then the outburst stopped just as abruptly, and a rainbow appeared behind the house, one end disappearing into the dense bush beyond the river. She stepped out into bright sunlight.

Evonne pulled up to park on Richard's circular driveway. The deciduous trees framing the gravel were losing their bronzed leaves; only a few stubborn ones remained after the rain. Three or four birds emerged from their hiding places and splashed noisily in an elevated bird bath, and Kelly could hear the laughter of toddlers from the garden next door.

'Turning out to be a beautiful morning after that storm,' said Evonne. 'Winter's coming at last.'

Kelly gave her sister a hug and they marched up to the house. 'I don't know why Richard couldn't have just spoken to us on the phone,' she said.

'I think he wants to feel on top of things. Wants to make sure he's in the loop about whatever's going on.'

Richard himself opened the door. Jemima was at work and the twins were at school. The house seemed silent without them. He led them into his study instead of the lounge room (Kelly rolled her eyes behind his back) and – rather ominously, she thought – closed the door.

'Right,' he began. 'So let's see where we are, shall we. Evonne, maybe if you go first.'

'Honestly, Richard, I don't know why we need all this rigmarole. I've already told you on the phone how things went, and I've seen you since then too.'

'Yes but we haven't all been together. I thought we should take stock, see how things are progressing.'

'Just humour him, Vonnie,' said Kelly. 'And it'll all pass more quickly.'

'Oh, all right then. Well, I've delivered two of my envelopes. The first, as you all know, was to Nigel Lawless. It turns out he's in a nursing home, in a pretty bad way, so Lib and I saw his son, Ivan Lawless.'

'And handed over a cheque for a quarter of a million dollars,' said Richard dolefully.

'What would you have done differently, I might ask? Held back the cheque? Just handed over the letter?'

'All right, all right. Just can't believe it's bloody legal. Right, moving on.'

'No, hang on a minute,' said Evonne. 'You opened up this

point of discussion. So let's discuss it. Whether you like it or not, Richard, it appears that Dad did do the wrong thing by Nigel Lawless all those years ago. And his family paid for it. Ivan told me how his father had to start again from scratch. That can't have been easy for him, or for his family. Now I don't know why Dad did what he did, or why he never saw fit to make amends before now—'

'Probably because he never had to,' interrupted Richard. 'I mean, if what he did was illegal, Lawless would have sued at the time, surely.'

'Maybe,' said Evonne. 'But he didn't. Dad must've felt it was a moral wrong even if not a legal one. I think it was weighing on his mind. In fact, I think a lot of things were weighing on his mind, and he decided to do something about them.'

'What I don't understand is why he couldn't have done something about them when he was alive to do it,' retorted Richard. 'Why leave all this messy baggage for us to clean up?'

'I don't know the answer to that.'

The three of them sat in silence for a moment.

'It's a hard thing he's done, writing these letters,' said Kelly. 'He's confronting his regrets and he's trying to set them right. Maybe he didn't have the courage to do it when he was alive, but I'm still proud that he's been brave enough to do it through these letters. It may not be the perfect way to resolve things – it may not be *your* way, Richard – but it's still an amazing thing he's doing.'

'Through us. He's using us, that's what he's doing.'

'Maybe we should look at this in a different way,' continued Kelly. 'I mean, Evonne and I have seen you more times over the last six months – since he died – than in the two years before that. Maybe Dad wanted to bring us closer.'

Richard scoffed and turned to stare out the French doors to the garden. A gust of wind ruffled the golden-brown leaves littering the lawn.

'Anyway. So that was Nigel Lawless,' said Evonne. 'And the other one we've delivered was to Audrey Blackson, or Windsor, as she is now.'

'Oh yes, Dad's childhood sweetheart,' said Richard.

'I don't know about that,' said Evonne. 'She hardly knew Dad existed. I think he admired her from afar. Anyway, it was a bit of an anticlimax. She was lovely, but …'

'No cheque at least.'

'No, Richard. No cheque.'

'And Kelly?'

'Well, I've met Irene, of course.'

'Ah yes. The infamous first wife nobody had ever heard of before. Except you.'

'She's actually very sweet, Richard. I've stayed in touch, you know. Evonne and I even met her family, didn't we, Vonnie?'

'We did. Lovely crowd. She's got four sons and I don't know how many grandchildren and great-grandchildren.'

'I thought you said she'd never married again?'

'She didn't. Common-law wife, she said she was called back then. Didn't want to make it official, not after the debacle with Dad. Her partner's dead now, anyway. But as I said, we met her children – the oldest one, Ryan, and one of his girls, and her two kids. He used to be a plumber, had his own business at Caloundra. Now his daughter runs it. Sounded like a big operation.'

'It certainly did,' agreed Evonne. 'Quite a few staff.'

'I'm thinking I might ask Irene down to stay sometime.'

'Oh, good grief,' said Richard. 'Don't let's all get entangled in another of Dad's prior relationships that we knew nothing about. She'll be wanting something from the will next.'

'You are such a cynic, Richard. She's perfectly nice. And overjoyed to get back her albums and tea set and stuff.'

'That'll have just given her a taste for it. If she gets a whiff of what his estate is worth, she'll be after more. You see if I'm right.'

Evonne gave Richard an exasperated look. 'For heaven's sake, Richard, it's not all about the money.'

'Anyway,' he continued, 'mine seemed fairly straightforward. That Jewish woman. Hardly worth the effort, if you ask me.'

'It might seem trivial to you, Richard, but clearly it meant a lot to Dad.' Kelly picked at a spot on her shirt: probably a bit of Eden's breakfast Weet-Bix. 'Makes you think, doesn't it.'

'No,' snorted Richard.

'Oh, come on,' said Evonne. 'You can't tell me this hasn't been playing on your mind. What you'd say to the people you've wronged.'

'Nope. Can't say I've given it a moment's thought.'

Kelly had had enough of her brother's stubbornness. 'So what have you got to report, besides meeting Ms Mosely?'

'I think I got the difficult ones,' said Richard. 'I'm having trouble tracking down this Jeffrey Upton character. I've found Leanne Young, though.' He sighed. 'Apparently she committed suicide, years ago. I'm meeting with her son in a couple of weeks. And I'm not looking forward to it. God knows what Dad's connection to her was.'

'It's probably unimportant,' said Kelly, but she knew she sounded unconvinced. 'Surely he can't have too many other skeletons in the cupboard.'

Richard looked away uneasily. 'Well, I hope you're right. Perhaps the hardest ones have passed.' She watched her brother rolling something small in his left hand, massaging the object like a stress ball, until he noticed Kelly's eyes on him. He slammed the smooth black stone onto the sideboard. 'Bloody mumbo-jumbo. Keep meaning to get rid of it.'

RICHARD HAD ARRANGED TO MEET Clancy Young at a cafe in Rosalie. The beeping of a reversing truck punctuated the general drone of traffic. He walked up the steps to the outside tables of Alter Ego as a waitress sashayed past, bearing two plates heaped with colourful food. Each table was decorated with a succulent or a cactus in a pot. The overhead heater was on, and patrons had blankets pulled around their shoulders or tucked across their laps.

Only one man sat alone, reading the newspaper, a half-finished coffee at his elbow. He was younger than Richard had expected, perhaps thirty. He raised his head and glanced at Richard, then gave him an uncertain wave. As Richard got closer, he could see that despite the man's youth, his face was etched with worry lines, and his eyes behind his glasses were those of someone whom life had disappointed.

'Richard Whittaker.' He extended his hand.

'Clancy. Clancy Young. Good to meet you.' They shook hands and Richard sat down.

'So. I believe your father knew my mother?'

'Yes, it would seem so,' said Richard. 'Your mother – Leanne – worked in real estate?'

'Yes, for quite a few years. Not happily, I'd have to say, from what my dad's said. It's a rough world. You in the business yourself?'

'No. I'm in the banking sector.'

'Oh. Right.'

'Your mother … she …?'

'She committed suicide, yes. Twenty-five years ago now. My sister and I were just kids.'

'I'm sorry,' said Richard.

'Thanks. Yeah, it was hard going. We had some tough years there for a while. Dad had to cope with being a single parent. And my sister never really came to terms with Mum dying. Took it pretty hard. Went off the rails in her teenage years.' He ran his hands through his hair. 'Anyway. You don't need to hear all that.'

Richard took a deep breath. A waiter delivered meals to the people at the next table. Bright beetroot hummus was smeared across one plate, alongside leafy greens and pulled pork. 'Have you eaten?' he asked Clancy.

'Yes, but you go ahead. Please.'

Richard got the waiter's attention. 'I'll have what they're having,' he said. 'And a black coffee.' He busied himself unfolding his napkin and straightening his cutlery. 'Look. I can't confess to knowing what this is all about. When my father died late last year, he left a whole lot of letters for people. People we don't even know, mostly. Seems to have been getting his affairs in order. He's left this one for your mother.' He retrieved it from his jacket. 'I suppose he didn't know she'd … taken her own life. Or he would've left it for you, instead, wouldn't he.' Richard felt like he was painting himself into a corner. The envelope's contents now seemed sinister, dangerous in a way he couldn't explain.

'I don't pretend to know what's in here,' he continued, as he passed it over. 'Going from the other ones that've been delivered, it's probably some grand apology for a slight made to your mother at some point in her career. Probably means nothing to you. Probably would have meant nothing to your mother, had she been here to read it. I suspect the old man's mind was going a bit, towards the end, you know.' Richard didn't know if he really believed this or not, but it seemed like the right thing to say.

Clancy Young had pushed aside his newspaper. He turned the envelope over in his hands, as if deciding whether to open it. Richard had the uncomfortable feeling that the other man knew more about the letter than he did.

After a few minutes, he opened the envelope and read the letter. He looked puzzled, and then relieved. And then merely sad.

Richard was again comforted to see there did not appear to be a cheque attached.

Clancy Young folded up the letter and slid it with care back into the envelope. He dabbed at his eyes with a paper serviette, and Richard realised with a sort of embarrassed horror that the man was crying. He turned from side to side, as if to summon assistance, but in the end settled for clearing his throat and handing the man his serviette as well. People about them continued to eat their meals, all tactfully ignoring the man's sniffles.

'Sorry. Oh, so sorry. Gosh, where did that come from. Sometimes the emotion just wells up and overwhelms me when I least expect it. Even now, so long afterwards.' He blew his nose. 'I still remember her: how she looked, how she smelt. The dress she was wearing that last day. I've lived more of my life with her dead than with her alive. A lot more. And yet … she's still there, in my memory.' His eyes filled again and he wiped at them with the crumpled paper napkins.

Richard didn't know where to look. He picked at a cuticle self-consciously.

'Have you …?' Clancy gestured to the letter. It took a moment for Richard to work out what he meant.

'Oh. No. I haven't read it.'

The man offered him the envelope. 'Would you like to? I find that anything to do with Mum, even after all this time, helps to give me some closure. Little things, you know. Recollections from people she knew. Old photographs. I know it's not the same for you, I mean, your father was quite elderly, wasn't he. And yet' – he gave Richard a sad smile – 'you can never have too many memories. Of your loved ones.'

Richard slipped the letter out. He recognised his father's close cropped writing. Although the letter was addressed to Leanne Young, he was surprised to see that it had been written after she had died, and it was clear that his father had been aware of that fact.

Daniel Whittaker – now dead – had, when he was still alive, written a letter to a dead woman.

Richard wondered if his father really had started to lose his marbles.

The letter was written in a warm and intimate fashion. When Richard reached the paragraph about his father gazumping Leanne in a real estate deal, he gasped. He looked up, but could read nothing in Clancy's posture or expression. His father apologised for his actions and then went on to apologise for Leanne's death – as if he had any part in that!

When he had finished reading the letter, Richard replaced it in the envelope with a firm resolve. 'Well, I hope you don't think my father was taking any sort of … responsibility, or whatever, for your mother's death. It sounded like he hardly knew her. And as for the business deal, to be perfectly honest, I wouldn't put too much store in what he says here.' He pressed on. 'He seems to have come to the end of his life and started apologising for all manner of things, to all manner of people he met over his life. Doesn't mean much, I can assure you.'

In his mind, he half-expected Clancy Young to correct him, to in some way apportion blame for his mother's death. Richard sat forward, ready to deflect any criticism that might be thrown at him.

But Clancy's posture stayed relaxed, his eyes unfocused. Finally, he spoke. 'I knew about the deal. It was a whole apartment block, I think. Fell through just before Mum died. She took it pretty hard.'

'Well, whatever business dealings my father—'

Clancy interrupted him by gently placing his hand on Richard's wrist. The contact felt unnatural, yet Clancy seemed unmoved, as if it was perfectly normal for two grown men, strangers, to be practically holding hands in public.

'My mother wasn't well, Richard. She had a lot of issues from her childhood, and after the birth of us kids. My father did what he could but he didn't know how to cope. With her. With her moods. Her ups and downs. She could be … I think she was quite difficult at times. I don't blame your father for her death, no more than I blame my own father. Mum lived with her own demons, Richard, as do we all. And eventually, hers killed her. There's no point assigning blame for that.'

He paused. 'But your father obviously felt responsible, in some way. He mentions that he should have noticed the signs. That he could have prevented her death if he'd only done more, or intervened. It's a shame he's not here himself to hear this, but I'll tell you instead. He's not responsible. There were plenty of people in Mum's life who might have stepped in, I suppose. And whenever someone takes their own life, those people always lead the way in regret. If only I'd done this, or said that. If only … But ultimately, each one of us is responsible for our own life, and for our own death. In hindsight it may have seemed to your father that he could have prevented what happened. But I doubt that. I really doubt it.'

He lifted his hand from Richard's wrist. Richard felt pinned to the spot under Clancy's gaze. He had not thought of his father as responsible; if anything, he had been ready to defend him to the last. And yet he suddenly felt the weight of culpability lift from him. He felt his father's words of apology being met by Clancy's forgiveness and quiet acceptance, and in some inexplicable way he felt lightened by his words, by his touch. He felt an unaccountable relief.

. . .

A week later, a letter arrived for Richard, marked *Personal*. On the back was written simply *Sender: Clancy Young*. No return address. Richard groaned at his naivety in thinking that he had been let off the hook so easily. Of course this man would want something from him, or from his father's estate. Of course he wouldn't let the suicide of his mother go by so meekly.

He opened the letter with a feeling of dread, and began to read:

Dear Richard

Clearly you didn't read between the lines. Perhaps your father didn't want you to.

The contents of that letter were a surprise to me, not because of what was said, but rather because of what wasn't said.

Since we met, I've done some thinking. And I've decided I don't see why you should be spared the details.

Your father wasn't completely honest. The truth was, he and my mother had an affair that ended just before she took her own life.

Richard groaned. He read on with reluctance.

When my father found out, he threatened to leave her if she didn't end it, and then that real estate deal fell apart, and it was all too much for her. I don't suppose he envisioned that would be the ending she would choose.

So you see, there were many reasons she could have taken her own life, which is why I choose not to lay blame at anyone's feet.

My father kept this to himself until about five years ago. He was diagnosed with prostate cancer: a big wake-up call, I guess. He sat my sister and me down and told us the truth. He said it nearly killed him, the thought that his rejection might have forced Mum's hand.

The only reason I can think of that your father didn't mention this in his letter is that he didn't want to hurt Dad and our family any further with the whole truth. I don't believe he ever knew that Dad had found out about him and Mum.

Still, the way your father took advantage of Mum was shameful, and it's unfortunate that he's only now owning up to his part in her unhappiness, and even then, only with this apology full of half-truths.

It didn't feel right to tell you all this at the cafe. I had no wish to cause a scene. But I do feel that if you and your family are going through some sort of process of finding out about your father now that he has gone, you have a right to know.

I'm hoping that your father became a different bloke. That he changed his ways and turned out all right. And ultimately, I still believe that he wasn't to blame for Mum's death. I don't suppose we'll ever

116

truly know what went through her mind at the end, why she decided to jump. But what I'm trying to say is that your father was a symptom, not the cause.

Yours sincerely
Clancy Young

Richard sat back in his swivel chair. He was tired of this mad quest of his father's: all he wanted was the estate to be settled, and then he could stop holding his breath and finally tell Jemima the truth about his retrenchment. But until then, until the financial aspects were resolved, he couldn't confide in her. It was too humiliating.

But his father's past was only coming alive in all its ignominy. Extramarital affairs. Illegal business dealings. First wives. Richard began to sweat, despite the chill of the air-conditioning. A sharp pain echoed somewhere in his chest. He got up and began to pace the room. *Bastard*, he kept thinking. *Bloody selfish bastard.*

He thought back to the time when his father was having an affair with Leanne Young. He would have been in his sixties, the same age Richard was now. Good Lord. How long had it been going on? Had there been other women? Richard had never thought so, but he clearly had a blind spot where his parents were concerned. What did he know of their relationship?

He struggled to recall a time when his parents had appeared content. If they weren't sniping at each other, or maintaining a cool distance, they were too busy with work or hobbies or other friends to spend much time together. A long line of women marched across his memory, women his father had worked with, played tennis with; the cleaners, the caterers, the secretaries, the woman from the corner store, the one from the local newsagent. They all loomed suspiciously in Richard's mind. Had his father been a serial adulterer? And had his mother known? Had she turned a blind eye, or had those occasional spectacular rows been about this very thing? His head whirred with the possibilities, with the not knowing.

Why, oh *why* had his father left them this enormous, ridiculous task? Why dredge up the past, when they had been perfectly happy wallowing in ignorance? And why on earth did it make him feel so sordid and alone, so powerless? So inexpressibly sad?

He retrieved the grieving stone from his coat pocket and stared into it, but it remained stubbornly murky and dark.

THROUGH HER KITCHEN WINDOW, KELLY watched Eden playing in the grassy backyard that rose steeply from their house. Several mature trees marked the fence line, including a poinciana that would flower with stunning crimson blossoms by the time spring arrived in a month or two. On its sturdy lower branches, Ben had constructed a wobbly collection of timber to make a haven for Eden, who laboriously climbed the short rope ladder and sat in his cubby, hidden in the dense foliage. Ben had wedged another wide wooden plank between the poinciana and the mango tree, which was covered in glossy green leaves. When it fruited in summer, Eden would emerge sticky with sap after gorging on the small, ripe mangoes not yet decimated by flying foxes. These trees, and the old wooden laundry, and the fence itself were surrounded by a dense mass of gnarled hibiscus and asparagus fern, by native ginger and yellow oleander. Persistent weeds – gorse and ragweed – grew indiscriminately, and the creeper that her mother had called bitter yam ran rampant through everything else, its stubby tubers shooting out roots, eager to find new ground to inhabit. Their yard was a bit of wildness flourishing amongst their neighbours' neat lawns and raked gravel, and Kelly loved it.

She watched as Kara offered Eden a snack of biscuits and milk. He climbed backwards down the trunk and then hung upside down from a low-hanging branch, his shirt covering his face and Kara tickling his tummy.

Kara walked into the kitchen and put the empty glass in the sink. She unfolded a piece of paper from her pocket and waved it at Kelly. 'As I was saying, I've got three possible Jennifer Ibsens.' She had wanted to accompany Kelly on her mission to track down Jennifer Ibsen, and Kelly was pleased to have the benefit of her daughter's technological skills. She saw it as a little project they could tackle together, and had asked Kara to get online and see what she could find out.

'Two were Ibsen before they were married, now they're … umm … Cole and Jessup. The other one was a Smith before she married an Ibsen.'

'Ages?'

'Jennifer Smith – now Ibsen – is only twenty-four. And she's only been married about two years.'

'Hm. Unlikely to be her, but not impossible. What about the other two?'

'Jennifer Cole, nee Ibsen, lives way out west, Birdsville or Charleville. I've got it written here somewhere. I think she's in her sixties. And the other one – Jennifer Jessup, nee Ibsen – is eighty-five and lives in a nursing home at Brookfield.'

'Sounds promising, you think? She's the closest, anyway.'

'Yes, probably the easiest to try first,' said Kara. 'Although if she's gaga I don't know what we'll do.'

Kelly merely raised an eyebrow.

The following week, she arranged for Eden to stay the night with Evonne and Libby, so that she wouldn't have to rush back from Brookfield to collect him from preschool. Eden was ridiculously excited to be having a sleepover with the Aunts VonLib, as he called them, and had packed his favourite stuffed elephant, his plastic dinosaurs, his colouring books and his scooter.

'You're only going for one night!' said Kelly, smoothing back his fringe.

'Yeah, but I'll be there for the whole day of tomorrow and I don't want to run out of things to do.' He cuddled into her arms.

'I'm sure you'll have plenty to do. Will you miss me?' she asked.

'Probly. Might be too busy, but.'

When she left him at Evonne's place, he was scootering around the back deck, scaring the birds and trying to spot lions in the jungle. Kelly was going to spend the morning at the shops with Kara, before driving out to meet Jennifer Jessup.

Mrs Jessup was about as far from gaga as they could have imagined. Her modest home was in a retirement village, not a nursing home, and she was as sprightly as the rainbow lorikeets that flocked to her small porch, where they were handfed honey-soaked grain and bread sprinkled with milk. She served Kelly and Kara strong tea in dainty cups from an eclectic collection displayed in a glass-fronted cabinet, and offered them homemade teacake dusted with cinnamon sugar. She didn't sit down herself until each of the birds had eaten their fill and flown off to perch in a nearby tree, denuded of leaves in the winter cold, the lorikeets colourful decorations amongst the bare branches.

Despite Mrs Jessup's animated manner, Kelly could detect the creeping signs of her old age. Her clothes smelt musty, and her mismatched socks puddled at her ankles. Something had recently been burnt on the stove; the acrid odour still hung in the air. Some of her plants had been overwatered and sat in saucers of stagnant liquid. And when Kelly looked closely at the dream-catchers and macramé plant holders around the room, she could see their thin coating of dust.

A black cat sat curled in a cardboard box; it opened one yellow eye and twitched its tail. Kelly wondered that it didn't scare away the birds. Perhaps it too was old, and past bothering.

'Now then, girls, more tea? Another slice of cake?'

'No, thank you, Mrs Jessup. That was lovely.'

'Please, call me Jennifer. Mrs Jessup makes me sound like an old person.' She chortled, covering her mouth with her hand, her eyes twinkling behind purple-framed lenses. 'You're only as old as you feel, isn't that right? Kara, how old do you think I am? Go on, guess.'

Kelly didn't have the heart to tell her they already knew. She and Kara exchanged a glance.

'Um, seventy?' Kara ventured.

'Oh, you're being silly. What about you?' She turned to Kelly.

'Seventy-four?' said Kelly.

'Bless you both for being so kind to an old lady. I'm eighty-five, eighty-six next birthday. Only got to hang on another fourteen years and I'll be getting a letter from the Queen.'

Kara smiled. 'We have a letter here for you, actually. From … well, it's from my grandfather, Mum's father. Grandpa Daniel died last year and he left a letter addressed to a Jennifer Ibsen, which was your name before you were married, right? We're not actually sure if it's you, but we thought we'd try and see if you remembered him. Daniel Whittaker? He was eighty-eight when he died.' She passed the old woman the cream envelope.

'Well, that's quite something. Let's have a look at this letter, hey?'

Jennifer Jessup removed her glasses and let them drop on the cord that hung around her neck. She fumbled on the side table and replaced them with a pair of reading glasses in lime green. She stared at her name on the envelope. 'Daniel Whittaker, you say? I can't say it rings a bell. Sorry, girls.' She held out the envelope.

'Do you think you *might* know him?' said Kelly. 'I mean, if you opened it up and read it, maybe it would jog your memory.'

'But what if it's not for me, dear? I wouldn't feel right opening somebody else's correspondence.'

'But ... well.' Kara looked to Kelly for guidance.

'I'm sure it won't do any harm to have a look,' she explained to Jennifer. 'If you still don't remember anything, then we'll just seal it up again and try the next one. We've got three Jennifer Ibsens on our list.'

'Well, if you're sure. I don't want to be doing the wrong thing. Can't afford a stretch inside at my age, can I?' joked the old woman. She took a long time to open the seal, trying to inflict the least damage possible. Eventually she retrieved a sheet of paper, and read it over several times. Kelly could still hear the lorikeets squawking from the trees.

'Well, I'll be a monkey's uncle,' said Jennifer finally. 'My word.'

Kara opened her mouth to speak but Kelly put a restraining hand on her arm. They waited.

Jennifer looked at each of them in turn. Addressing Kelly, she said: 'This quite takes me back. You've lived a bit more of life than this young lady,' she glanced at Kara, 'but even so, I hope what I've got to say won't shock you.' She folded the paper and took a sip of tea. 'Let me tell you a story. Once upon a time there was a young girl with her head full of mischief and nonsense and her heart full of dreams. She was born an age too early, into a life where girls did what they were told and women followed suit. She was considered flighty. Cocky. *Not* very lady-like.' She peered at them over her glasses. 'This girl taught herself to drive on the family farm. Roped her brother into giving her lessons. All in secret, of course. It wasn't the done thing for ladies to go gallivanting about in vehicles in those days. But her brother was kind, and loved showing off, so it suited him fine to demonstrate his skills to his baby sister. That's the first part of the story.' She took another sip of tea. 'The second part concerns a lad with yellow cornfield hair and eyes as blue as sapphires. He was a neighbour's son. Fine, strapping boy with brown skin on his arms from working all day in the sun. He was trouble, though, that boy. But the girl didn't know it yet. And when he kissed her, and more, she thought it meant they were always going to be together. She took it as a promise. Whereas for him, it was only a diversion. A bit of fun.'

Despite wondering where this was going, Kelly kept her gaze resolutely on the woman before her. She saw the wrinkled folds of her neck. The skin on the back of her trembling hands was pale, almost translucent. Kelly could see the veins tracing crisscross paths, a roadmap, across her wrists and up her forearms. She concentrated on the mellifluous tone of Jennifer's voice, and silently urged her daughter to do the same.

'One day, the girl was making a dress. A party dress with yellow and blue ribbons. And she had miscalculated and run out of ribbon, and so rather than bother her mother – who was heavily pregnant with her twelfth child, and feeling the heat – or her father – who was out on his horse tending cattle – the girl decided to borrow her father's car for a trip into town. It was an old heap, bought fourth-hand from a neighbour. But she'd practised with her brother and she was full of confidence. So she slipped out of the farmhouse and down to the shed, and she started it up and drove it away, down the long, winding lane of their property, and onto the road proper. She felt a special thrill, driving for the first time, just herself, without her brother there to guide her.

'She came to the intersection of two roads, the one on into town, and another that led out to the Mulvaneys' place. There, she stopped like her brother had told her, to make sure there was no-one coming in either direction. But then the car stalled, you see. She tried and tried to get it going again, and she was so focused on trying to get the car started, not wanting to appear a fool, that she didn't notice another car trundling along at quite a speed. And the other driver must have thought she'd stopped – well, she *had* stopped, but all of a sudden the car launched itself into action again. The other car was going much too fast to stop and it ploughed right into the girl's car and carried it off, away over the side of the road and into a ditch.'

She was silent. Kelly felt her spine tingling, goose pimples shivering her arms. Kara was rapt.

'What happened?' her daughter whispered.

'There was a lot of blood,' said Jennifer, her own voice also soft now. 'An awful lot of blood, although the girl couldn't really see where it was coming from. She'd hit her head, and that would ripen into a right bruise in the coming days, but it wasn't bleeding. And she'd cut her arm, but the blood was too much to be coming from such a small injury. No, she was remarkably lucky to escape with no serious wounds.'

'But the blood?'

'Ah yes. The blood. She sat in the car for quite a while, you see, waiting for help. And she kept bleeding. It was soaking through her dress and wetting the seat and she kept thinking, *That'll be a bugger to get out of the upholstery. Dad's going to be furious.'*

'Did help come? What about the other car? Did the driver help her?'

'No. No, he – or she – didn't. The other car hadn't gone into the ditch; it had stopped just shy of the edge. He reversed and backed up, and then took off.'

'What, like nothing had happened?'

'Yes. That's exactly right. Like nothing had happened. But the girl was too concerned about the blood to notice at the time. She was worried that she was hurt quite badly and for some reason couldn't feel it.'

'So, what happened?'

'Eventually a tractor rolled along, old man Beavis, returning the tractor to his son who lived further along, and he stopped and helped the girl out. She said she wasn't in too much pain, so he propped her up on the tractor seat next to him and drove her to the local doctor's surgery. There wasn't any hospital there in those days, of course.'

'And were you … I mean, was the girl all right? Was she okay?'

Jennifer Jessup cleared her throat. 'Well, that depends, I suppose.'

'Depends on what?'

'Depends on your definition of okay. She had a mild concussion and she needed a couple of stitches in her arm. No broken bones, though.'

'But where was all the blood coming from?'

Jennifer laid her hand on her stomach in a protective gesture. 'Well, I suppose you could say she had an internal injury. The blood was a baby. A baby.'

Kelly heard the sharp intake of her daughter's breath. 'A baby?' said Kara.

'The girl was pregnant, you see, with the yellow-haired boy's child. She didn't even know it herself, not then. She was not much more than a child herself. Hadn't noticed the signs of her changing body. Hadn't even known what to look for. When the doctor told her, after he'd examined her injuries and asked her some questions, well, she could barely believe it. How could all that blood be that baby? How could she have lost a baby she didn't even know she had?'

They were all quiet. Kara reached out and laid her hand on Jennifer's, which was now curled into a fist, emphasising the paper-thin skin, the veins strung around her knuckles.

'I'm so sorry,' she whispered.

The old woman took a deep, shuddering breath. 'No-one ever spoke of it,' she said. 'My mother, my father. Oh, they talked about the accident. I was in so much trouble for taking the car. When my injuries healed, my father gave me one heck of a beating with his belt buckle as a punishment. But the blood … they never spoke about that. My father got rid of the car. Sold it or what, I don't know.

'I went back to the place it happened, a month or two later. I could still see the broken brush where the car had gone over the side, the flattened-down grass. I tried to find some blood. I tried, so hard, to find some evidence of that baby, there on the hard ground. But it had rained since, and it was all washed away. There was just a patch of soil.'

Kelly felt unable to speak. The words were lodged in her throat and would not come forward. Finally, she found her voice. 'Daniel Whittaker was the driver of the other car.'

The older lady met her eyes. 'It appears so. I never knew – or even thought much about – who it was. He was just a stranger. According to this,' she held up the letter, 'he knew he'd done the wrong thing and felt guilty, but he didn't have the courage to come forward. Seems to think it was all his fault. I don't know about that. For me it was an accident. Just an accident.'

'But it must have affected you.'

'Oh, it certainly did affect me. It's amazing how one incident – one accident – can have such an effect on your whole life. I don't know. Maybe I would have lost the baby anyway. My parents would have found out about the pregnancy sooner or later. They blamed my wicked behaviour, and told me it was God's way of punishing me, of trying to teach me a lesson. By placing that accident in my path and causing me to lose the baby. They only said it the once, mind, and then never mentioned it again. But I knew. I knew. I had sinned. And I had been punished.'

She leant across to reach a silver-framed photograph of a dark-skinned man in a stockman's hat. She shone the glass on her skirt and passed it to Kelly.

'This was my husband, Jack. He grew up in Cherbourg and worked on my father's property. I was thirty when I married him. An old maid. No-one wanted me, not after what had happened. Except for him. He'd lost his first wife young, in childbirth. Both dead, his wife and his baby. He carried around a lot of sadness in him. He and I both. His was more entrenched though, long before I met him. Lost his parents when he was only a lad. His dad to TB. His mum went out to work for the government and never came back. He had a lot of aunties and uncles, though, and they were always very nice to me. I never felt judged by that mob.' She sighed. 'It was different for my side of the family. A few eyebrows were raised when we got married, I can tell you. We did it quietly, in the office in town. He was a good man.' She took back the photo and rubbed her thumb across the surface. 'Gentle. A decent man. He had large hands. Skin colour didn't matter to him, nor the fact of all that blood. He just accepted everything in his stride. We loved well, that's for sure. We loved well.'

...

When Kelly took up Jennifer's offer to read the letter, she was unprepared for the detail it included. Her father's description of the day was as sharp as if it was yesterday.

He knew he was going too fast on a strange road in a strange town. But road rules were elastic then, especially in the bush. He did see the car that had stopped. He thought someone had pulled over to take the air, or check a tyre, or *take a piss* (his words). And so he was barrelling on through the intersection when the other car lurched forward and he collected the front end. Pushed it sideways along the road, clods of earth flying; a sickening, scraping sound. The other car dipped down and he realised it had gone over slightly, just the side wheels. Both cars dangled there for a moment. A jet of steam puffed from an engine. The side mirror hung by a thread.

These tiny details her father had held in his mind for seventy years. He had filed each one carefully away.

He had sat for a minute. Caught his breath. Slung his car into reverse and backed away, the two cars disentangling with another shocking screech. He could see a woman in the driver's seat. She was moving about. Holding her head. He'd had half a mind to go to her then. At least he conceded that, thought Kelly.

But then he remembered the beers he'd had at lunch. The speed at which he'd been racing along that road. And he remembered his new wife at home, Irene, whom he was desperate to see in his short leave. And he remembered his place in the army, for which he'd fought so hard. He continued:

Like so many of us do in these situations, I thought: my life is more important than this. My world and my role in it is more important than this dusty outback road, and this careless other driver, who is now stretching and rising and looking around.

And so I continued to reverse, and my car roared back into life – remarkably undamaged (another sign, I would later think, when I was justifying my decision). I drove off.

The next day, I read in the newspaper that the police were looking for the other driver, to question him or her. But the girl, Jennifer Ibsen, had made a statement that it was her fault, that she had stopped and then pitched directly into the path of an oncoming vehicle, that she was inexperienced, that she didn't see. Her injuries were relatively minor, the report said. It was her father's car. She'd taken it without his permission. She wasn't even licensed to drive.

It seemed to Kelly that there was so much blame and wrongdoing accorded to Jennifer Ibsen that her father was quickly forgotten. A bit player.

You would have been about the same age as my grand-daughters, he wrote. *And when I think of someone doing to them what I did to you – driving off and leaving you alone that way – it makes my blood boil. I'm so sorry.*

He'd apologised for what he'd done, but there was so much he hadn't known. The baby and the blood. The beating and the judgement passed by pious parents. The dark-skinned man with large hands and a gentle soul. All of this came afterwards, like a series of dominoes falling, one after the next; the first one pushed by the nose of his car.

Kelly looked up from the letter. Kara stood on one side of Jennifer, holding a bended arm, accompanying her down the concrete ramp to a well-tended garden. The older woman was talking in an animated fashion once more, although Kelly couldn't make out her words. Kara was gesturing at something high up in one of the gum trees. She was taking such care.

From the silver frame on the table, Jack's warm, brown eyes stared out at Kelly, his smile bright. She thought of second chances, and the infinity of consequences.

EVERY FEW WEEKS, WHILE TIDYING the house, Evonne would find one of the printouts from her father's memorial service, as if they were multiplying. On the front was a formal shot of him taken at a studio about ten years earlier. Their parents had sat for a photographer, together and separately, and Evonne wondered now whether this had been the purpose they'd had in mind. Below that was a shot taken last Christmas – her and Kelly on one side, Richard on the other, all with their arms entwined, and smiling. A rare, light-hearted moment: Evonne vaguely recalled Eden and the twins performing an amusing parody of the manger scene from the nativity. Their father looked frail though, the expression on his face forced and unnatural. In the year before his death, he seemed less able to take pleasure from their silly antics. On the back was a montage of shots from when he was younger – with Aunt Mary by a creek bed; standing proudly outside his real estate office; a sepia photograph of her parents' wedding day; her father cradling one of his swaddled children. Evonne had dug out that one from a box of loose black-and-whites; they hadn't been able to agree on which sibling it featured.

In the pit of her stomach, she still harboured a knot of resentment towards her father. And yet those feelings were tangled up with warmth, and tenderness, as she saw his need to make amends, to connect. As she looked at the photos on the printout again, tiny, unrelated details gnawed at the edge of her memory. Holding tight to her father's arms as she walked up his bended knees and somersaulted backwards onto the floor. The times he had got up in the night and soothed her sore throat with knobs of butter rolled in white sugar. The loud buzz of the lawnmower on the weekend; the pungent smell of the manure and compost he dug into the soil. His one attempt to create a kite from paper and bamboo rods; her embarrassment at his acute disappointment that it refused to lift off the ground and fly. She remembered shutting the door to her bedroom on the pretext of homework, while she listened to the top-forty countdown on her bedside clock-radio, straining her ears for the sound of her father's footsteps in the hallway.

She had been so young then, too. Photographs and memories now all that remained as proof of that time.

. . .

Evonne had finally managed to track down the correct Michael Adamson. He was buried under six feet of earth at Resthaven Memorial Park – *A Place To Calmly Be*, its motto claimed. Evonne thought that surely all those interred had no choice other than to 'calmly be' – and what was so great about 'calmly being', anyway?

Had Michael Adamson not been residing at Resthaven, he would have been approaching the age of one hundred and thirty. Evonne had found the dates of his birth and death, and that of his marriage to Ellen Wandsworth, of Adelaide. The couple had four children born between 1910 and 1921. He had served as a signalman in World War One, and Evonne wondered how he'd managed to father four children in between fighting the Germans. All four of Michael Adamson's children had survived and gone on to have countless other children and grandchildren; Evonne had become hopelessly mired in the searches until she lost the thread of her original query. She backtracked to his youngest son and followed the paternal line until she reached Tarquin Adamson, Michael Adamson's great-grandson, born in 1970 and coincidentally employed as a primary school teacher, which was the occupation listed on Michael Adamson's marriage certificate, presumably when he wasn't off fighting a war.

As it turned out, after Evonne had searched through four generations of relatives around the country, Tarquin lived only a ten-minute drive from her house. His home was small and neat, bordered by a two-toned box hedge and a tidy white picket fence. Evonne could hear the whisper of a train from the direction of the station, then the clattering vibration as it rattled over the bridge.

When he opened the door to Evonne, it was obvious what Tarquin Adamson did with his time when he wasn't teaching – model trains of every variety littered the entryway and the living room, tiny tracks heading off through doorways, under couches and across halls. Evonne stood mesmerised.

'Wow,' she said eventually. 'That's quite a hobby.'

'It's become much more than a hobby,' he replied, with a proud and sheepish grin. 'I've been chair of the National Model Railroad Association four times now, and I'm a member of the Australasian association, too. I suppose these are my babies.'

Evonne squatted down to get a better look. At eye level, the detailed workings of the trains themselves and the minutiae of the buildings and signs and landscapes surrounding them were incredibly intricate.

'You make all this yourself?'

'Most of it's pre-purchased, but yeah, I put it together myself. Assemble the models, paint the scenery and the backdrops.'

Tarquin made them both a cup of tea and Evonne explained the reason for her visit, chatting to him as he pottered about his cosy kitchen. They took their mugs out to the covered back deck, where train paraphernalia in various stages of assembly was heaped in tidy piles. Tiny trees and mats of grasses and foliage sat next to miniature houses and factories; figurines were gathered around a collection of road signs, animals, bridges and gravel. Tarquin had not asked her how she preferred her tea; he had made strong Earl Grey, served with fresh lemon. Evonne appreciated the waft of bergamot steam that rose from the surface.

'So this is the envelope here,' she said, passing it over. 'It's addressed to your great-grandfather, although of course I know he died some time ago.'

'Yes, in the 1950s, well before I was born. I'm impressed that you managed to track me down, with my father gone as well.'

'Yes, last year, wasn't it? I'm sorry.'

'Not even seventy. Out gardening one minute and the next minute dead. Stroke. At least he didn't linger. He wouldn't have liked that, being paralysed or unable to speak. Would've been a living hell for him, so I suppose it was a blessing it was quick.'

Evonne felt a pang of voyeurism. She had seen Robert Adamson's death certificate, and knew the details, before his son – to whom she was a perfect stranger – had told her.

'Yes. Well. You can access all sorts of information from the Registry. I didn't realise myself until I had cause to use it. And, of course, the date helped.' She pointed out the 1935 written in black ink on the corner of the envelope. 'My father would have been ten, and I knew he'd attended Milton State School …'

'… and you found a record of my grandfather teaching there,' Tarquin finished. 'Astounding, isn't it.' He turned the envelope over in his hands. 'Any idea what's in here?'

'No,' said Evonne, 'none at all.'

'Shall we find out, then?' He placed his mug on a round mosaic table.

A perky willy wagtail bobbed up and down on a low branch, chirruping at the ginger cat that lay rolling in the dust at the foot of the trunk. The cat swivelled and sat on its haunches, very still, and stared at the bird. From its throat came the same chittering sound that Evonne's cat made when stalking prey. The bird, safe on its perch, chattered back in reply but did not fly away.

Tarquin pulled out a folded sheet of paper and a smaller folded piece of yellowed cardboard. He read the letter, then studied the card, then reread the letter, before giving them both to Evonne. 'Well,' he said. 'See for yourself.'

Evonne's eye was drawn first to the cardboard: it had *School Report* emblazoned across the top in heavy, old-fashioned type and, printed underneath that, her father's name – *Daniel Jeremiah Whittaker, Grade Five*. Her father had received uniform marks of Average or Good for most subjects, and the comments were written in the singular style of the time: *Young Daniel needs to spend more time on preparation of his lessons; Daniel must practise his multiplication tables; Daniel has a talent for self-expression that should be encouraged.* On the back of the card was a space for a general comment, and Daniel's teacher – Mr Adamson – had penned: *Considering Daniel's circumstances this year, I think he has done as well as could be expected in most areas and*

I am pleased to report that he has excelled in language. I hope that next year will be less tumultuous for him and will result in better scores.

Evonne wondered what had happened that year to cause her father to be distracted from his schoolwork. She perused the letter:

Dear Mr Adamson,

As I sit here writing this letter to you I am aware that you are almost certainly not alive to read it. Perhaps it is the foolishness of an old man, for I am seventy-three myself and so not a young man anymore. You taught me in Grade Five at Milton Primary School in 1935 and I thought you were an old man then, although you were probably only in your forties. My forties seem such a long time ago already. Anyway, I do realise that I am probably writing this to a deceased person, but I hope – if my wishes are carried out correctly after I myself die – that one of my children will deliver this to one of your children or grandchildren, and that way I will feel better for saying what I've got to say. Better that someone hears it, even if I never said it to you.

You were the best teacher I ever had. You were supportive during a difficult time in my life and I've never forgotten it. You listened to me. You didn't expect more of me than I could give. You nurtured my studies. But most of all, you were kind, a commodity not in plentiful supply in those days, when school was considered a place of learning and rules and regimentation, and not of compassion or understanding, particularly. Or perhaps that is only my interpretation. In any event, when my world seemed to be falling apart around me, you remained my teacher, my mentor and, dare I say it, my friend, and I shall always be forever grateful. To whoever is reading this, I hope you feel a sense of pride that your ancestor Michael Adamson, whether he be your father, grandfather, uncle or whoever, was a good and decent man, and that I, for one, appreciated his kindness.

Evonne let the letter rest on her lap. 'That's a lovely tribute to your great-grandfather,' she said to Tarquin. 'He must've been a wonderful teacher.'

'From what I've heard, yes, he was. In fact, at West End Primary they've got an award named after him. He was promoted to Head Teacher there in the early forties. Very special to have something this personal in writing, though. Don't often get that, do you. Dad would've been chuffed. And my grandfather, too.' He looked at Evonne. 'So what's your father on about, then? What happened to him back then?'

'I don't know,' said Evonne. 'I really haven't got a clue.'

...

She phoned Richard as soon as she got home but had no joy.

'How on God's green earth should I know what happened when Dad was ten? Could've been anything. Maybe he was sick, missed a lot of school. Maybe his dog died. Honestly, Evonne, you're getting way too invested in this whole palaver. You've delivered the letter, you've made some mad keen train enthusiast happy by telling him nice things about his dead relative, and now we can move on to the next one. It's been over eight months already. The sooner we're finished, the better, as far as I'm concerned.'

Evonne could hardly conceal the irritation in her voice. 'Don't you want to know if I kept it?'

'Kept what, for God's sake?'

'The report card.'

There was silence at the end of the line before Richard muttered, 'Oh, for the love of God, Evonne,' and hung up.

...

Evonne wasted no time in bringing Libby up to speed and planning what to do next.

'Ring Kelly, that'd be the first thing,' said Libby. 'She knew about Irene White, remember.'

But Kelly could shed no light on the situation, either.

Evonne could almost hear her thinking, through the phone line. 'Umm … Nup, sorry. Nothing springs to mind,' Kelly said. 'You're going to have to do a bit more poking about, I think, if you want to find out any more.'

'Right then,' said Evonne. 'Back to Births, Deaths and Marriages I go.' She thanked Kelly and hung up.

Libby was stirring a pot of potato and leek soup; the rich aroma made Evonne's mouth water. 'You don't have to, you know, Vonnie. I mean, loath as I am to agree with Richard on anything, you have done what your father's will stipulated. You've delivered the letter. You don't have to go any further.'

'I know. But I feel like Dad wants us to find out more. I mean, from what he wrote, it's like he imagined we might dig around to work out what he meant.'

Libby ladled the soup into bowls and they took their lunch out to the spring warmth of the deck.

'Maybe it *is* nothing,' Evonne continued. 'A dead pet or something, like Richard said.' She broke off a chunk of bread and dipped it into her soup. 'But I feel like he's given us a window into his life as a boy, and as a young man, that we didn't have before. A clue. I'd like to know where it leads.'

'Of course you do.'

'It's funny, you know. When all this started out, with the letters, and approaching strangers and everything, it all felt a bit weird.'

'Still does.'

'I guess. But at first it was all about them, wasn't it? Now, somehow, it's beginning to feel like it's more about us.'

...

Evonne had a potted history of her father's family. His brother, Geoffrey, had predeceased him, while his sister, Mary, lived in the dementia unit of a nursing home on the Gold Coast. Evonne had last seen her at the funeral – her grandson had collected her and brought her to the service.

'Aunt Mary would have been about four when Dad was ten,' she said to Libby. 'Unlikely she'd remember anything from back then. Most of the time she doesn't even know what day it is.'

'You never know. Could be worth a try. Talk to her, see if you can get anything out of her. Or what about her kids? There're a few of them, aren't there? Maybe they know something?'

'There's Xavier, he's her youngest. He's about my age. Lives in Melbourne. You met him at the funeral, remember? And she has a daughter in London and another in Dubai.'

'Gosh, they really flew the coop, didn't they.'

'Xavier's kids are pretty good. They check in on her. And Margot's son, he lives on the Gold Coast, so I think he keeps an eye on her too. Most of the time, she doesn't even recognise them, or that's what I've heard.'

They had scraped the last of the soup from their bowls and sat companionably on chairs facing out over the reserve. Cumulus clouds scudded across the sky, playing hide and seek with the sun. The pungent fragrance of the lemon-scented gums had intensified after the morning's rain. The bush echoed with the ticks and vibrations of unseen animal life.

Evonne closed her eyes and allowed a series of images to scroll

140

through her mind, disconnected memories, pictures flashing across her retinas. A much younger Aunt Mary showing her how to hold a pencil, how to feel the weight of it in her fingers, how to let it fall lightly onto the page. Holidays spent with her cousins, the younger ones tearing around their grandparents' house, their feet slipping and sliding on the protective plastic hall runner laid over the Axminster carpet. The musty smell of her grandfather's armchair in the corner and his library of well-thumbed books with gold-stamped spines. The fantasies they had spun about the fireplace, that it contained a hidden trapdoor that led to a secret passage below the house. She remembered collecting chokoes from the vines that wound around her grandmother's trellises; picking armfuls of fresh mint and helping stir the mint jelly as it thickened on the stovetop; stealing pieces of coke from the ancient coalbox and using them to scratch black lines on the concrete. She could see the outside toilet at Nana's house, the spare toilet roll under the crocheted dress of a Kewpie doll, the cloying aroma from the air freshener that never quite masked the stench from the septic tank, the door that never quite closed properly. She recalled barking dogs, and aviaries full of canaries, and cats who left litters of kittens in the darkness under the house.

So many memories.

But thinking of her youth returned her mind to one singular image: a time soon after Kelly's birth. Her father pacing the bedroom with Kelly swaddled and squawking in his arms. Her mother silent and watchful, the room dim and the curtains drawn. Those few months she had seen a rare side to her father – gentle and considerate. Richard said that Aunt Mary had called their father a good man at the funeral: this memory was her clearest proof of that, but it was complicated by the knowledge that once her mother reappeared from under the cloud, her father was back to stalking through the house, shouting instructions, slamming doors, demanding quiet. She tried to turn back the clock of her mind even further, to her father's childhood. Tried to imagine his memories of growing up, with Geoffrey and Mary, a different generation. Still, she struggled to recall any mention of a significant event from that time, to make sense of what her father had said in his letter to Michael Adamson.

Evonne knew Libby was right. She knew she didn't have to follow this thread any further. She had done what her father had asked.

But she was curious.

...

While Xavier didn't have any further information about his mother's early life, and felt certain Aunt Mary herself would be unable to be forthcoming, he promised to look into it. A week later, Evonne got a phone call.

'I've found something,' Xavier said. 'The old family Bible. It was in a box of photo albums I took from Mum's old house. I've been meaning to sort through it for ages, ever since she went into the nursing home, so I can scan the old photos and give everyone digital copies. Your call pushed me to have a look. It's an old King James Version. And at the front, there's a list of handwritten names, family members going back a couple of generations. There's our great-grandparents, our grandparents and our parents.'

Xavier paused. Evonne could hear him breathing hard. 'But get this,' he said, 'there's another name there.'

'What? Where?'

'In between your father and my mother. *Brian, 1927.* That's all it says.'

'You mean they had another sibling? Are you sure? Dad certainly never said anything. Did your mum ...?'

'Not that I can recall.'

'Well, whoever Brian is – or was – he was never spoken about. Perhaps he died as a child?'

'Must've, I suppose. Unless he was the black sheep or something. Locked away in an asylum or excommunicated from the family.'

'Well, the way this has all been going so far, I wouldn't cross any possibility off the list. Thanks, Xavier. I'll let you know what I find out. If anything.'

And so Evonne returned to searching the Registry of Births, Deaths and Marriages. She entered her uncle's name, Brian Whittaker, along with his parents', Evelyn and Timothy. She hazarded a guess and typed in 1935 as the year of his death. In only a few minutes she had confirmation, and it was easy enough to purchase a copy of the historical records. It was emailed through to her – a scanned image of the ledger where the details of his death were recorded.

Brian Whittaker, aged seven. The cause of death was listed as *dehydration; fractured skull; injury suspected to be inflicted by cattle.* Evonne wasn't sure what to make of this – had little Brian died of dehydration, or from being kicked by a cow? The two hardly seemed compatible. She decided to turn to the newspapers of the day to see if she could find any record of an accident matching the description from the Registry's entry.

Brian's death was recorded as the seventeenth of July, 1935. Evonne started scanning the pages of *The Courier-Mail* from after that date, zooming in on each page, trying to find a link. She was distracted by the events of the time. The country had almost recovered from the Great Depression; the headlines touted economic growth rather than concerns about unemployment. Floods in China at the end of the month killed tens of thousands. Amelia Earhart was in the news for two more solo flights in the Americas after her epic journey across the Atlantic three years earlier. But the news was mostly parochial, related to events much closer to home, the copy filling the pages in densely packed columns. The prominent advertisements stood out: a new Belling piano for ninety-six pounds; an offer of travel to Sydney by sea with 'every Comfort and Amenity' on the TSS *Ormiston*; ads for furriers and tanners, for widowed farmers looking for companionship, for 'bone-dry wood'; announcements for shows at the Tivoli, the Theatre Royal, His Majesty's and the Lyceum. Honey and beeswax were for sale at the Roma Street Markets, along with poultry and eggs, Carmen potatoes and lucerne chaff. A loaf of bread cost five pence.

After reaching August with no luck, she backtracked to the start of July. Perhaps little Brian had received his injuries some time before he died from them. Bingo.

The first of these, from the tenth, was headed *Mystery of Missing Child – Local Lad Lost*. The copy went on to report that *Brian Whittaker (aged 7) has been missing from his Milton home since late yesterday afternoon. Brian was in the care of his brother Daniel (aged 10). The two boys were doing the afternoon milking when Brian wandered off. Police and local men are searching nearby bushland.*

And on the thirteenth: *Missing Lad Found with Severe Injuries – Milton boy Brian Whittaker (7), missing since Tuesday, has been found several kilometres from his home suffering severe head injuries and dehydration. He remains in the Royal Brisbane Hospital in a serious condition.*

And the final entry, which she'd somehow missed, from the eighteenth: *Injuries Fatal, Child Dies – Brian Whittaker (7) has died*

*in hospital from a combination of head injuries possibly inflicted by a kick
from a large animal, and his generally weakened condition sustained from
three nights alone in the cold without food or water. The boy's ten-year-old
brother, who was with him at the time of his disappearance, has been
questioned but the police say no charges are to be laid and there are no
suspicious circumstances.*

Evonne removed her glasses and rubbed her eyes. 'Libby,' she
called. 'Come and look at this.'

...

'God. No wonder that was a tough year. Imagine being only
ten years old and having to mind your little brother, then him
wandering off in the middle of nowhere.'

'But it was Milton. There must have been houses around, surely.'

'Yeah, but mostly farmsteads back then, I reckon. People
would've still had acreage – paddocks, crops. It's quite feasible a
little one could have wandered off and got lost in the scrub.'

'And then he gets kicked in the head by a cow.'

'Or a bull. Or could've been a horse, or anything I suppose.
They don't seem sure.'

'And then to be lying there, injured, in the middle of
winter … God, it doesn't bear thinking about.'

'Poor little mite. And your poor dad. Lot of responsibility for a
ten-year-old.'

'I can't believe we didn't know anything about this. I mean, Dad
had another brother who died, and we were never told about it.'

'You've got to think of the time, Vonnie. Farm accidents
probably weren't all that rare back then, plus kids dying of all sorts
of things – influenza, measles. And the whole family probably felt
pretty damn guilty.'

'Yeah, especially Dad.'

'Of course. I mean, it says in the paper, *Brian was in the care of his brother Daniel*; they even name him. Not sure they'd be allowed to do that today.'

'I can't get my head around two little boys heading off to some remote corner of the homestead to do the milking, all by themselves. Dad never mentioned anything about having cows.'

'Yeah, well. Probably a bit too close to home.'

Evonne glanced again at the pages on the screen. She tried to imagine her father as a frightened child, looking up from a pail of milk to discover an empty space where just moments before his little brother had stood. She imagined him calling Brian's name, and hearing only birdsong and the great quietness of the land in response. Perhaps he thought his little brother was playing hide and seek. She pictured her father getting increasingly desperate when he couldn't find him, debating whether to stay and keep looking, or to run back to the house and sound the alarm.

She imagined the look on her grandmother's face when Daniel had returned to the house alone, out of breath. The helpless feeling as she stood there in the doorway, shushing Mary on her hip, instructing Daniel and Geoffrey to run to the nearest neighbour, to find their father.

She envisaged dusk falling, with still no sign of Brian; Daniel sitting in the dust, exhausted from looking, exhausted from the not knowing. She saw the bobbing lights as locals with torches combed the outlying fields, the deadly quiet that descended once it was too late to keep searching. The men returning home with weary fallen faces, their own families waiting in trepidation and relief, sorry for the tragedy but glad it was not visited upon their own doorstep.

Three nights little Brian was out there, in the dark. Alone. Injured. Hurting. Her father had let him wander off. Had lost him. She imagined Daniel lying awake in his bed, his heart racing with fear.

And when they found Brian – bleeding into the dirt, his head half stoved in from whatever rogue animal had had a go at him – perhaps her father would have been too young to realise the significance of his condition. He might have just been relieved his brother was alive. Even with the blood and with him not talking or moving about, he might have figured Brian would go off to hospital for a day or two, like their mother did when she had the babies, and be back to help him with the milking before he knew it.

But in another five days his brother was dead. And not even a chance to say goodbye.

Evonne imagined her father's guilt. He would've been so, so sorry for losing Brian. Sorry about those damn cattle. Sorry he didn't lend him his green marble when he'd asked to borrow it. Sorry he'd teased him about being afraid of the dark. Sorry he wasn't a better big brother. A small part of him would have shrivelled up inside, into a seed of grief and loss. A physical pain he could feel his whole life. A presence to remind him of his brother's absence.

Evonne wondered how it was possible for this to have happened to her own father, and for her never to have heard about it. The mantle of culpability that had settled on his young shoulders; a cloak of blame, heavy and suffocating. She thought of her father growing into adolescence and adulthood, finishing school, getting a job, being married, having children. And all with the shadow of his dead brother hovering in the background, forever seven years old.

She opened the Bible that had arrived by overnight express. The words were inscribed in black ink. She ran a finger over the names of her uncle and her aunt, and her father, and then of her other uncle, Brian. A slight indentation in the thin, onion-skin paper. The fine, spidery writing hinting at his existence.

THEY HAD ORDERED THAI TAKEAWAY and now Jemima was reading the girls a story and settling them for the night. Richard turned the envelope over and over. He sipped from his whisky and water, one of several he'd had over the last few hours. October already. His father in the ground nearly a year. He thought again of his sisters' words, describing their father as thankful and forgiving and compassionate. That was not how he remembered his father at all. He saw him as gruff, and determined, and demanding – slightly bullying when the circumstances warranted it.

How strange to have entire chunks of his father's life about which he knew so little. He wondered what had gone on during the war. His father had hardly spoken of it. He had never displayed those medals they found packed away under the stairs. Changed the channel to avoid watching war movies. Richard had once toyed with the idea of joining the army, but now he couldn't imagine what he had been thinking. He couldn't picture himself donning a uniform and kissing Jemima and the girls goodbye, all the while thinking *maybe this will be the last time*. Boarding a train with thousands of other men – or boys – all of them shouting farewells to mothers and baby brothers and grandparents. No, Richard couldn't see it at all.

He wondered what his own children would think of him when he was gone, how they would view his life. And if he were to leave his own letters behind, who would he write to? How would he address his regrets? How would he right his wrongs?

...

'They're off, finally.' Jemima flopped onto the sofa.

'Want one?' Richard held his glass aloft.

She shook her head, one eyebrow raised. 'Is that your last letter?' she asked, pointing at the envelope in Richard's hands.

'Yep. For me, anyway.' He passed her the thick packet, full almost to bursting with whatever it enclosed, the sides reinforced with sticky tape. 'The mysterious Jeffrey Upton. It's bloody nigh on impossible. No other information, no date, place, nothing. Just the name. There's hundreds of J Uptons listed, and that's just the ones that are still alive. Most of these letters have been addressed to people who've already died, or at least have one foot in the grave.'

'At least you're near the end.'

'Except for the three that Hardcastle is *withholding*. God knows what's in them. I dread to think.'

They were silent for a moment. A kookaburra chortled outside, as the tree branches scraped against the window in the dark. Suddenly Jemima sat up straight.

'What about your dad's notebooks?' she said.

'What notebooks?'

'You know, that box of journals and things Evonne found in the unit. I think there were old school books, maybe a diary from when he was younger, some workbooks from real estate courses … Evonne said she'd go through it and keep whatever was worth keeping. Chuck the rest. I don't know why we haven't thought of this before.'

Richard could think of nothing worse than rifling through some dusty old boxes. 'It's a bit of a long shot, hoping that one name might pop up there after all these years.'

'Worth a try, though? Can't hurt.'

'Maybe.' As he sipped his whisky, he noticed Jemima raising an eyebrow again.

'That should be the last one for you, Richard. Time to put the bottle away?'

'Don't tell me when I've had enough,' he glowered. 'And I didn't appreciate you leaving that article out, either.'

'What article?'

'The one about what constitutes a standard drink. I'm not a child, Jem. I know my limits.'

'You can't deny you've been drinking more since your father died. It's not good for you. Think of your heart.'

Richard drained his glass and refilled it, staring at her defiantly over the rim. How easy it would be to confide in her, to explain his behaviour. He was so tired of pretending.

But he foresaw the bewilderment on his wife's face. The derision. The pity.

'I'll be the judge of how much I drink,' he said coldly. The call of the kookaburra sounded again, its piercing laughter mocking him.

Jemima stood up and tried to take the glass from his hand. He held firm. 'For heaven's sake, Richard. Your mood these last months has been terrible. And you *are* drinking too much. If you don't want to be treated like a child, then stop acting like one.'

In an explosion of movement, Richard stood and wrenched the glass from her grip. Whisky splashed over his shirt. He hurled the tumbler at the brick mantelpiece of the fireplace. The glass shattered. He took Jemima's face in his grasp. His grip was tight.

'Richard, you're hurting me,' she whispered.

'Don't. Tell me. What to. Do.' He pushed her head back and turned away, his hand now on his own face, running over his closed eyes. *My God*, he thought, *what have I done?* He was not that kind of man. He *was not*. He wiped his hand over his damp shirtfront; he smelt like a distillery.

When he turned back, Jemima was kneeling on the carpet, picking slivers of glass out of the pile and placing them in a shallow ceramic bowl. She was shaking.

'I'm sorry,' he said. 'Jem, please, look at me. I'm sorry. I didn't mean to be so rough. I shouldn't have pushed you. Sorry.' He noticed his own hands trembling. He clasped his fingers together, still not quite believing they had been capable of such force. The tang of whisky rose from the wet patch where it had splashed onto the carpet as well as his shirt.

Jemima spoke in a small voice. 'You've had too much to drink, Richard. You should go to bed.'

'Look, I said I'm sorry. I'm very stressed at the moment. All this, with Dad leading us up the bloody garden path.'

'That's no excuse and you know it.' Her voice stronger.

'I said I'm sorry. What more do you want? Jesus Christ, if you don't want a reaction, don't start telling me what I can and can't do in my own home!' His words slashed the air between them as sharply as the shattered glass. Why could he not help himself? He felt nauseated; a bubble of bile rose in his throat.

Jemima rose. She put the bowl on the table.

Richard approached her, but she flinched. 'I really am sorry, Jem. It won't happen again. Forgive me? Please?' He could hear his voice wavering.

Her eyes were clear but pained. 'It'd better not. I won't put up with it, Richard. Not again.'

. . .

Jemima hardly spoke to him the next morning, apart from a curt reminder to call Evonne about the box. 'I'm going out,' she said as she was leaving the house. 'The girls are going straight from school to a sleepover. I won't be home for dinner.' She slammed the door with more strength than he thought necessary. Contrite, he rang his sister as soon as he was alone in the house.

'I'd completely forgotten about it,' she said. 'It's been under the house since we cleared the unit. I haven't had time to look through it properly yet. I don't want stuff thrown out willy-nilly. Thought the kids might be interested in keeping some of the old notebooks.'

'Yes, yes. Don't worry. I won't throw anything away. I'll do a quick search for any reference to Jeffrey Upton and return the box intact.'

He hung up and listened to the quiet of his home mid-week, the girls at school, Jemima gone, most of the neighbours at work. Where he should be. Where he *was*, should anyone ask.

He had been stupid yesterday. He had drunk too much and lost control. How long could he keep up this charade? He'd thought his position at the bank was secure. With a pang, he recalled the 'voluntary redundancies' he had been forced to manage before he himself had been given the chop. Unbelievable. The top brass had waited until he'd done all their dirty work and then given him his marching orders.

Before he knew he was doing it, Richard found himself with a glass of whisky on ice in front of him. He felt a momentary twinge of something like guilt, but he thought again of his bosses at work and all those bloody letters, and he sat back and sipped gratefully, feeling the warm liquid slide down the back of his throat and settle in his gut.

...

The following Friday, Richard sat at his desk, the contents of the box from Evonne spread across its surface. There were reams of paper relating to real estate – courses, accreditations, copies of old contracts. There were a couple of folders containing university course notes, and Richard realised with a start that his father had completed some tertiary studies as an adult, subjects in business and accounting and economics. Received good grades, too. Richard remembered arguing with his father once about the value of a university education; he recalled barking at his father that he wouldn't understand, as he'd never studied further than high school. Had his father pursued extra studies to prove a point to Richard? Or had he been in possession of these documents the whole time – proof of his thirst for knowledge – and simply not wanted to contradict his son? Richard remembered shouting his father down. But perhaps his father had merely chosen not to disabuse him of his youthful notions of self-importance.

There were school notebooks, marked in red. A diary in childish scrawl. Richard flipped through the pages. Descriptions of marbles and Matchbox cars. Some drawings on pieces of lined paper, previously stuck in with sticky tape but now yellowed and loose. The drawings were quite good – a child leaning over a railing, a baby chicken, a dog. Richard wondered if they had been done by Aunt Mary. Towards the end of the book were more loose sheets – notes and old letters, order forms and lists. And, suddenly, there it was – the name Jeffrey leapt out at him from the page. It was a list of boys' names, written in looping script in blue ink. Classmates? Friends? Richard peered more closely at the other papers, trying to find the name again.

An hour later, he slammed shut the diary. No further mention of Jeffrey, and no mention at all of anyone named Upton. He glared at the mess of papers and books and journals, and began sweeping them into a pile.

As he dumped the papers into the box, the dog-eared corner of a photograph peeped out from the cover of an exercise book. Richard wasn't sure how he'd missed it earlier. He tugged until the photo came away – a group of boys in three neat rows, dressed in football uniform, the seated ones with their legs apart, their hands on their knees. He turned it over. Written on the back were the names of the fifteen boys pictured. He found D. Whittaker (seated, first on the left) … and J. Upton (second row, in the middle). He slapped the desk in triumph.

Richard found a magnifying glass to look more closely at the photograph. The boys' bodies were adolescent, their faces marked with acne. His father looked about sixteen. Some of the team looked much older – bulging biceps, a casual strength. Rough and ready, thought Richard. Typical public-school issue. Thank God he'd had the sense, foresight and – well, to put it bluntly – the money to send the girls to a good private school, where they didn't have to mix with riff-raff like the boys in this photo. But then his eyes fell on the adolescent face of his father, and he felt ashamed of his ungenerous thoughts.

As he stared at the boys in the photograph, he pondered again the things his father had known and never shared. This naive-looking boy in the photo would live through the carnage of war; he would witness brutality and barbarism that Richard could only imagine. His manhood had been forged through inconceivable times of conflict and hate.

In comparison, Richard's own life appeared inconsequential. Trivial.

. . .

A few days and a couple of phone calls later, Richard found himself in the Archives Library of his father's old high school. A helpful young man had pointed him in the direction of the year-book collection, and said he was welcome to photocopy anything of interest.

It didn't take him long to find his father. Here a class shot of barely pubescent boys in Grade Nine, his father staring out grimly from under a thatch of untrimmed hair. Here – and this was a surprise – a description of the Junior drama production of *Hamlet*, his father mentioned as performing one of the minor roles. Richard had never thought of his father as having an interest in drama, or in any of the arts, actually. There was a staged photograph of a group of students in white lab coats huddled around a Bunsen burner; Richard couldn't see his father's face, but the title suggested he was there. He was mentioned as one of the organisers of the Grade Eleven end-of-year dance. Pictured at that same dance with a pretty girl in a gingham dress with a tightly cinched waist. Richard wondered if this was Audrey Blackson, whom Evonne had met.

The background hum of school life continued around him. A photocopier whirred, a disembodied voice made indecipherable announcements, a bell dinged from the front counter, students' chatter rose and fell from outside the windows. Richard shut his eyes as his own memories came flooding back. The whiff of body odour and unwashed gym clothes in a locker; the haze of smoke drifting over the oval as the groundsmen burnt off the rubbish. Spilt ink blotting the pocket of his shirt, staining his hands. He saw his mother standing stiffly at a parent function, her hat slightly askew, gripping her handbag in front of her like it was a shield. His father's reluctant appearances at sporting events, arriving late and leaving early. He remembered school lunches, rowing and fencing, community service events. His whole life had been contained within the life of his school, his identity subsumed by its parameters.

Strange how he had never before considered that his father's life had been the same.

Eventually he turned a page to see the same photograph that had grabbed his attention days earlier in his study – that of the rugby team. And there was J. – presumably Jeffrey – Upton, staring out at him from the second row.

Richard realised that he had become distracted by looking for evidence of his father's place in the school, and had lost sight of his task: to find clues about Jeffrey Upton. He went back through the record books, looking this time for Upton rather than Whittaker, or, preferably, for the two names connected in some way. Jeffrey Upton had as many references as his father, maybe more. He was a member of the debating team; he played cricket and tennis as well as rugby. He was a founding member of a committee formed to support the war effort – it appeared that the boys collected bottles, newspapers and old tyres (for what purpose, Richard couldn't fathom), while the girls knitted socks and scarves for the soldiers. Jeffrey Upton was certainly busy.

The photograph of the Senior Class of 1941 had been taken outside, the tips of trees showing in the background, various shades of grey. He checked the names under the black and white shot – and there was J. Upton, near the back right. Richard searched for his father's name but it wasn't there. Richard flicked back through the year books. The last mention of Daniel Whittaker that he could find was his name in the Honours List for Academic Achievement in Science in Sub-Senior, 1940. He checked again. Nothing.

Then it hit him. The war. Of course.

Kelly had said something about their father lying about his age in order to enlist. Sixteen, she'd said. Their father had enlisted for service at the tender age of sixteen, but had somehow managed to convince the military personnel that he was nineteen, at least. Richard supposed he must have forged his parents' consent.

If their father had enlisted at sixteen, he wouldn't have finished his Senior year.

Without quite knowing how it got there, he noticed in his hand the grieving stone that the Mosely woman had given him. It seemed to cleave perfectly to the shape of his palm. Its smooth edges curved into the hollow of his clenched fingers. Rubbing it made a comforting, rasping noise on his skin.

Richard flicked back to the photograph of his father at the Grade Eleven dance. A young man – a boy, really – stared back at him. A boy with his whole life ahead of him. A boy who'd just been awarded an Academic Achievement in Science (*fat lot of good that had done him*, thought Richard grimly). A boy with the wild fantasy of war and adventure in his head. Richard thought back to himself at the age of sixteen. The most responsibility he had to manage was his paper run. He tried to imagine himself marching up to army personnel and bluntly lying about his age. Lying for the privilege of putting on a uniform and marching around in the heat with a heavy pack. The privilege of travelling to foreign shores to defend his country. The privilege of being shot at. Of aiming his own rifle at the face of a stranger, and pulling the trigger.

He tried to envision himself doing all those things, but he failed.

He had never even held a gun.

In his mind's eye, he saw his father, watching his family as they stitched together the pieces of his life that he didn't have the nerve – or the capacity – to mend himself.

Surely his father had changed because of the war. It must have loomed large in his consciousness, an intense experience scaffolded by a profound silence. A black time. Death and sorrow. Unswerving loyalty. Unforgivable cowardice.

Forgivable cowardice.

Richard had only one clear memory of his father speaking about the war; it shone because it was so rare. The two of them had been alone at home, and his father had consumed almost two bottles of red wine. There had been something on the news about a Japanese soldier found on a remote island in the Philippines; apparently, unaware that the war was over, he had been in hiding for over thirty years, surviving in the dense jungle. He had wept when surrendering his rifle, anxious he would be court-martialled for desertion.

'I shot a Jap in the forehead,' his father had said calmly. 'Bam, one clean shot.'

Richard had stared at his father, incredulous.

'It was either him or me.' He had gulped down the dregs of his glass and walked over to turn off the television. That was the end of the discussion.

Richard now wondered if his father had thought of the other man's family. His wife and children, if he had them; his parents. Or had he been overtaken by fear? He thought of the Japanese soldier, isolated for those long lonely years, in constant anxiety that he would be discovered by the enemy, captured and imprisoned. Yet it would have also required an immense inner fortitude to survive such an ordeal. Just as his father would have needed grit and resolve to shoot at another person. He wondered how such monumental aspects of human character were to be spoken of with mere words. The failure. The surprise. The depths of despair. The ability of the human heart to keep beating in the most horrific circumstances, when surely it should give up.

Could he blame the war for his father's nature? For his silences and his emotional distance? For his intolerance? Or perhaps that was a coward's excuse, a blanket to throw over all that came afterwards. The enormity of war used to camouflage bad behaviour, to hide one's inadequacies.

It was all so long ago.

And yet the reverberations rippled across the years.

...

Tracking down Mr Jeffrey Upton – or at least, his descendants – proved to be surprisingly easy. Between the school's historical records, the electoral roll, and a few searches done through the Titles Office and the Office of Births, Deaths and Marriages, Richard was able to trace a line to Jeffrey's grandson Hunter, who lived in Stanthorpe. Jeffrey himself had died over twenty years previously, and his son had succumbed to cancer not long afterwards, but Hunter Upton said he would be pleased to meet with Richard and receive the letter.

Richard decided to take Jemima and the girls and make a weekend of it; he was trying to make amends. Crossing from Brisbane to the Southern Downs was like passing into a different country – as soon as they reached Cunningham's Gap, heralded by bellbirds, they felt the cool change in the air, the atmosphere thin and clear. They stopped at a roadside stall at Applethorpe to buy early-season nectarines and apricots, leaving their money in an honesty box made from an old fruit-packing carton.

Their accommodation was at a boutique winery on the other side of sleepy Stanthorpe. As evening settled, the girls spotted kangaroos outside the window of their villa, which was open to the aching isolation of the fields. The animals were there again the next morning, a sizeable mob grazing on the fresh, tender grass cultivated around the cottage. Victoria and Violetta sat motionless at the plate glass, staring at this wildness brought so close to their door.

The silence was encompassing. No traffic, no neighbours; even the bugs were quiet, with only the sporadic *whop* of the kangaroos' tails slamming into the earth as the animals bounded away into the brush.

'Come on, girls. Are you finished with your toast? Get your coats. Might be chilly out.' Jemima brushed hair and adjusted buttons and hustled them into the car. She and the girls planned to explore the second-hand shops and craft stores along the main tourist strip, after dropping Richard off in the town centre.

He had agreed to meet Hunter Upton at the tea house, which was decked out to mimic a domestic living room. Odd sofas and an eclectic mixture of chairs dotted the room, the framed work of local artists gracing the walls. Old kitchen utensils had been given new life: a rack of hanging cheese graters were illuminated by tea light candles; a mobile or wind chime made from forks and hand beaters and battered metal spatulas was hung in every doorway. A different salt and pepper set adorned each table – the one not matching the other. Wine barrels served as side tables, wine bottles as vases. The effect was strangely comforting.

Hunter stood to greet Richard. His handshake was firm and warm.

'Down from the big smoke, eh?' he said. 'Heard it's been getting warm. Bet you're enjoying this cooler weather. Where're you staying? Oh, that's right, you did say, The Drunken Grape. They make a nice drop. Last year's pinot was superb. Now, cup of tea? Coffee?'

Richard found it hard to get a word in edgeways, but eventually Hunter Upton's mouth was busy with cake and Richard managed to turn the conversation to the purpose of his visit. He placed the packet on the table between them.

Hunter swallowed. 'So this is it, hey? Well, will you look at that. Jeffrey Upton. Strange to see his name written there like that, after he's been gone so many years. Dad's gone too, did I tell you that? Only me and my sister left now, and she's over in New York, living with some American guy who builds installation art, whatever the hell that is. Does something with old cars. Not my cup of tea, but there you go, different strokes for different folks, hey. Should I …?'

'Yes. Please,' said Richard. 'Go ahead.'

Prising open the packet was not a simple task – the tape was yellowed with age but stuck fiercely to all four sides of the large envelope. Eventually, Hunter resorted to the use of a butter knife, and the envelope's contents spilt forth onto the table. Newspaper clippings, dozens of them, the print grey and faded, the edges brittle or curling with age. A couple of old-fashioned mimeographed copies; Richard recognised the spreading stain of the purple ink, each letter having long ago lost its clarity and bled into its neighbour. A folded sheet of white paper sat atop the pile. Hunter Upton fanned the mound of documents across the table and picked up the letter. It was all Richard could do to restrain himself from delving into the clippings and copies, but he waited patiently. After a good five or six minutes, Hunter refolded the paper and tapped it on the tabletop, two fingers to his lips, apparently deep in thought.

'Well?' said Richard. 'What does it say?'

The other man appeared to consider whether to pass it over. With an arrogant shrug, he threw the letter down onto the pile of papers. 'Doesn't mean much to me, mate.'

Richard recognised his father's hand.

Jeffrey –

The years we spent – I won't say 'together' – that sounds as if we were friends – at school now seem very far behind me. I look at myself now, the man I have become, and what I see is in some ways far removed from what I was, and yet in other ways is so much still the same.

Those were unhappy years for me, those secondary school years.

We played at being men of course, in those early years of the war, hoarding precious materials and co-ordinating care packages. 'Doing our bit', as we thought. How could we have known the horrors that were to come? Perhaps nobody knows, not truly, not until they are embroiled in it themselves, standing in the muck and mud, levelling a rifle at a stranger's head, holding together the pieces of your best mate's face as he wails with what's left of his throat.

I heard you were called up. So no doubt you've seen as bad as me. Possibly worse, although I find that difficult to imagine. But I suppose I've learnt that there is always something worse.

But before those days of battle, we were merely two young men just out of short pants, studying Shakespeare and memorising the periodic table as if verse and the elements would make a difference, as if they would matter at all. Still, even sixteen-year-old boys have unseen struggles. Your father drank, they said. Belted your mother black and blue. Belted you too, when you didn't get out of the way quick enough. So I guess you didn't have it easy at home. (But why am I making excuses for you?)

Whatever dreadfulness you endured at home inured you to violence. By the time I met you, you were accustomed to being the big man, the tough guy. And I was an easy target.

Your bullying was so intense, so relentless, so brutal. It shames me now to think of it. You shoved my head into dirty lavatory water more times than I can remember. I can still hear the roar of the water around my ears as I struggled to hold my breath. You had boys pin me against a wall while you pummelled me with your fists. You stole my shirt when we were at physical training, and my gym clothes when we were not. I found my tie wound around bathroom pipes and strung across doorways. I lost count of the many times I saw something of my own — a new pencil, an unmarked notepad, my worn card deck — carried about your person as if you had owned it forever.

Yes, I have thought of you often over the years, Jeffrey Upton. I have remembered your bullying. Not that it was seen as such. Back then you were just a high-spirited boy from a rough background who knew how to handle himself. You were feared and venerated in equal measure. Despised and revered.

I saw enlistment as a way out. An escape.

I can hardly believe that now, but it was true. I thought that being in the army and going into battle would be better than remaining at school to face you and your ilk every day. How deluded I was. I escaped one sort of hell only to find myself in another.

I've done a lot of research since into the correlation between boyhood conflicts and acts of war. They're not so far apart. The bullied take it out on those weaker and more vulnerable, and the bullies move on to bigger prey. War is merely an excuse to legitimise the tactics.

So many times over the years I was determined to confront you, to challenge you on what you did. I spent hours at the library, copying down statistics and anecdotal evidence to explain your abuse and your power over me, to validate my all-encompassing fear of you, to justify my hatred of everything you represented.

But I am reduced to this: to confronting you in a letter that will not be delivered until after my death. Perhaps you have passed before me, and in that case this will be no sort of confrontation at all. In any case, I enclose the research I have collected over the years, in part to make some sense of your actions in the schoolyard. But it is also my attempt to coax some meaning from the madness of war. For what we all did was inexcusable.

Sincerely
Daniel Whittaker

Richard felt a profound humiliation on behalf of his father. He felt an unreasonable dislike for Hunter Upton, his mind somehow blending the two Upton men into the same bully. He reached for the topmost newspaper article. 'May I?'

Hunter Upton sat back in his chair. 'Go your hardest, mate.'

He read the article, then the one under that, and the one under that. The first headline blazed across the page in bold font: *'Analogy between Playground Battles and Wartime Disputes'*. Underneath that was a copy of an article that looked to be clipped from a business journal: *'Teaching Our Children to Wield a Big Stick – the Psychology behind Power and Might'*.

Snippets and phrases caught his eye: *'The attitude of a country's citizens towards a whole war is a direct reflection of the state of that nation's public institutions.' 'How people approach confrontation provides helpful insights into their historical relationships and resolution of conflict.'* 'Social *chronology, biology and intellectual history all relate to masculinity in schools.' 'Post-colonial "bullying" is mirrored in society's places of learning.'* The list went on and on, touching on juvenile delinquency, truants, suicide and criminal behaviour.

'My God,' said Richard. 'This is incredible.' When he received no response, he pushed further. 'Don't you have anything to say about all this?' He clutched a handful of articles and waved them about.

Hunter Upton held up his hands. 'Looks as if your father was a bit obsessed, if you ask me.'

'Obsessed?' Richard stuttered. 'Your grandfather was a bully. He sounds like a monster. My father … my God, my father actually joined up rather than stay and face him.' He slapped the articles back on the table and held his head in his hands. He thought of his father as a young man, being harassed and humiliated – *tortured* – to the point where he enlisted. Richard had always assumed his father had joined up out of duty, and because he believed in the cause. Could it be true that he had been merely running away from his own problems?

Richard gave Hunter Upton a cold, hard stare.

'What?' Hunter replied, unfazed. 'Your father and my grandfather didn't get along. So what? Plenty of schoolyard shenanigans back then.'

'Schoolyard shenanigans?' Richard could hardly believe the words he was hearing.

'Yeah, hijinks, tomfoolery. Whatever. Clearly your old man didn't cope. All this …' Hunter swept his arm across the scattered papers. 'Well, it's not normal, is it? He's fixated on it.'

Richard spoke through gritted teeth. '*My* father was being

bullied by *your* grandfather, and this is a message to let him know he hadn't forgotten. Enlisting changed the course of his *life*,' he snapped.

'Well, we only have his word for that, don't we. My grandfather's not here to defend himself. Easy to lay recriminations at the feet of a dead man.' Hunter clasped his hands behind his head. 'I mean, maybe your father felt guilty over whatever he got up to during the war. Maybe this is him trying to make excuses for what he'd done.'

'I don't have to sit here and listen to this.' Richard pushed the pile across the table. 'I've done my duty. I was asked to deliver the letter and I've delivered it. Do what you like with the stuff – burn it, for all I care.' He stood to leave, collecting his coat from the back of his chair. He anchored a ten-dollar note under his teacup, still half full.

'No skin off my nose, mate. You're the one who drove all this way.'

Richard pushed his way past an overstuffed couch and a pink plastic flamingo, Hunter Upton's voice calling out behind him.

'*You* arranged to meet *me*, remember? Maybe your old man had a message for *you*!'

. . .

Later that evening, Richard sat by the fire in the cottage and poured himself another glass of red wine. He had lashed out at Jemima on the way back from dinner. She was driving, of course. She always did. But she had made some comment this time about how it would've been nice if she could've had more than one glass with dinner, and he had barked at her. He wanted to snatch back the words as soon as they were out of his mouth, recalling his intention to make things up to her, but she ignored his stammering apology. The girls had grown wary and silent, and Jemima had turned in soon after them once they arrived back at the villa. So now Richard sat alone, contemplating Hunter Upton's parting shot.

Perhaps it was true; perhaps his father did have a message for him, and for his sisters. The uncomfortable parallel between Jeffrey Upton's behaviour and Richard's own was not lost on him. He thought of how he had taken out his frustrations on Jemima: his anxieties about work and money and his father's will. He winced as he remembered his acts of selfishness and anger and hurtfulness, his cruel and unkind behaviour. The times he thought only of himself, and put his own needs first.

Such a litany of regrets. Such a shameful burden of wrongs.

And now, when it was all too late, his father had left these flimsy letters, some written half a lifetime ago. Many of them now rendered meaningless. Why didn't he just send them at the time? Richard didn't know. All he recognised was the irresistible urge for atonement, for reparation.

Richard wondered if his father was watching the three of them as they followed his instructions. What would he see? They had been disparaging, yes, sometimes. But they were also gaining some measure of understanding towards him: the bullied adolescent, the errant husband, the grieving brother. Perhaps that was a small gesture of hope.

When he held the grieving stone in his hand, the flames reflected from its black surface. But when he raised it to the firelight, it seemed a little less cloudy, a little less opaque. A little clearer.

KELLY AND HER FRIEND SALLY were on their third drinks at their local, which ran as a cafe in the daytime and as a bar with live music at night.

'So Richard says,' she continued, her words slurring slightly, '"let sleeping dogs lie, I reckon".' She imitated her brother's pompous tone. '"Obviously Dad had to get something off his chest, and he did, and that's that. Move on, I say."'

'God, he's an irritating prick. Probably just pleased there wasn't another cheque attached.'

'Exactly!' said Kelly. 'That's exactly what he said. "At least there was no cheque." I wish I'd told him what I *really* thought. Why do we spend so much time saying what people want to hear? Women, I mean.'

'That's your third G and T talking.'

'No, I'm serious. We never say what's in our hearts. What we say doesn't at all resemble what we feel. We don't want to hurt other people, or open ourselves up to a vulnerable position …'

'We don't want to reach out in case our feelings aren't reciprocated …'

'We don't declare our fury or our shame or our sense of powerlessness. None of those things. Our words don't come from our true emotions, but the emotions that we feel other people can bear.'

'It's about what we think people *want* to hear.' Sally rolled her eyes and took a gulp of her gin.

A heavy-set man with a bushy beard and a man-bun had begun setting up amps and his acoustic guitar. Background music throbbed through the crowd.

Kelly leant towards her friend. 'How many times have you pulled up short, in case you say something you'll regret?'

'Engaging my brain before putting my mouth into gear? Not often enough, probably.'

'But what if that's all a mistake? What if allowing your emotions to flow freely is the only true expression?'

'Yeah, it's like it's bred into us to tread carefully. Do you know that it's scientifically proven that women are far more likely to suggest than to demand? We're more likely to assist rather than to expect assistance. We grow up expecting to be the ones placating and generous.'

Kelly held two fingers up to the waiter and he nodded at the request. 'It's true. Men are allowed – no, *encouraged* – to say what they like. To ask for what they want. My father was always so direct in all his interactions – with Mum, with our family, with people at work. He had no fear of what people might think. Or that's how I'd always seen him in the past, anyway.'

'And now?' asked Sally.

'Now ... now I'm not so sure. It's not always black and white. I read these letters, or hear about the others from Evonne or Richard, and I try to imagine him lacking the courage to stand up to Jeffrey Upton, or to say what he thought to Irene, or to any of them. But it's so difficult to think of him as being less demanding, less confident.'

'I dare say we remember our parents as how they were when we were growing up. It's a formative time, after all.'

Kelly felt light-headed from the combination of alcohol and not enough food in the last few hours. The first time she had drunk too much gin, she was seventeen and supposed to be at the cinema with a group of girlfriends. But Darren Webb, a boy she fancied, an apprentice mechanic with oil-slicked hair and permanently grimy nails, had persuaded her to sneak out early and sit with him in the local park. He was twenty-one, long finished with school, and had a bottle of Beefeater in a brown paper bag. He pushed her on the swing until she was dizzy. She lost track of time. It was only when she saw her father, marching along the pebbled path towards them, that she realised the movie had finished an hour earlier. He would have been waiting for her outside the cinema. Her friends wouldn't have known what to tell him.

Her father had moved with the fury of a contained animal. He strode up to Darren, grabbed the bottle from his hand and smashed it against the path. He grasped the boy's collar and practically lifted him off the ground. Their faces almost touching, he growled that if the boy ever so much as looked at Kelly again, he would regret it. After Darren took off into the night, her father stomped towards her, and for a terrible moment she thought he was going to hit her. But he didn't.

'I thought I'd lost you,' he said simply. She saw tears in his eyes.

Then he turned from her, and tramped to the car.

He never mentioned the incident again, and neither did she.

How could that indomitable man also be so wary of speaking his mind?

Again she saw her father as he was in his last weeks. A husk of his former self. He had winced as he stood, and sighed as he settled into his chair. He continually wiped at his one watery eye, and his thin, dry lips stuck together as he spoke. He had not said no when she offered to walk out to the mailbox to collect his post. He had reached the last page of the sports section before realising that it was yesterday's paper, and then laughed and said it didn't matter.

He had called her Shirley when she left.

...

'Anyway,' Sally ventured, 'back to business. As I said on the phone, I think I may have found your elusive Monteray Max.'

Sally volunteered on a coffee van for the homeless in the city, doing the weekend shifts.

'So I'm working the Sunday-morning slot with Gina, you know the woman who runs the shelter over at Windsor? I was telling her about this wild goose chase you're on, having to give letters to strangers, then I mentioned that you were still hunting one fellow down. I couldn't remember if his name was Max Monteray, or the other way around. Anyhow, Gina's eyes grew so large I thought they were going to fall out of her head, and she said, wow, that's a real coincidence, 'cause there used to be a disabled guy at the shelter, years ago this was, before Gina ever worked there, and his name was Monteray. Gina remembered because he used to do a magic act and his nickname was Monteray the Magician.'

'No way.'

'I kid you not. He was in a wheelchair, I don't know why. Maybe he had polio – anyway, he couldn't walk, couldn't work either, and so he was a regular fixture at the shelter. Gina even said that there's a photograph of him. They have all these photos from the past, and they have one of him with a dove on his shoulder. Monteray Max the Magician.'

'Are you serious. You're not bullshitting me?'

'That's what she told me. She said I could take you to see the photo if you want. I mean, he's probably dead by now, it was that long ago, but I'll bet it's the same guy. How many guys are walking around with the name Monteray Max?'

'Or not walking around,' mused Kelly. 'Being pushed around in a wheelchair, maybe.' She sat back in her chair. 'You might have just saved me a whole lot of time and trouble.'

'Guess you're getting the next round then, hey.'

...

Gina led Kelly and Sally through the shelter to the main activity room. A flat-screen TV showed a muted cricket game. A woman with green hair sat at a laptop in one corner; three middle-aged men played cards in another. A woman with a very young baby strapped to her chest in a sling was folding washing on the dining table. She gave them a shy smile.

'Just over here,' said Gina. She headed towards the far wall, which was covered with framed photographs. Most were recent shots, but some were older. Gina pointed at one in a plain wooden frame.

'See? I told you.' She squinted to read the fine print underneath. '"Fun and Games! Monteray the Magician and Singing Sue Provide Sunday Entertainment for the Residents, 1948."'

The man in the photograph looked to be in his twenties. He was seated in an old-fashioned wheelchair. He was dressed in a formal suit and there was indeed, as Sally had said, a dove on his shoulder. A woman in a tailored skirt and jacket with a trim peplum stood behind him, her left hand on his right shoulder. They both stared directly into the camera. The woman – 'Singing Sue' – had an enigmatic smile on her face. Monteray the Magician wasn't exactly frowning, but he didn't look too jolly, either.

'Wow,' said Sally. 'This must be him, surely.' She turned to Kelly. 'How old was your father in 1948?'

Kelly calculated on her fingers. 'He was born in 1925, so … twenty-three? That would fit. He and this Monteray Max would have been about the same age.' She turned to Gina. 'Do you have any more information about him? Are there any records here at the hostel?'

'Way ahead of you,' she said, smiling. 'Already looked. Come through to the office and I'll show you what I found.'

They went back through the main room. Gina had a quiet word to an older lady buttering toast on the bench, and bent down to say something to a young man squatting on the floor, a tattered backpack at his feet.

'Give me ten minutes,' Kelly heard her say. The new arrival stretched out on the floor, his pack under his head, his eyes closed, his arms folded across his chest as if he was dead.

Monteray Max's real name was indeed Max Monteray. His stage name for his role as an amateur conjuror and illusionist had been Monteray the Magician. He had been a guest at the hostel on and off between 1944 and 1952, when he had died from consumption.

'Consumption,' said Sally. 'You don't hear that very often anymore.'

'Another word for pulmonary tuberculosis,' said Gina. 'TB. Very common after the war. Lots of soldiers returned home from the fighting already infected.'

'So was he in the army, then?'

'Infantry. Fought in New Guinea, I believe. That's how he lost the use of his legs.'

'Dad fought in New Guinea. That could be the connection. What happened?'

'Well, according to what I could find out, he took some shrapnel to his spine in a ground attack in … let's see, when was it … oh, yes, here we are … late 1943. Medically discharged and sent home. Only trouble was, he had no home to go to. Both his parents had passed away. I believe he had a sister in Cairns, but she was busy with little ones, and her husband was away in the war, too. Monteray Max spent a few months at a repat hospital but they had to discharge him eventually – needed the beds. Steady influx of wounded coming back from Europe and the Pacific. He had nowhere to go, so he came here.'

'What, he lived here permanently?'

'Oh no, they weren't allowed to stay indefinitely, even if they had nowhere else to go. I think back then …' She glanced at her notes. 'Yes, they could stay for up to two weeks at a time. Then they had to be discharged for at least twenty-one days, before they could come back.'

'But where would they go for those three weeks?'

Gina's smile was a sad one. 'There are no records about where the men lived when they weren't here at the hostel. It was only men then, no women allowed. And mostly returned soldiers. Lots of them suffering not just terrible physical injuries, but mentally as well. Depression, post-traumatic shock, although of course it wasn't called that back then. Even psychotic episodes, some of them. The worst cases were put into asylums or psychiatric hospitals, but there weren't many of those around. The others … well, the others just muddled through, I suppose. Did the best they could.'

They were silent. Eventually Kelly spoke. 'So he died in 1952, did you say?'

'Yes. Of tuberculosis. He must've had a relapse.'

'He wasn't married? Not to Singing Sue here?' She gestured at the photograph.

'No, but as I said, he had a sister.' Gina opened a dusty ledger to a page she had previously bookmarked. 'Here, you see? Under next of kin they've listed: Carrie Birch, sister. Must be her married name. There's an address in Cairns. Perhaps you could try starting there?'

Kelly copied out the details. 'Thanks so much, Gina. You're an angel. I was putting this one off. The name sounded so strange, I wasn't sure where to begin.'

. . .

Kelly's calls to Cairns led to the news that Carrie Birch had died in 1963. Her surviving children were scattered around the globe – two sons in the United States, a daughter in England and another in Japan. This last was the only one who answered Kelly's emails with anything approaching affability; not surprising, Kelly thought, when she was searching for details about their long-dead mother's brother, who was even longer deceased. Phillipa Reynolds – Pip – was almost seventy and worked as an English teacher on the island of Shikoku. She had long set aside her life in Australia, but in one email, told Kelly that she did remember her Uncle Max: *I was only a child when he died, maybe six or seven years old? I recall him being in a wheelchair, and I wasn't to ask him about it. But the thing I remember most clearly is his magic tricks. He used to make things disappear – a coin, a handkerchief – and then they'd reappear from behind my ear or out of his empty hat. And he had a bird, a dove I think, grey, that always sat on his shoulder. He used to let me pet it. We didn't see him much, only visited him on a handful of occasions.*

176

I don't think he ever came to the house. I got the sense my father wouldn't allow it, I think he said Uncle Max wasn't quite right in the head. They can't have been very close, my mother and my uncle. We hardly saw him.

Kelly asked John Hardcastle whether she could simply forward the letter to Pip Reynolds, but he was firm in his reply.

'Sorry, Kelly, but all the letters need to be hand-delivered. In person. Any chance she plans to come back to Oz in the foreseeable future?'

She held the phone between her ear and her shoulder as she picked up Eden's toys and stowed them in a wicker basket. 'No, I've asked her. The last time she came back was ten years ago, for a niece's funeral. It seems she's firmly entrenched.'

'Right. Well, I'm sorry, Kelly, but it looks like one of you will have to go over there. I could talk to Richard or Evonne if you don't feel able to do it yourself?'

'There's no way I can afford a trip to Japan.'

'Could you make the time, if money wasn't an issue? Your father stipulated that if hand-delivering any of the letters required travel, then a certain amount of money was to be made available from his estate. Your expenses would be covered.'

'Okaaay. That puts things in a different light.' She turned it over in her mind. 'I suppose I could go. Take a week's holiday. But what about Eden? Could I take him?'

'Certainly. There's a total amount of ten thousand dollars available. I'm sure you could manage it quite comfortably.'

Kelly hung up and sank onto Eden's three-quarter-sized bed. She smoothed the Thomas the Tank Engine sheets and collected an assortment of things from under the pillow: pencils, a *Star Wars* figurine, a quartz rock and a broken snail's shell. *Japan*, she thought.

...

Once the decision was made, Kelly began to feel excited. She and Eden would have one night in Tokyo, then Pip had offered to host them in her home for three nights in the small mountain village of Yanase. Afterwards they would visit Kyoto for four days. Richard was predictably dour about the whole exercise. Evonne was delighted for her, though, and asked her to bring back some Japanese pottery as a surprise for Libby's birthday. Eden was most thrilled about the prospect of getting on a plane, something he had never done.

'Will we be up higher than the clouds, Mummy? Will we see birds up there? Will we see the sun? Is it night over there when it's day here? Will I have to eat lots of rice? Can I bring my dinosaurs?'

Kara was equally enthusiastic, even though she wasn't going. 'It'll be so great, Mum. So good for you to get away for a bit. Eden will remember it forever.'

'I feel a bit bad leaving you two here.'

'Are you kidding? The house to ourselves for ten days? Party time.'

'Oh God, Kara. I want the place still standing when I get back.'

'I'm only kidding. Honestly. Have a little faith – you can trust me.'

Kelly hugged her daughter and willed herself to relax.

The travel agent had assured her that she was travelling at the best possible time. 'Of course, cherry blossom season is lovely, and very popular, but to my mind the autumn leaves in November are absolutely the peak time, especially if you're visiting temples and gardens. The whole country will be alive with colour.'

...

And so, only a few weeks later, Kelly found herself navigating a large wheeled suitcase and one very tired four-year-old through the maze of Narita Airport as she tried to find the right train into the city. Neon signs blazed. Plastic replicas of meals were exhibited in glass cases outside the never-ending array of food stores. Announcements poured out of the loudspeakers. And there were people, people everywhere, asleep on chairs, frantically checking tickets, maps and phones, hurrying through the throng, talking in a dozen different languages.

She swung Eden onto what she hoped was the right train, with only a moment to spare before the doors hissed closed, and the carriage moved off at a brisk but effortless pace. Kelly lay her head back against the seat, but kept her eyes open, too scared to allow them to close in case she nodded off and missed their stop.

After falling into an exhausted sleep at their hotel, they spent most of the next day travelling by train to Shikoku, the island where Pip lived. She would collect them from the station in Kochi for the three-hour drive to her village.

Pip was sprightly and energetic, with a mass of frizzy grey hair and kind hazel eyes. She seemed to speak Japanese fluently, and spent the entire trip pointing out landmarks and sightseeing spots. They stopped for an early dinner at a dark, smoky restaurant, and Eden was most amused by having to take off their shoes and leave them in wooden cubes, 'just like at kindy!' It was the best Japanese food Kelly had ever tasted – fresh, piquant vegetables, delicate meats and fish, fragrant miso soup and pearlescent rice. Eden was a magnet for curious onlookers, and many people came over to their table to say hello. 'Wait until you get to Yanase,' Pip said. 'When I first moved there, oh about twenty years ago, some of the locals had never seen a foreigner, other than on television. This little fellow will get some attention, that's for sure!'

Pip's house was small and neat, set into a small yard of white gravel and stones enclosed by a wire fence. Each window was bordered by heavy, hinged panels. 'Typhoon shutters,' explained Pip. 'Not necessary now; the season's finished.'

In the entrance way, they again took off their shoes, and Pip gave them each a pair of slippers. Eden struggled to keep his on his feet as they shuffled down the narrow hallway, at the end of which was a compact kitchen. Pip turned on the heater and the acrid smell of oil warmed the air. She showed them the bathroom, which Kelly found a little dank and musty; mould collected in the grouting and the damp corners. Next to the bath was a wooden stool under a shower head that was only waist height. 'Look!' said Eden delightedly. 'It's a little person's shower, just my size!' The toilet, in a separate room, looked like something out of a space station, with more buttons and levers than Kelly's car.

At the other end of the hallway were two tatami-mat rooms, used as living rooms during the day and bedrooms at night. Kelly and Eden had to take off their slippers to enter their room, and the tatami felt both slippery and textured under their socked feet. One wall was taken up by a massive cupboard with sliding doors, from which Pip took out their futons. Kelly admired the beautiful embroidery on the coverlets of the thick, soft mattresses. Pip explained that, each morning, they would hang their futons over the fence and beat them with a special stick, to release the dust and allow the sunlight to infuse the bedding, then pack them away again in the cupboard until the following evening.

A loudspeaker on the wall crackled into life and made an announcement in Japanese.

'Don't worry,' said Pip. 'That's the nine o'clock announcement, reminding us to turn off all our fires – gas and oil heaters mostly – and go to bed.'

'Really? That gets piped into every house?' said Kelly.

'Oh yes. You get used to it,' said Pip. 'There's another one at 6 am, exhorting us to get up and do our exercises! Now, you two unpack, and I'll go and run the bath for young Eden.'

...

They spent the next day exploring the local area. Yanase was a logging village built beside a large dam on the top of a mountain. The travel agent had been right – autumn was the perfect time to visit. Trees and shrubs of every variety were clothed in rich reds, burgundies, chocolate browns and burnished gold. Eden had great fun racing through the ankle-high carpet of fallen leaves, crunching them underfoot.

Pip took them to the kindergarten where she taught, and the students – in neat uniforms and matching caps – performed two songs for Eden, Kelly and Pip. They applauded loudly at the finish. Pip then pointed to objects around the room and asked the children for the English words. *Chair*, the group recited obediently. *Flower* or *teacher* or *ball*.

Once the group was dismissed from the formal activities, the children attempted to teach Eden a complicated game involving running, tagging, chanting, and dense cloth balls filled with raw rice. When they arrived back at the house, Eden fell promptly asleep on the tatami, his head on a pillow, his arm thrown over his face.

'He's exhausted,' said Kelly, smiling. 'He's had such a lovely day. Thank you so much, Pip.'

'You're welcome. The kids loved seeing you. They'll be expecting him to drop in again tomorrow, you know. Do you want to have a rest too? Remember we've got that enkai tonight, the party, at the Mayor's house.'

'Yes, I'm so looking forward to it. You've all been so generous and hospitable. It's amazing. We won't want to leave. But while he's asleep, perhaps it's a good time to give you the letter.'

'Oh, of course! Let me get my glasses and some tea and we'll have a look.'

Pip returned with steaming cups of green tea and a plate of sweet biscuits, each wrapped individually in rice paper. She picked up the envelope reverently, turning it over in her hands. Of all the envelopes John Hardcastle had given Kelly and her siblings, this one was the most aged.

'Incredible,' said Pip. 'To see something addressed to my uncle. Most people would be lucky if their headstone was still being looked at after sixty years. I almost don't want to open it.'

'Yes, I know what you mean. While it's still sealed up, the possibility of what's inside remains endless. But as soon as we open it …'

'The mystery ends. Yes.'

She and Pip held each other's gaze, and they seemed to come to an unspoken agreement. Pip prised apart the envelope – it wasn't difficult as the glue had dried and the paper was brittle.

Inside the envelope was another, also yellowed with age. Written on the front in her father's handwriting was a date – *24th of October, 1983* – and the words *Correspondence to Monteray Max, given this day to John Hardcastle. May God Protect Our Souls.* The enclosed letter was nestled inside two layers, and was dated *15th of June, 1950.*

'Wow,' said Kelly. 'He must've kept this stored away for over thirty years.'

'Come sit by me,' said Pip. 'We'll read it together.'

Dear Max

 I hardly know where or how to begin this letter. Even as I write, my hand is shaking. But nightmares have claimed my sleep and even during the day I imagine I see the ghosts of the lost, shadowing my every move. I cannot escape them. I cannot escape the memories of what we lived through, or the vivid pictures of what we were called upon to do in the war. I cannot forget the faces of those who didn't come home, or those who returned as broken men, in body and spirit. Vacant shells. War does funny things to a bloke. Brings out the best and worst of us.

 I write this now because I have become aware of your living conditions and because I am deeply ashamed, not only because of what happened in New Guinea, but also because now, despite all my good fortunes, I still cannot bear to contact you in person. I am a weak man, Max. A better man than me would pull you out of that hostel and give you a room in his own home. A better man would try to make amends. A better man would not allow shame of his own shameful behaviour to dictate his decisions.

 But I am not a better man, I am just the same man I was when we served together, and you know as well as anyone that I've nothing to crow about.

 All I know how to do is to write down my feelings. My doctor suggested it. A good man; he fought in the first war. Knows a thing or two about the evils of the world, and about the damage that goes on in our heads. I told him about my nightmares. About waking with my blood boiling, the sound of artillery fire in my ears, flashes all around me as if I were in the midst of battle. He told me it might help to write things down. So that's what I'm doing. I don't know even yet if I will have the guts to send this to you.

Do you still have nightmares, too? Do we dream the same dreams?

The smell, that's what I recall most strongly. That goddamn awful smell around Lae. Rotting food and decomposing bodies, and those bloody shallow trench latrines, full of dysentery, that flowed right into the creek. And the air so thick with mossies you could open your gob and chomp on a mouthful if your rations ran low.

That five-day march nearly killed us. Cutting through all that bloody grass as we went, thick as your finger and tough as nails. The rain, the swollen rivers. I heard later there were over a thousand casualties at Salamaua. We could see with our own eyes our boys were dropping like flies, from fevers and the runs and the bloody heat, let alone once the Japs found us. Day raids, night raids, it never bloody let up. And commands from the shiny arses on high that seemed completely unachievable, especially when our rations ran out.

I can still hear the artillery salvos, so loud you couldn't hear the bloke next to you if he was yelling in your ear. The metallic smell of mortars and heavy machine guns. The ever-present fear of unexploded mines.

Sometimes I wish I didn't remember. Or that I could make new memories and paper them over the old.

I heard you're still doing magic tricks. Mate, you were bloody brilliant with cards. There were some nights, hunkered down in the trenches, when – I don't mind telling you – some of us were near to tears with the exhaustion of it all. The vigilance. And your card tricks, mate, they worked wonders. Took our minds off our troubles. You'd have us laughing and holding our breath and slapping each other on the back in disbelief. You worked magic.

I can't imagine how it must be for you, mate, without the use of your legs. There. I've said it. Said what I've been scared to think until now. Frightened to think about you in your wheelchair because it leads to thoughts of how you ended up that way, and that's a path my mind doesn't want to travel, towards that particular day in my memory. But it's etched on my mind like an engraving.

I'd banged my shin the week before on a ruddy steel peg when I was trying to find my way to the latrine in the dark. Took a chunk of skin off and all I could think about was whether it was going to ulcerate. The medic kept an eye on it but he'd started talking about digging out the bad flesh with a spoon, and I don't mind telling you, I was scared half to death. I even sat with my leg in the river one day, hoping the fish would come and eat away the rotten bits. Point is, I was distracted. Not that that's an excuse. Plenty of blokes had worries, injuries and illnesses, bad news from home. Shouldn't have made a blind bit of difference to the kind of soldier I was.

It was bloody hot that day. We were up at dawn. The mossies and flies were swarming, the birds were calling – the jungle chorus, we called it, hey. We loaded our packs and headed for the rendezvous point.

We were a few men down that day. Dengue fever, malaria, parasites. But we soldiered on, tramping off to sneak up behind the Japs. Or so we hoped. We had to patrol along the ridge; hopefully do an ambush raid. We split up into two groups, remember? Hardy took his men to the right, and our men took the path on the left. Although it was hardly what you'd call a path. Just more bloody jungle to cut through.

So there we were, the six of us, single file. Rosenburg signalled halt and we all froze. I remember peering through the bushes, trying to see what he'd seen. And there he was, one lone Nip, his trousers lowered, squatting to relieve himself. I suppose they got the runs as bad as we did. Next thing I know, Rosenburg's fired a shot and the Jap's up and running towards us, one hand grabbing his pants. Towards us! Heading bloody straight for us, his gun raised. Rosenburg's gun jammed, and before I knew what was happening, the two of them were in arm-to-arm combat, tussling on the ground. By the time the others shot the Jap, he had his bayonet sticking out of Rosenburg's chest. Poor bugger didn't stand a chance. Then suddenly we heard the Japanese mortars and it was raining metal. The almighty crashes as they exploded nearby, sending up mountains of flame and ash and debris, the noise echoing around us until we could hardly tell which way was up. We retreated, running every which way, trying to find cover. It was bedlam.

Smith, the medic, wanted to go back and get Rosenburg's body. I heard you offer to help. But I said we should wait a bit. No sense walking straight into the belly of the beast, I thought. So we waited there until it quietened down, and in the end we decided we'd all go, seeing as our mission was to push on in that direction anyway. Lo and behold, when we got to the two bodies, there were another three or four Japs within spitting distance, holding their hands in the air and waving at us. 'Course, we all knew how bloody unlikely it was that they were surrendering, but we had to do the right thing.

So over we went, to collect them, and then the bastards opened fire on us. Must've had reinforcements hiding further up the hill. Smith went down, the back of his head blown away. The four of us scattered, and you and I ended up flat to the ground. That's when I saw that you'd been hit. The back of your shirt was all torn and bloody. Looked like you'd taken a fair amount of shrapnel. The longer we lay there, the paler you got. Your face was all sweaty, and when I grabbed your hand it was clammy and slick.

I knew I shouldn't have moved you. I knew the drill. I should have opened my pack of sulpha powder and shaken it all over the wounds, and insisted you stay still until the stretcher came. But all I could think about was how we were sitting ducks. All I could hear was that warning by Tokyo Rose that any captured Allied men would have their leg muscles cut out so they couldn't walk, and how they'd be left to die a slow and *horrible death. I heard the POW stories replaying in my head and all I knew was that I didn't want to end up in a Jap camp.*

If I'm honest, all I could think of was myself.

And so I made you get up. I made you stand and I half-dragged you along, even though I could see the blood soaking through your uniform and dripping down into your boots.

Sometimes, in my nightmares, I imagine I can hear the shrapnel moving inside your flesh, the hard metal rubbing against your spine.

If you'd been lying still, the bloody stuff might have been harmless. You might have gone home with a few scars. But I see me pulling you along, and the shrapnel digging in closer and closer to your spinal cord.

And then suddenly – as if you were a puppet and someone above had cut your strings – you dropped to the ground.

I can remember screaming at you to get up.

I can't, you said. I can't move my legs.

Those five words haunt me still.

I lay in a shallow ditch full of water for three or four hours before they came. They got to you first. Poured water over your face, stuck a needle full of morphine into your stomach, lifted you onto a stretcher. When I could see the coast was clear, I dragged myself out of the stinking puddle and joined the rest of them. I must've looked a sight. They slapped me on the back and said it was my lucky day. No-one asked me what had happened. Not then. Later, after you'd been sent off to the divisional clearing station, I heard talk that because of the long evacuation time, you'd probably lose the use of your legs permanently. I didn't like to think I could have done something to prevent that. All I could fathom was that I was okay, that it was not my day to die.

I put you out of my mind.

I heard you were medically discharged. Heard you had a hard time when you finally made it back. Heard you never got back on your feet.

That's seven years ago now. Seven years and I haven't been able to show my face, not to you or anyone else from that platoon. Always afraid that someone would ask what really happened that day. Afraid of the truth.

Afraid to look you in the eye because of the resentment or disappointment I might see. Even more afraid in case all I see is understanding and forgiveness. That I could not stand. Your forgiveness, or your kindness, or your pity.

There. I've written it down. Do I feel better? I feel lighter. My burden lessened. So I suppose the exercise has done its job. It's done nothing for you, though. Selfish, this was.

For what it's worth, I am sorry for what I did. Or what I failed to do. I'm sorry your life has been diminished as a result.

I'm sorry this blasted war ever happened, and that we were ever involved in it.

Good luck and God bless.

Your erstwhile mate,
Dan Whittaker

Pip and Kelly sat very still. The afternoon sun had crossed the sky and now laid stripes of shadow across the tatami. Eden was beginning to stir; he rubbed his eyes and straightened his legs, a frown of consternation on his face.

'Mum?' he whispered.

Kelly rubbed his foot. 'I'm right here, sweetheart.'

He slid into her embrace and popped his thumb into his mouth.

'You're all right, love. You've had a big sleep. We're at Pip's house, do you remember? In Japan.'

Eden's heavy lids closed again. 'Mmmm …' he murmured.

Kelly's gaze returned to the pages in Pip's hand. Pip reached across and squeezed Kelly's shoulder. 'I really don't know what to say, Kelly. Where to begin. What an intensely private and intimate correspondence.'

'I'm so sorry,' Kelly muttered. 'I'm so sorry that happened to your uncle. That my father ... left him that way. That was unforgivable.'

'Oh, my dear. Nothing could be further from the truth. It sounds to me as if your father suffered some sort of post-traumatic stress, from the war. Not that it was talked about then. They probably all did. Goodness, the things they had to see, what they had to do. How any of them made it back to their families, back into any sort of normal existence is quite beyond me.'

'That's no excuse,' Kelly said.

Pip looked at her gently. 'Kelly, my Uncle Max was as damaged as any of them, and not only because of his paralysis. He had a whole lot of demons, probably from the atrocities he witnessed in that war. Anyway, perhaps your father did the right thing, trying to get Max moving. Perhaps – if they'd waited for help – they might both have been killed. Who's to know? Sounds to me like he's blaming himself for a situation that was out of his control. And it's certainly nothing for you to be sorry about. Good heavens, if women ran the world, there probably wouldn't be any wars in the first place, right?' Her eyes twinkled.

Kelly snuggled Eden closer. 'He wrote that in 1950. But he never sent it. Why? I mean, why wait until the eighties, and then only give it to his solicitor to keep, with instructions to send it after he died?' Her mouth dropped open as the realisation dawned on her. 'This must have been the first of them. Out of all those envelopes John had, this must have been the very first one.'

'He mentioned writing as a sort of catharsis,' Pip mused. 'Perhaps it worked for him that way. That's why he continued on.'

Kelly imagined her father writing a letter every time he couldn't talk about his feelings. As her gaze drifted around the tatami-mat room, taking in the calligraphy on the wall and the smoky incense rising from the shrine in the alcove, another thought occurred to her.

'It's uncanny, isn't it?'

'What?'

'Reading about the "Japs" as he calls them. When we're here, in Japan. There's no way he could've known, seventy years ago, that the very people he was fighting against would be welcoming his daughter into their homes and spoiling his grandson. Life is so strange and unpredictable. Impossible, really. And yet, the impossible seems to happen, every day.'

'I think,' said Pip, 'that you've been given a very special gift, through these letters. A glimpse inside his heart. Most people never get that from their parents, even when they're alive, let alone after they've passed.'

'A gift,' repeated Kelly. 'It is, isn't it? I'm not sure I recognised that until now. But I think you're right. A unique and precious gift.'

EVONNE AND HER SIBLINGS WERE gathered in John Hardcastle's office once more. The blind had been lowered to block the blazing sun. Three envelopes lay on the desk.

'Well,' said the solicitor, 'from what I can gather, you've all had quite a year.'

'You could say that,' replied Richard. He stared at John, but Evonne noticed that he looked away first.

'Wild goose chase,' her brother continued. 'Thank God we're nearly at the end of it. Only those three and then we're good to finalise the estate, am I right?'

John nodded. 'That's correct.'

'Well, don't keep us in suspense. I've had about enough of this game.'

Evonne put her hand on her brother's arm. 'You don't have to keep up that act, Richard.' She gave him a gentle smile. 'I think we're all in agreement that no matter what "game" Dad set up, it's definitely been an interesting experience, wouldn't you say?'

'No. I wouldn't say.'

'Come on, Richard,' said Kelly. 'We've all learnt things about Dad that … well, things we couldn't know. It's been enlightening.'

'Yes, well, makes little difference now that he's dead and buried, doesn't it?'

'What about his brother? What about—'

Evonne interrupted her sister. 'Leave it, Kelly. If the past twelve months hasn't sunk in under that hard shell, then I don't know what will.'

Richard sighed. Kelly sank back in her chair, biting her lip. Evonne stared out the window at the ever-present pigeons, squabbling over position. All about power and place, in the animal world. *Not so different from our own lives*, she thought.

With a certain solemnity, John Hardcastle handed each of them an envelope. To Richard he gave an envelope labelled *Ryan Mossman*. Evonne and Kelly exchanged a puzzled glance. To Evonne, he passed one labelled *Ronald Linklater*. Evonne didn't recognise the name. But Kelly's was a different matter. As soon as John passed her the third envelope – with, Evonne would later think, a moment's hesitation – Kelly blanched. In their father's handwriting were the words *Simon Radley*. Kelly's ex-husband.

Her sister moaned something inaudible then found her voice. 'Why …' she croaked, before clearing her throat to begin again. 'Why would Dad be writing anything to Simon? What could he possibly have to say to him?'

'Calm down, Kelly.' Evonne fanned her sister with her own envelope. 'It could be nothing. Some of the letters haven't turned out to be about much at all, have they.'

'Yes, and some have turned out to be world-shifting.' Kelly held the envelope in her hands as if it might bite. 'Do we really have to do this, John?'

'I'm sorry, Kelly, but yes, I'm afraid you do,' he replied. 'This is the last condition of the will.'

Evonne wondered, too, what secrets their father had to share with Simon. She looked again at the name on her own envelope – Ronald Linklater – and speculated about this stranger's connection to her father. As for Ryan Mossman …

The insight danced around the edges of her consciousness, tantalising her. Slowly, it dawned on her.

'Kelly,' she said. 'Irene's son. Ryan. The plumber. What was his surname?'

SHE WASN'T GOING TO PUT it off any longer. Simon had sounded reluctant on the phone. She knew that Kara and Ben had been keeping him updated on the letters, and Simon sounded wary that his name had been brought into it.

They had decided to meet at the Botanic Gardens. Neutral territory. Well, almost neutral, in the sense that it wasn't home ground for either of them, but it was a place they both loved. Nestled at the foot of Mount Coot-tha, the last barrier between civilisation and the rugged tracks that led up into the mountain's wild bushland. The gardens, in comparison, were tame. A haven.

A favourite place of escape.

She got a sick feeling in her stomach when she thought of the times she had fled, barefoot, driving erratically, going over the speed bumps too fast, taking the corners too wide. Arriving at the gardens in a state of hollowness and rage and anguish. But no matter how she felt, how angry their words had been, how quick his temper, it would all fall away once she stepped into the cool foliage. The tension in her body dissipated into the atmosphere.

She headed directly for the Japanese Gardens – past the cafe decked out in white and pink ribbons for a wedding banquet, along the winding paths, and through the heat of the cactus house. The famous landscape architect Kenzo Ogata had designed the Japanese section, *tsukiyama-chisen*, merging stone, water and greenery to create a meditative space. Memories of her recent trip to Japan flooded back; she had passed through similar gardens, and now this one seemed even more laden with reflection and meaning. If the Botanic Gardens had a heart, a church, a sacred place, this was it.

She sat on a long wooden bench, overhung with a bamboo shade. As she breathed in the crisp air, the colours around her seemed clearer, the edges more defined, the tiny details of each leaf, each twig and each pebble, more vital, more significant.

The water in the pond was barely moving, fallen leaves floating on the surface. Clusters of lily pads were gathered around the base of a stone lantern, and dragonflies darted across the water, their wings a blur.

The large stand of bamboo at the entrance was a recent addition. She remembered the previous bamboo flowering about ten years earlier, a sight much feted in the media. Apparently, some people waited their whole lives in Japan to see a stand of flowering bamboo. Then the plant had died, and been replaced by this new stand. The one spectacular flowering, and then death.

Kelly retrieved the envelope from her bag. The fine striations of the linen paper felt delicate under her fingertips, like braille. She lifted it to her nose and inhaled, trying to recapture some of her father's scent, that distinct combination of peppermint and barley. But all she could smell was the clean wash of the gardens.

These blasted letters. She and Simon had separated over ten

years ago. Her father had been dead for twelve months. What could he possibly have left to say? To Simon, of all people?

He was very late now. Kelly willed her lungs to slow her breath, and concentrated again on the scene before her: the steady sound of the sprinklers; the birds calling to each other in the treetops; the rustlings of unseen creatures; the scattering of floral colour – confetti amidst the green.

A screech pierced the air. She looked up to see a flash of red and black moving amongst the leaves of a eucalypt. The bird hopped from foot to foot, its head bobbing. A red-tailed black cockatoo. Surely it was unusual to see one this far south? Weren't they endangered? Kara had once told her that red-tailed black cockatoos accompanied the dead on their journey to the Dreamtime. She thought again of her father. Maybe it was a sign.

So many people had once lived on the land beneath her feet. The Indigenous children who had roamed the area, hunting their dinner, picking native fruit. The Elders who had danced their ceremonies and loved their kinfolk and buried their dead. Mount Coot-tha had once been called One Tree Hill, because the colonists had displaced the Turrbal People, cleared the mountain, and left only a huge eucalypt on top. Later, the mountain was renamed in honour of the ku-ta, the native bee honey collected by the Turrbal.

The first people, who had left such light footprints on the land.

She thought about her own ancestors, some of them buried in the adjacent cemetery, and the rich history of this place before a white face was ever seen.

Since she and her siblings had been distributing her father's letters, she had begun to consider her own situation, the deeds embedded in her history, the actions of the people of her past. What did she know of invasion and occupation? Of atrocities and massacres? A profound and unfathomable shame lay deep in her belly; realisation of how little she understood of her own people's complicity, of her scant knowledge of Aboriginal affairs, or the local Indigenous customs. She loved the gardens, but surely this very spot had once been revered by others, its beauty sung in song, its bare earth pounded by dancing feet, its native flora and fauna celebrated.

She started at the sound of Simon's voice in her ear, the touch of his hand on her shoulder.

'You were miles away.'

He reached down to kiss her cheek. They sat in companionable silence.

'Always so peaceful here.'

'Yes.'

'Did it look like this? Japan, when you were there?'

'Yes. Just like this.' She sighed. Held out the envelope.

Simon was hesitant to take it. 'You really don't know what's in here?'

'Nope. No idea.' She waited. 'Do you?'

He paused. 'No,' he said. 'I don't.'

'But?'

'But … I can't be sure.'

'Well, that's helpful.' A beat. 'Are you going to take it? Open it?'

Simon deflated, the air rushing out of his body. Then he took a deep breath, as if steeling himself. 'All right. Give it to me.' He took the envelope and ripped it open. He glanced at it and then returned his gaze to the tranquillity of the garden.

'Well?' she asked. 'Are you going to tell me what it says?'

Simon stared at her as if he was seeing into her soul. It was a long time since he'd looked at her that way. Kelly saw that a tear was making its way down his cheek.

'Sorry. Sorry, Kelly. I'm so sorry.' He handed her the letter. Wiped the back of his hand roughly against his face.

On the sheet of paper were written only a few words.

She deserves to know the truth.

'Me? What truth? What's this about, Simon?' Kelly's heart was racing.

Simon rose to his feet and began pacing back and forth along the path. He kept running his hands through his hair.

'Simon?'

He turned to face her. She wasn't sure what she anticipated him to say. He didn't even seem sure that he himself knew. His eyes darted from left to right; he stared up at the arc of the roof and finally met her gaze.

'I had an affair,' he said. 'With Charlotte. That's why I left.'

The unexpectedness of the statement winded her. She inhaled and her chest hurt. Charlotte was the woman Simon had been dating when they met. The woman he left, to be with Kelly.

'I still don't know how your father found out, or how long he'd known, but sometime after Kara was born, he spoke to me. Threatened me. Said if I didn't do the honourable thing and leave, that he would tell you, and then find the best lawyers that money could buy and make sure I never got to see the kids.'

Kelly's voice, when it came, was small and quiet. 'When did you start seeing her again?'

Ben dropped onto the bench, his head in his hands. 'I never really stopped.'

'But ... but when we got married?'

'We got married because you were pregnant with Ben. It was

the right thing to do. I still think it was the right thing to do, even though I was in love with Charlotte.'

'You said you were in love with me.'

'I was. I thought I was. I don't know, Kel, it was so confusing. The idea of becoming a father was amazing. I knew I could never abandon our baby. Or you. And Charlotte … well, she's never wanted kids.'

'But you kept seeing her.'

'Yes. I kept seeing her.'

'All along?' Kelly's eyes widened. 'Even when I was pregnant with Kara?' A sob escaped her lips. Simon gave an almost imperceptible nod.

'I grew to love you. And you know how much I love the kids. There was no way I could give them up.'

'But you couldn't give her up either.'

'No.' His voice sounded hollow. 'I couldn't work out how to extricate myself.'

Her laugh was bitter. 'But you worked it out eventually. With my father to change your mind.'

'Daniel told me I didn't deserve you. And he was right. I didn't.'

Kelly opened her mouth to say something, but closed it again.

'He told me that Kara and Ben needed to be raised in a home of honesty, not a house of lies.' He grimaced. 'His exact words.'

That was rich, coming from her father, given what she now knew about his own infidelity. 'But … I don't understand. All through the divorce, the mediation … you never said a word.'

'Of course I didn't. Why would I? I didn't want to hurt you any more than I already had.'

Kelly leant her head back against the bamboo wall. Sunlight streamed through thousands of tiny holes in the thatched roof, piercing the shade with shafts of light.

'That's why you never fought for shared time,' she said slowly. 'That's why you settled for every second weekend. Why you never argued about it.' She wiped at her eyes. 'I thought you didn't want them. I thought you didn't care about the kids enough to fight me for them.'

Simon sighed again, so deeply the seat seemed to collapse a little. 'Kel, don't you see? It was *because* I cared. I knew what a great mother you were. Are. I knew I could never take that away from you. And after what your father said to me, honestly I felt lucky to be seeing the kids at all.' He stood up and began pacing again. 'I couldn't be with you anymore. I was so ashamed about seeing Charlotte. I felt completely humiliated that he knew about it. I felt ridiculous. I *was* ridiculous.' He clutched her hand. 'I tried so hard to love you,' he whispered. 'I loved our life, our family. But once I realised that your father knew I was being unfaithful, I didn't know what to do. I was terrified of losing the kids. I could hardly bring myself to look at them – they reminded me of all we had, all that I was choosing to throw away. I couldn't *function*.'

'But why didn't you talk to me about it? We could've … we could've …'

'What?' Simon said gently. 'We could've worked it out? I was still seeing her, Kel. I wasn't prepared to give her up. Telling you was only going to make it worse for me. Your father and I agreed that not telling you was the kindest thing.'

Kelly swallowed her hurt and her pride, and her voice came out stronger as she pictured her father speaking to Simon. 'That bastard! Who did he think he was, plotting and scheming behind my back? About my life. About our life … God, Simon, you should've said something!' she hissed.

Simon's expression was now the one she'd become used to since he'd told her he was leaving her: disappointment and, she realised, a little despair.

'It was hopeless,' he said, and she could hear the resignation in his voice. 'Once he knew, I couldn't pretend any longer. I had to make a decision.'

'And you chose Charlotte.'

'Yes. I chose Charlotte. But I also chose Kara and Ben. I wasn't prepared to put them through a sordid custody battle. I knew they'd be okay with you. I knew you'd be okay. And I realised I'd have to accept whatever contact you allowed me. It seemed the best way out. For everyone.'

'Well, thank you very much, you and my father both, for making life choices on my behalf,' she said sarcastically. 'I can't believe he said nothing to me. Why didn't he keep his bloody nose out of it? And why this, now?' She crumpled the page in her fist. 'Why open up old wounds?'

'Maybe he knew those wounds had never healed. For both of us,' he added. 'I think he was hoping I'd eventually leave Charlotte and try and make it up to you. And when I didn't, I suppose he thought that I would've told you everything myself, well before now. At first, he thought it was best you didn't know. But later, maybe …'

'He thought you'd come to your senses.' She caught his eye and held his gaze. 'That you'd respect me enough to tell me.'

He cringed, and looked away. 'Yes. He probably thought this letter would never be necessary. But I'd started to think your father was right. Why hurt you any more than I already had?'

'Because I would have had a *choice*,' she snapped. 'You never gave me a choice. You never gave me a chance to forgive you.'

'I'm sorry.' His voice softened. 'It could have been Eden, you know. That prompted this letter.'

'What? What do you mean?'

'I know he had a really hard time accepting Eden. He had a go at me once. Said that if I hadn't had an affair with Charlotte, and ruined your life, you wouldn't have gone on to have a child out of wedlock.'

'But what happened with Billy ... with Eden's father ... had nothing to do with you.'

'He thought you refused to acknowledge Eden's dad because you still had feelings for me. That was the only way he could understand why you didn't want him involved in your life. He took it very hard, you being a single mum. Maybe he thought if I came clean, you'd finally move on.'

She stared at him, resolute, before she felt something soften inside her. She closed her eyes and leant her head against his shoulder. It was so evident now. She had always thought it was something in her, some lack, some deficiency, that had made him leave. She had thought he wasn't committed to seeing the kids, never pushing for more time, never arguing when she changed arrangements, never complaining when she told him the kids were too tired or sick to see him that weekend. And yet they seemed to have such fun when they were together.

She had always blamed him for the breakdown of their marriage. *He* had left *her*. But how had she not noticed that Charlotte might be in the background? How had she never questioned her own story?

'Do you still see her?' she muttered.

'Yes. On and off. She ... she's never wanted to commit.'

'Friends with benefits.'

'Something like that.'

They stayed propped against each other, neither of them speaking, for a long time.

Kelly heard her father again, asking her endless questions about Eden and his father, trying in his own muddled way to bring some measure of stability to Kelly's life. Perhaps he had been tunnelling down to the truth; perhaps he had wanted for her what he had never had for himself – a relationship based on honesty, rather than lies.

On her second date with Billy, they had gone back to her house, which was silent with the children's absence. Kelly had rushed ahead of him, collecting stray shoes and toys, moving a basket of clean laundry from the sofa, but he had taken the basket from her and dropped it to the floor. The strange feeling of release as he took both her wrists in his right hand and pinned them above her head, pushing her back against the wall. His body wiry and firm. A dancer's physique. She could see the tendons in his neck as his face came towards hers, until they were so close that only their breath came between them, his smelling of the joint they had shared.

That afternoon, they had made love so tenderly she had cried.

She had thought of Simon, and wondered if she was crazy to let another man into her life. Crazy to let someone new catch at her emotions like kite strings, to be foolish enough to hope he would not let go.

The fathers of her children.

One had been disloyal; they shared a history that was painful and raw, and yet in an odd way she found it easier now that she knew the truth. Simon had rewritten the story of their marriage, and their separation. He had held her aching heart.

And the other? Billy had never had a chance. She had never given him a chance. She had denied him the opportunity to make his own choice about his own life. About his own child.

The irony felt like a barb in her chest.

Billy deserved to know his son. She thought, too, of her son's paternal ancestry, the important stories he should hear, the languages he should learn, the Elders to whom he should pay his respects.

Perhaps she had been selfish.

But here was a chance to set things right. A new age of sincerity and integrity. History marching forward; the past bursting forth like bright, new growth on a gnarled and ancient tree.

THE MORNING DAWNED CLEAR AND bright; the previous night's storm had washed the landscape clean. Through the large bay window, Evonne could see the black wattle and the huge Moreton Bay fig hunkered over the house, their branches distinct, their leaves glossy and luminous. A golden orb spider was busily restoring its tattered web, the fine silk still strung with water droplets like beads on a string. Evonne blinked the sleep from her eyes and focused on a spot of colour: an azure kingfisher was perched on the verandah railing, the intense violet of its back and wings contrasting with its pale-orange underbelly. Its slender bill stabbed the air as it cocked its head in quick, jerky movements. The mournful cry of a curlew echoed, farewelling the night, heralding the morning. From the heart of the reserve, the revegetated area around Enoggera Creek, to the open forest on the hillsides, and the gullies still in shadow, the birds and insects and small native animals were greeting the day; the night creatures – owls and nightjars, possums and flying foxes – disappearing into their holes as the sun rose.

Libby appeared at the doorway. 'Getting up anytime today?' she teased. 'That letter's not going to deliver itself, you know.'

Evonne groaned. She had racked her brain, trying to comprehend a link between herself and Ronald Linklater.

'It can't be anything good, Lib. I've got a bad feeling about it. Dad's left these ones until last for a reason.'

'But Kelly's experience wasn't all bad. It sounds like it might lead to some positive changes for her.'

Evonne thought back to her sister's visit yesterday: Kelly had by turns been circumspect and hopeful. Simon's revelations had stung, but their meeting also appeared to have opened a door on her emotions, and she was cautiously optimistic about the future. 'I hope so. She's still upset, though.'

'Well, she's got a right to be,' observed Libby wryly.

'I know. She and Simon have a lot to work through. God, fancy Dad speaking to Simon all those years ago. Should have minded his own bloody business instead of getting involved in their marriage. I'd be bloody furious.'

'Yes, well, that's no reason to think that this letter to Linklater is going to be anything more than the others.'

But Evonne wasn't convinced.

...

After almost twelve months, Evonne was well used to the methods of tracking someone down, and familiar with the websites and agencies set up to help. After several dead-end queries, she found a Ron Linklater in his mid-eighties, living in Brisbane. They had a difficult phone conversation in which it became apparent that Mr Linklater was hard of hearing, but Evonne managed to arrange a face-to-face meeting.

He resided in a large unit at West End with an expansive view of the river. The building was in an older style but had been recently renovated. Evonne made her way through the spacious foyer and took the lift to the eleventh floor.

The first word that came to her mind about the man who opened the door was *dapper*. He stood tall, without stooping, and wore smart casual chinos and a soft, pale-blue buttoned shirt. His skin was tanned, and any signs of his age served only to enhance his appearance. His apartment was furnished straight out of a catalogue – expensive and tasteful, thought Evonne. Every wall was adorned with huge canvases of modern art. Ron showed her through to the balcony, where he had set out a pot of tea.

'Wow,' said Evonne, as she took in the view.

'Yes, it's quite something, isn't it? Never get tired of looking at the river. Always something to see.' He poured the tea. 'Now, I'm sorry I couldn't catch what you were saying over the phone. Something about your father? Lost the hearing completely in my left ear in a mining explosion when I was a young chap, and I'm afraid my right hasn't compensated.' He fiddled with his hearing aid.

And so Evonne began her explanation, of the unexpected path that she and her siblings had travelled in the year since their father's death. She asked questions about Ron's life and his past, hoping to find a connection.

'Well, I've always lived in Brisbane, except for a few stints out west. And I'm about your father's era, aren't I, so it's possible we knew each other, I suppose. What did you say his name was again? Daniel. Daniel Whittaker. Hmmm. At school, perhaps?'

But they had attended different schools, and not served together in the forces. 'I was deemed medically unfit, 'cause of my hearing. Blessing in disguise, I reckon. Not sorry I missed all the action.'

'Nor should you be. Terrible time.' Evonne drank the last of her tea. They watched a ferry chugging by on the river, leaving an eight-seater boat rocking in its wake. The coxswain called commands; the rowers' arms rotated in fluid unison. A flock of birds flew in formation before spreading out into a black streak, a shifting stripe across the sky.

'It's so peaceful here,' she said.

'Yes, it is. The *serenity*,' he replied with a chuckle. 'Can't go past the serenity.'

Evonne excused herself to use the bathroom, stopping on the way back to look at some of Ron's photographs on a shelf. She picked up a framed shot of Ron and another man, heavy-set and hearty, their arms around each other, the same twinkling eyes.

'That's Andrew. My partner. Fourteen precious years we had together.' He took the photo from her and brushed it gently.

'He has very nice eyes.'

'He does. Did. And a personality to match. But I've been on my own since his death. Fifteen years ago next February.'

'Oh,' said Evonne. 'I'm sorry.'

Ron replaced the photograph. 'Nothing to be sorry about. We had a good life together. He's responsible for all of these.' He gestured at the paintings. 'A passionate art collector, he was. "That's our superannuation", he used to say. Not that I've been able to part with any of them.'

'They're stunning,' said Evonne. 'I do some art therapy at the childcare centre where I work. We have lots of migrant kids, refugees many of them. English is their second language, and sometimes when they arrive they can't speak a word. They can all draw and paint, though; they can all understand each other's work, if not each other's words.'

'Art is the universal language, as they say.'

'Right. Mind you, it's usually only a matter of months, or even weeks, before the kids are translating for their parents! They're quick learners.' She stepped back to admire a large, square oil in primary colours. 'This is exquisite. You have good taste.'

'Well, Andrew did. He gradually educated the philistine out of me.'

Evonne laughed. They returned to the balcony and to the subject of her father, but they seemed to have exhausted the possibilities of a past connection. She drew out the envelope from her tote bag.

'Well,' she said, 'I suppose you could just open it and see what it says. I'm sure it will be obvious if it's meant for you. And if it turns out it's not, then I'll seal it up and start again.'

Ron rubbed his hands together. 'Do you think we should? Right. Let me get my reading glasses, then.'

He was careful to tear open the envelope neatly. They began reading the letter inside, and Evonne soon found herself compelled by the words swimming before her.

Dear Ronald

As I come towards the end of my life, I am drawn to consider my actions and behaviour throughout the years. I am remembering much of my youth (although I can't often recall what I had for breakfast yesterday ... such is the stuff of ageing). I have been trying to account for my life, for all the things I did and didn't do, the things I should've said, or those I shouldn't. If you are reading this, then you have outlived me, and I am glad of that, for you always seemed an honest and true fellow, and I hope you have had a fulfilling life with work that has satisfied you and people who have loved you. Forgive me if I ramble. It is the right of the aged, is it not, to speak our minds.

If all has gone to plan, then my daughter Evonne will be with you now. She is a good girl, faithful and determined. I think you will warm to her, if you haven't already. She certainly has tolerance and understanding in spades, much more than her old man, I'm afraid.

We knew each other so briefly that you probably don't even remember me. Let me remind you. It was 1948. The war had ended and everyone was trying to get on with a new way of life. I found it difficult to do so – my first marriage had been very short-lived and she had left me for an American soldier. The horrors I had witnessed during my service had left me cold and empty. I spent much of the time confused and without purpose, trying to fit in to my old life but feeling the futility of it all.

Like so many others, I sought refuge in alcohol. I began to frequent the city bars, full of ex-servicemen like me, all attempting to make some sense out of what we'd been through.

I first met you at Lennon's, and after that a few times at the Grand Central Hotel and the Gresham. There was something about the convivial atmosphere that drew me to those places – men gathered together to gossip and exchange ideas, intent on fixing the problems of the world. There were always two distinct groups at the start of the evening: the squares (I counted myself as one of those) and the fellows who were known, even amongst themselves, as the queens, or the pansies. Men who seemed to me to be so much more certain of themselves, unashamed to flaunt their proclivities. Secure in their enjoyment of life.

Towards the end of each night, the two groups would begin to merge. There were always a few fellows from our side who were swept up by what was forbidden.

At first, it seemed like harmless fun. A few drinks, a laugh. Sharing intimacies in a way that I hadn't done since the war. Fellows opening up to each other. I began to feel safe, with you and your friends. Understood. Recognised.

The night you drew me aside and we slipped into a darkened corner and you covered my mouth with your own, I was nervous and excited, terrified and completely at ease, somehow all at once. I didn't stop to think about what it meant. All I knew was that, for the first time in years, I was in a comfortable place.

We met several times after that, drinking at one of the bars and then proceeding along to public – but more private – spaces: Wickham Street, the Botanical Gardens, Albert Park, under the Victoria Bridge – these locations are seared into my brain. All scenes of intense pleasure, quick and furtive, satisfying a physical need but somehow also touching something deeper, more passionate.

The urge to meet you, to engage in our trysts, was something I could not understand, never mind explain to anyone else. After all, I was told daily, by the newspapers and the reports of arrests, that what we were doing constituted an act of gross indecency. Sodomy. Sexual perversion.

And yet, when I was with you, it felt as far from that as possible. It felt honest and true.

I continued my double life for several weeks. A Christian boy by day, a deviant by night. An honourable son, returned from service, who created excuses to sneak off into the city and engage in unspeakable acts.

For those few weeks in 1948, I craved your physical attentions so severely that you were all I could think of, night and day. You were so handsome, in a totally unaffected way. You wore your clothes naturally, but with flair, and I remember how you would blow cigarette smoke out of your nostrils like twin clouds of steam.

Of course, I know that for you I was merely a dalliance, one in a long line of partners. I didn't begrudge sharing you because, despite the strange combination of shame and excitement, I admired your honesty.

You knew who you were, and you had no compunction in staying true to yourself. You were careful, you had to be, but you never lied to yourself, of that I'm sure. I have always remembered that, and admired that about you. So much wisdom in one so young.

The stolen hours spent with you over those few weeks unlocked something in me. My nightmares came less often. And when I began to write down my thoughts and my feelings, spurred on in part by the honesty I saw in you, the bad dreams became fewer still. But I truly believe this: you released me.

Then there was the night of the big round-up. We'd been expecting it, after the public inquiries: the police were determined to improve their charge rate. I had been drinking at the Gresham, hoping you would turn up, and managed to escape as the chaos began. All those officers charging in, and entrapping others in the lavatories of our favoured parks in the city. I heard that many of our acquaintances were imprisoned, beaten, and charged with base offences, and I hoped you were not amongst them. I was so frightened by that close call that I never returned to our usual haunts. I told myself I had never really been one of you. Just a ring-in from the other side of the pub.

The following year, I married again. Shirley, her name was. She died a few years ago. We were together more than half our lives.

I never again looked at another man like that. And to my great shame, and this is the crux of this letter, I began to expunge the experience from my mind. I listened to the hate-mongers and the God-spouters. I blocked out you and the friends I'd known and the things I'd done, as surely as if they had been figments of my imagination. I aligned myself with intolerance and hatred.

And I fear — no, I know — that this attitude has served me poorly, most importantly with my own flesh and blood.

I have asked Evonne to deliver this letter because I hope that you

will share it with her. I have something important to say to her, and this
story explains it far better than I could ever have done in person. You
are perhaps the only one who can understand the times we lived in, the
pressures, the release. And you are perhaps the only one who can explain
all of this to my daughter. She is a good person. She deserved a better
father than the one she got. She deserved my love and understanding,
but she got so little. And I have never had the guts to say as much to her.

I want her to meet you. To know what you meant to me, even if for
only a short time. I want her to understand why I behaved towards her
the way I did, for all those years.

Perhaps it was not because I didn't understand – but because I did.

Yours,
Daniel Whittaker

She turned over the last page of the letter. 'That's it?'

'I would say that's quite a lot, my dear. Quite a lot to take in.'
Ron was looking at her thoughtfully.

Evonne realised she was shaking, her whole body racked by a
convulsion, and for a moment she thought she was going to burst
into tears. She had risen from her chair, and Ron pressed on her
arm.

'Sit down.' He took the pages from her hands. 'Let me pour you
some water. You've gone quite pale.'

Evonne took small, quick sips, willing her throat to swallow
without gagging.

'You're shocked,' said Ron.

'Of course I am. Not because of … because of all that.' She
pointed at the letter. 'Not because of you or my father. Not because
of whatever you meant to each other.'

213

Ron raised an eyebrow.

'I mean, I'm surprised, yes. Of course I'm surprised.'

'He was unsure. Plenty of men were then – and still are, of course. But I can't begin to tell you how different it was. It was an offence, as your father wrote. People were gaoled, humiliated, threatened. Their livelihoods and families put at risk. You shouldn't blame him at all for what he did. There were plenty of men who needed physical release and emotional strength, and our community accepted them. We prided ourselves on allowing people to be themselves, on not being judgemental or preachy.'

He paused.

Evonne laughed then, a full-throated, cheerless laugh. 'You don't understand.' She reached for her tote bag and pulled out her wallet. Extracted a photo of her and Libby, their arms around one another, their noses touching, a shot taken at Peregian Beach. She handed it to Ron.

'My partner,' she told him. 'Libby.'

She wanted to say more, but she was struggling to reconcile the words on the page with the barrage from her father's mouth, which she could hear still; the way he railed at her, as though describing something foul, something soiled. Terrible words that not only affected her but that tainted Libby too, her Libby, with her kind eyes and her gentle manner, Libby who offered such a comforting embrace. She heard her father utter the word *lesbian*, sounding so condescending. Or *queer*, a word her mother had used in a haughty, disdainful way, as if her daughter was indeed odd and peculiar.

She much preferred the word that meant happy, lively. Those were the feelings she had around Libby, although it didn't in any way evoke the complicated history of her sexuality, and the relationship she had tried for so long to navigate with her parents.

Ron Linklater watched her, expectant.

'I'm gay,' she said. 'And my father made my life bloody hell over it.'

RICHARD WAS FUMING. HE COULD not believe what Evonne had told him about their father's letter to Ron Linklater.

'I may as well throw everything I know about him out the window,' he railed to Jemima. 'He wasn't the man I thought he was. He wasn't the father or the husband I thought I knew. He was a bloody stranger.'

'All of us hide secrets, Richard. You shouldn't be so harsh to judge.'

'All of us have secrets? What's your secret, then? Tell me that. What's mine? I'll tell you – nothing. I have absolutely nothing to hide, from anyone, least of all my family.' He hoped Jemima wouldn't hear the hypocrisy in his words, and ploughed on. 'But that's all Dad did. He lived a whole double life that none of us knew about. And this … this … *homosexuality*' – he growled the word as if it hurt him to say it – 'is the last straw. I tell you, if Evonne hadn't read it with her own eyes, I would never have believed it. Not in a million years.'

'Richard, please …'

'Don't you Richard me! My father was not gay! He was not. I don't care what he said. Those men must have preyed on soldiers after the war, when they were damaged by all the fighting, from risking their *lives* for everyone—'

'That's enough,' snapped Jemima. 'You can't talk about gay people that way. I heard Evonne too, and from what she had to say, your father met a group of men who welcomed him, made him feel comfortable. For the first time in a long time, he felt supported. Irene had left him. He'd had those awful experiences overseas. He found physical and psychological release—'

Richard groaned.

'Yes, Richard, your father was a man, like you. Flesh and blood and bone. He had needs and desires, much as you don't like to think about them.' She took Richard's hand in her own. 'So he batted for the other side for a bit. Tried it out to see what it was like. So what?'

'So what? Oh, my God, Jem. How can you be so flippant about it?'

'I wish you'd lighten up. It's not like other people haven't done it.'

A beat. 'What? You … wait, what? What are you saying?'

Jemima gave an exasperated moan. 'Most people experiment when they're younger. I did it, maybe you did; it's just not that unusual.'

'I most certainly did *not* do it! And … and that's different. You're a woman. That's entirely different,' he stuttered, trying to find solid ground. 'Girls are naturally more curious, and open with each other, and—'

Jemima interrupted, enunciating slowly. 'Richard Whittaker. That is a rank pile of horseshit. It's all right for girls but not for

217

boys? Some girl-on-girl action is okay, but sex between blokes is a step too far? I can't believe you would say that. Your own sister's gay, for God's sake!'

'People make different choices, I understand that.'

'Oh, you are kidding me. Is that what you think Evonne's made? A choice? A choice to be criticised and humiliated for half her life by her own parents? A choice to be thought less of by her own brother? A choice to be laughed at and discriminated against?'

'No, no. I didn't mean that. I meant that she ...' He stopped. He didn't know what he had been meaning to say.

'Well?'

Richard still felt a roiling anger inside him, even though it wasn't directed at his father, or at Jemima. 'All I know is that I'm sick of this. Everything keeps changing on the spin of a coin. At any time. Without warning.' Almost by impulse, he lifted a vase from the windowsill and smashed it on the floor. 'There. Like that. Completely out of the blue.' He leant against the wall, panting hard. Sharp coloured shards littered the tiles.

Jemima stood with her hand drawn to her mouth, her eyes wide. Eventually she spoke.

'I don't know who you are when you're like this, Richard. I don't know you at all.' Her voice was a barely controlled whisper. 'Get yourself together. Get a grip on your temper, calm down, and ... and clean up this mess.' She stalked away.

Richard closed his eyes. 'Fuck.'

...

An hour later, Jemima appeared at the door with two cups of coffee. Richard looked at her sheepishly. He had given her the vase for her birthday two years ago. Now it sat in fragments, wrapped in newspaper, inside the wheelie bin. He had found the vacuum cleaner (though he couldn't recall ever noticing that cupboard under the stairs, and had certainly never had a need to search there for cleaning implements) and gone over the floor several times. He hoped he seemed suitably chastened.

'Coffee?' she said.

'Yes. Please.' He took the cup. 'And, sorry. About before. The vase ... I'll get you another one. I'm sure I can order one.'

'I don't care about the vase, Richard.' She placed her palm on his cheek. 'I care about *you*. I'm worried about you. I don't like the person you've become over the last twelve months. The things you've been saying, these petty violent outbursts. That's not the man I married.'

'I'm not sure I know who that person was,' he croaked. 'Everything's changed.'

'Nothing ever stays the same. Surely you can come to terms with that.'

'It's all so hard,' he whispered. 'These bloody letters. They're all I've been thinking about. What's in the next one? What other aspect of Dad's personality are we going to discover, that we never knew existed?'

'You're almost at the end, darling. There's only one left now.'

He squeezed his eyes shut. 'That's the one I'm most worried about.'

Ever since he realised the last letter might be addressed to Irene White's son, Richard had slept fitfully, thrashing amongst the bedsheets until Jemima woke him one night and told him to go into the guest room. There couldn't be another Ryan Mossman, surely. That would be too improbable, and too much like good news. To his consternation, Kelly and Evonne had found Ryan thoroughly agreeable when they had met him. Richard didn't know why that worried him even more.

And he still hadn't spoken to Jemima about his retrenchment. Money was getting tight. If only the estate could be finalised, then at least his financial worries would be over.

But first he had to confront Ryan Mossman. He didn't know what was worse: not knowing what was in the letter; or knowing, with everything that knowledge would bring.

'Evonne's livid over the letter to Ron Linklater,' he said. 'And Kelly's still angry with Dad for interfering. I want to throw this last bloody letter in the bin and be done with it.'

'You know that's impossible.'

'Yes, I realise that,' he replied, resigned. 'Ryan Mossman will open the goddamned letter, and its contents will be there for all to see. And there's not a damn thing I can do about it.'

...

Towards dusk they were out in the garden, the twins taking turns on the tyre swing. Richard had arranged to see Irene's son the following day; to relieve his tension over the meeting, he was pulling stray weeds from around the bamboo. Jemima was dead-heading spent flowers, the secateurs snipping and snapping as she pruned. She added a straggly bunch to the weeds under the lime tree, and tossed the whole lot into the compost bin. Richard watched her fluid movements; she was too young yet to suffer from stiff knees and an aching back. He envied her easy grace.

Violetta and Victoria called for him to push them on the swing. He took off his gardening gloves and walked over. The girls balanced like cats on either side of the rubber tyre, and their laughter rang out over the garden as he propelled them further and further into the air.

Kelly appeared from the side path with Eden, who ran towards the twins, shouting for them to let him have a turn. Jemima gave her sister-in-law a kiss and stood back, holding her arms, to look at her face. 'How are you coping with everything, Kel? How are things going with Simon?'

'Oh, you know. Baby steps. We're taking it one day at a time.' Kelly grimaced. 'At least it's all out in the open now.'

'Exactly. It'll take time, but you'll get there.'

'I know. Hey, I wanted to talk to you and Richard about something. Have you got a minute?'

'Of course. Violetta! Victoria!' she called to the girls. 'Take Eden inside and get him a biscuit and some milk. One each!' She grinned at Kelly. 'The girls made them this morning and they're absolutely huge. Like cookie cakes or something.'

Richard came over to greet his sister, whom he still felt awkward hugging. 'Has something happened?'

'No, just something I wanted to share with you both. I've already spoken to Evonne. It's about Eden. Well, about his father, really.'

Richard was taken aback. In his mind, it was almost as if Eden's father didn't exist. Kelly's pregnancy had seemed to appear out of nowhere: she hadn't been dating anyone, or not that he was aware of, anyway, and she had never mentioned the man.

They sat on the grass as Kelly began to explain. 'I've been doing a lot of thinking lately. About Simon, of course, and everything brought up by Dad's letter to him. But also about Billy. That's Eden's father. Billy Henderson.'

And so Richard heard about this Billy, with whom his sister had

221

only gone on two dates. Her dilemma when she discovered she was pregnant. And her decision to have Eden, never telling Billy that he had a child. Kelly had slipped off her shoes and Richard noticed how small and bare his sister's feet looked, nestled in the grass.

'Now, I think it was wrong of me not to inform him,' she said. 'Not to give him a choice as to how he wanted to react. I made that choice for him.'

'Just like Dad and Simon made for you,' said Richard.

'Yes.' Kelly dug her toes into the soft grass. 'I shouldn't have. I know that now.'

'So what are you going to do about it?' Jemima's voice was gentle and reassuring.

'Actually, I've already done it.' Kelly beamed at them. 'I reconnected with Billy through Facebook. He's becoming quite well known. He's a dancer,' she added. 'Anyway, we had a coffee yesterday. Just the two of us. I took lots of pictures of Eden to show him.'

'How did he take the news?' asked Jemima. 'That must have been quite a shock.'

'Oh, it was. I hadn't told him beforehand over the phone. I thought it was something I needed to do face to face. He was shocked, yes. Took him a while to process what I was saying.'

'Was he angry?'

'A little, I think, at first. Yes, a little. But once I started showing him all the photos, his mood changed. I think he could see so much of himself in Eden. He just sort of sat there in wonder.'

Richard couldn't help himself. 'He didn't question paternity?'

'Oh, Richard,' snapped Jemima. 'Honestly.'

'It's all right, Jem. I'm used to it,' said Kelly. 'I'd already thought of that. I've told Billy I want to insist on a test anyway, just to clarify things. Make sure there's no room for doubt. Now that I've decided to make him a part of Eden's life, I want to make sure I do things the right way. Billy's determined to make up for lost time.'

'Are you sure this is wise?' Richard interjected. 'He's basically a complete stranger. Do you know anything at all about his life? His family? What did you say he does for a living?'

His sister regarded him coolly. 'He's a performer in the Bangarra Dance Theatre. He travels a lot. To be honest, I don't know a lot more about him than I did when we met five years ago, but I figure I'll work it out as I go along, just like I would've had he stayed and found out about Eden then.'

'She's doing what she thinks is right, Richard. That's the main thing,' said Jemima.

'Would you like to see a picture of him?' Kelly addressed this to Jemima, but Richard looked over as she held out her phone and swiped through the photos. There was one with the two of them together, smiling at whoever was taking the shot.

Richard squinted at her phone. 'He's very dark. Got some Maori blood, has he? Indian?'

He saw Kelly and Jemima exchange a glance. 'Actually, he's a proud Wiradjuri man,' said his sister.

'For heaven's sake, Richard, surely you've heard of Bangarra? It's a famous Indigenous dance group,' said Jemima. 'Don't mind him,' she said to Kelly. 'Sometimes it's like he lives on the moon.'

At that moment, Eden and the girls ran out from the back door and across the yard, chasing each other and screeching at the tops of their voices. Richard stared at his nephew. Never for a moment had he thought the boy might be part Aboriginal. With a guilty start, he thought of all the comments he had made over the years, to Jemima, to Kelly even, to anyone who would listen; his rants about the Indigenous population and all their problems. He felt a jolt of remorse at his uncharitable words, words that – he recognised now – could be seen to be mean-spirited, or even cruel.

The only person Richard knew who had any sort of connection to Aboriginal people was Kara. For several years she had hit him up for an annual thousand-dollar donation to support Indigenous literacy; it was one of the causes she was passionate about. One Christmas she had lectured him about his lack of respect for 'this country's first peoples'. Her phrase. He had said he didn't care much for history, that the whites were here now and that everyone should just get used to it and carry on. Kara had called him an ignorant racist.

'Billy Henderson. Not a very traditional-sounding name,' he mused, without realising he'd spoken out loud.

Kelly rolled her eyes. 'A lot of the traditional names were lost along the way when the Europeans arrived.' She ticked off the list on her fingers. 'White pastoralists renaming their workers, giving them names whites could pronounce; children born to mixed-race couples and taking the father's surname; Indigenous people denied the right to use their traditional names so as to erase their identity; kids forcibly removed from their parents and placed in foster care … Could be any number of reasons.'

He tried to back down. 'Okay, okay. It's all a bit of a shock, that's all.'

But his sister leapt to her feet, furious. 'For heaven's sake, Richard. When will you learn that it's not all about you. It was a shock for Billy to hear he has a son. It was a shock for me to learn about Simon's infidelity.' She stalked away, Jemima following her.

224

'Though no doubt it'll be a shock for you when you hear whatever Ryan Mossman's got to say to you. *Then* you can feel sorry for yourself!'

Alone on the grass, Richard thought about his father's letters, about all his father had felt he had to atone for. Richard had once considered his own life to be free from guilt and regrets. But of course it wasn't – he thought again of how he'd treated Jemima. He made a quiet resolution to be more honest with those he loved, but also to open his mind – to be more accepting and less judgemental.

...

He'd arranged to meet Ryan Mossman at Tognini's in Milton. Richard arrived early and ordered a cappuccino and a large piece of orange and almond cake. A cluster of small girls in pink tulle were squealing and chattering, which only served to heighten his tension as he waited.

The man who approached him was about his age, balding on top and sporting a well-trimmed moustache. He wore a glaring Hawaiian shirt and bright blue thongs. His handshake was firm.

'Good to meet you at last, Richard. Your sisters have mentioned you. I've seen them a few times now, at Mum's.'

'Yes. Your mother knew my father ...'

'They were married, yes. Short-lived affair, but there you go. There was a war on. These things happened.' The other man settled into his chair.

Richard did not want Ryan Mossman to gain the upper hand. 'Actually, I believe your mother left my father. Abandoned him while he was off fighting, risking his life for the likes of her.'

But Ryan merely smiled enigmatically. 'Yes, well, who are we to judge the actions of our oldies, hey? I certainly don't know the ins and outs of whatever went on between Mum and Daniel. Do you?' He waited for a response, as if it wasn't a rhetorical question.

'Well, no,' Richard mumbled at last. 'No, I don't.'

'Best not to speculate then, hey. Anyway, you said you've got a letter for me?'

Richard sighed. 'Yes. Well, I'm assuming it's for you. Although we won't be certain until you open it, of course.'

'Better get on with it then.'

The envelope looked flimsy in Ryan's large hands. 'I've always wondered,' he said, almost to himself. Richard was about to ask *wondered what?* when the other man continued. 'I've dragged myself up by my bootstraps, you know that? Didn't take to school too well. Left when I was only fourteen. Kicked around for a year or so, not knowing what to do with myself. But then I got my act together. Took on an apprenticeship with a local plumber.' He chuckled. 'Never worked so hard in my damn life. Dawn till dusk we laboured. And I drank it all in. Soaked up every last bit of learning I could about the business. Struck out on my own when I was only twenty-three. Mum was worried, said she didn't think I could do it. But I proved her wrong. I proved them all wrong, all those naysayers who thought I wouldn't amount to anything much. These days, the business has over twenty employees. Leigh, my daughter, she mostly runs it now. Don't even need to get my hands dirty anymore. Mostly sit around doing paperwork.' He glanced at Richard's hands. 'I hear you're a banker. Suppose paperwork's all you've ever done.'

Before Richard had a chance to reply, Ryan opened the envelope and retrieved the paper from within. When he had read it, he spoke in a low voice. 'Better late than never, I guess. Not that I need it now, but it's nice to be acknowledged.' He looked Richard in the eye. 'That's all any of us ever want, in the end, isn't it? To be acknowledged.'

Richard wasn't sure how to respond. Handing over the last letter after all this time was remarkably freeing. Finally, the burden of carrying out his father's instructions was over. The estate could be finalised, and they could all move on.

And yet something in the other man's expression gave him pause. The notion that had been niggling at the back of his mind made its way forward. Like watching a car crash in slow motion, he could see the inevitability of what was to come, how he and Ryan Mossman would be inextricably joined by the thinnest of threads.

Ryan drained his water glass. He answered Richard's unasked question. 'Just so you know, I never asked for this. Heading for seventy years old and I've never expected a damn thing. That clear?'

Richard nodded. He took the paper with a shaking hand. The letter contained only a few lines:

Dear Ryan,

I find myself wanting to make amends in my old age. It is a great sorrow to me that I did not know of your existence from the beginning; and to my great regret that even when I found out, I did nothing to acknowledge you.

Your mother had her reasons, I'm sure. Regardless of whether she has explained them to you, I wish to formally recognise you in my will as an equal fourth beneficiary of my estate, along with my other children.

My solicitor, John Hardcastle, of Hardcastle, Braithwaite and

Turner, has the necessary details. My son Richard shall offer you all the assistance you require. It may be too late, but I hope this gesture of acknowledgement is one you can accept in the spirit it is offered.

Yours
Daniel Whittaker

Richard stared at the letter. It was as he had feared. 'My father …'

'Is my father.' Ryan Mossman sat back in his chair. He fixed Richard with a firm glare. 'I'm your half-brother.'

…

Richard had to excuse himself to go to the bathroom. He knew it appeared rude, but he couldn't help it. Despite having an inkling all along, he still felt physically sick with the shock.

When he eventually returned to the table, Ryan was tucking into a plate of pasta. 'Thought you weren't coming back,' he said, and then frowned. 'Are you all right? You've gone all white.'

'Yes, I'm … sorry. Sorry. Um,' he cleared his throat. 'I just never knew.'

'Didn't know meself for quite some time. When I reached twenty-one, Mum sat me down and told me the story. Told me I was a man and deserved to know the truth. Up until then, I'd always thought Dad, Bob, was my real father. He and Mum were all I'd ever known. They went on to have three more kids together, your sisters might have mentioned it, and I had no reason to suspect I wasn't a regular part of the family.'

'Bob … was that the American serviceman that your mother went off with when she and Dad were married?'

'God, no. That guy was a fling.' He cast a worried look at

Richard. 'Listen, are you sure you're right to hear all this? We don't have to go on.'

'No, I'm fine. Please.' Richard wiped his forehead with a serviette and gulped some water. 'I need to know.'

'Well, Mum liked to say that she and Daniel Whittaker married in haste and repented in leisure. Soon after she got down to Sydney with the Yank, she realised she was pregnant. He cleared off quick smart. Poor Mum had to come back to her parents in Brisbane. Within the space of a year, she'd got married, left to live with the Yank, and then arrived back home alone and knocked up. Don't think she got much sympathy. My grandfather was a Baptist minister. It was a wonder they even let her stay in the house.'

'What year was all this?' asked Richard. He wiped his forehead again. He could feel the sweat trickling down the back of his shirt and collecting at the base of his spine. He drank some more water.

'I was born at the end of '45. December baby. Mum had me in one of those lying-in hospitals. I think her parents wanted her to give me up, you know, have me adopted out to some rich family in the church. But Mum wouldn't hear of it. She clung on to me, she said. Barked at the nurses to bring me to her for feeds, and ignored them every time they put the paperwork in front of her to sign. She sent the adoption people packing when they came. Told them nobody was taking her boy away from her. I'm just fortunate she was such a determined and feisty bugger.' He laughed.

Richard was having trouble getting enough air into his lungs. 'Why didn't she ever tell Dad about you? Why didn't she try to reconcile with him when he got home from the war?'

'You'd have to ask her. But look at it from her point of view – after all she'd been through, with the American and her parents and the adoption authorities, I imagine she didn't have the energy to be pursuing your father again. Even if she'd wanted to, which I don't know that she did. All her time would've been taken up with caring for me.' He placed his hands on the flat of the table, as if to emphasise his next point. 'She never gave him a bit of trouble about it. She raised me as well as she could. And soon after that, she got together with Dad, who, as far as I'm concerned, raised me as his own son. She did the best she could with the circumstances of the time, and I never felt a jot of difference from my brothers. Dad died ten years ago. Stroke. Before Mum lost her sight.'

Ryan extracted his phone and pulled up some photos. 'Here. Want to see my kids? My grandkids? Guess they're your, what, nieces and nephews.' He twisted the phone around so that Richard could see the screen. 'This here's my oldest, Danny. His full name's Robert Daniel, after the two men who fathered me. This here's his youngest two, and that's my middle one, Lilly, and that's Ryan Junior, and that's a few more of the grandkids.'

'Very nice,' managed Richard. He tried to collect his thoughts.

Behind his eyelids he could sense a determined pounding, the beginning of a migraine. He tried to look interested in the photographs, but all he could see were the words *Ryan, 1945, First-Born Son*, as if they were inscribed across his retina.

Everything he thought he knew, about his father, and about himself, was a lie.

ONCE AGAIN, THE SIBLINGS WERE gathered at John Hardcastle's office, with all its familiar sounds and smells: pigeons squabbling on the window ledge; the odour of the leather couches, worn smooth by hundreds of clients; the tick of the carriage clock as time moved relentlessly forward. Once again, John Hardcastle regarded them over the rim of his spectacles, his solid wooden desk between them. But this time there were no more letters.

Kelly stared at John's fingernails, neat half-moons clipped with precision. He wore a watch with a gold band that she hadn't noticed before. He seemed a little older. As they all were, she thought.

At last the solicitor spoke. 'Thank you all for coming today. I thought it fitting to give proper closure to your father's last wishes.'

'Closure,' her brother harrumphed. 'Bet the old man's having a bloody good laugh, that's what I think. Had us all running rings, hasn't he.'

Kelly and Evonne remained silent. 'I'm sorry you feel that way, Richard,' said John. 'I know these last twelve months have been hard on you. But I'm sure your father would be proud, of all of you.'

'I keep expecting you to bring out another letter,' said Kelly. 'After all this time, somehow it doesn't feel like it's really over.'

'There are no more letters, Kelly. I can assure you of that.' John blinked behind his glasses. 'Daniel would have been proud,' he repeated.

Evonne grimaced. 'I still don't understand why he couldn't have addressed those issues when he was alive. It would've made such a difference. To me. To Libby. To our relationship.'

'Or not,' muttered Richard. 'Just because he decided at the eleventh hour to tell the truth about his life, doesn't mean he would've been any different towards you, towards any of us. He was a coward. A coward and a liar.'

Evonne had begun to respond when John pushed back his chair and rose to his feet. 'I have some papers to fetch,' he said quietly. 'Some documents for you to sign. I'll leave you three alone to … talk things through.' He paused at the doorway. 'Take all the time you need.' The door closed with a gentle click.

'For God's sake, Richard, give it a rest, will you?' hissed Evonne. 'What's done is done. We can't change anything now. You're just upset to discover that you're not the golden child.'

'What the hell's that supposed to mean?'

'You know very well. The fact that Dad had another child before you were born – another *son* – makes you livid.'

'A mistake. That's what he had. A mistake.'

'Don't you start, Richard!' Kelly would not stand for this. She heard her voice echoing in the cavernous room. 'Ryan and his family are lovely. And Dad obviously cared a lot about Irene.'

'Yeah, well, apparently she didn't care much for him,' he sputtered. 'Not enough to tell him about his own son.'

Kelly exchanged a glance with her sister. Richard had only grown more indignant since meeting Ryan's family. At the dinner that Evonne and Libby had arranged, Kelly and her sister had shared childhood photographs with Ryan, his wife and one of their daughters. They had swapped stories of growing up, reminisced about their early lives. But Richard had remained aloof, seemingly unable to cede ground with their newly discovered half-brother, unwilling to share his memories of their father. He was still stunned that an equal portion of the estate had been left to Ryan, but Kelly knew it was about more than just the money: the security of his position in the family had been shaken.

'I feel like I don't know who he was at all,' Richard mumbled, his head in his hands. 'Maybe he wasn't even our father. Any of us. Maybe Mum had affairs. Maybe we were all adopted.'

'Now you're being ridiculous,' said Evonne.

'Really? Ridiculous? Could you ever have imagined that Dad had a homosexual past? And you,' he said, glaring at Kelly. 'Have you conveniently forgotten that he ruined your marriage?'

'No, Richard, of course I haven't forgotten. I haven't forgiven him either, for interfering. But at least now we've been forced to confront the truth.'

'Rubbish. You'd have been happier not knowing.'

'And I suppose you would have been happier not knowing about Ryan.'

'Absolutely. One more complication I don't need. A quarter of our inheritance siphoned off to the product of one of Dad's flings.'

'Richard, how can you say that? How can you begrudge that man anything? You saw how he lives. He's an honest, hardworking bloke. That sort of money will change his life. And not just his, either. His whole family's.'

'I'm glad he included Ryan in his will,' added Evonne. 'Really glad. My share is still more than I know what to do with.'

'Well, you don't have private-school fees and an ex-wife to worry about, do you. I'll find plenty of uses for my money, I can assure you.'

Evonne grinned smugly at their brother. 'Oh, I'm sure you will, Richard. I have no doubt about that.'

'What?'

'Oh, nothing. Just wondering if you've said anything to Jemima yet.'

'No, and I'm not going to either. No need, now that the estate's been finalised.

A beat.

'Wait a minute. What do you mean? How do you ... what do you know?' he demanded.

Evonne erupted into a huge belly laugh, and Kelly joined in. Eventually they took his arms, one on each side, and held him close.

'Jemima told us months ago,' said Kelly. 'About your work. She was so worried about you.'

'Yeah, you goose, why didn't you say anything?'

Richard was flabbergasted. 'What ... when ... How long has she known? Who told her?'

'She's very smart, your wife,' said Kelly.

'Not much gets past her,' agreed Evonne.

Richard freed himself from their grasp and looked frantically around the room, as if expecting Jemima to materialise. 'But why didn't she say something? Oh my God, how am I going to face her now?'

Kelly took his arm again. 'She was waiting for you to tell her yourself. She was hoping you'd confide in her.'

'But she's okay that you didn't,' said Evonne. 'Apparently, she sees more in you than both of us put together.' She laughed again.

'I'm teasing you. She's fine about it, really. Thinks it was high time you retired.'

'Yeah,' said Kelly. 'She thinks you'll make a stellar stay-at-home dad. Don't know that I agree with her, but hey, what do I know?'

Richard shook himself free again and stomped over to the window. Kelly watched his back; it trembled, though whether from anger or sadness or some other emotion, she couldn't tell.

'Do you think Richard's right?' she whispered to Evonne. 'About Dad? Do you think we really know the whole story?'

'Could there be more, you mean?'

'More. Or something different. If you'd asked me a year ago to tell you about Dad's life, I would have done so without even thinking about it. But that version wouldn't have been true, would it, or not the whole truth, anyway.'

Evonne shrugged. 'Stories change according to who's telling them. And who's listening. And the point at which they're told. The truth is only ever the story from one perspective.'

Richard wheeled around at that moment and announced he was going to the bathroom. Kelly noticed his eyes were red-rimmed. After he left the room, she took her sister's hand in her own.

'Do you think he'll ever change?' she said.

Evonne squeezed Kelly's fingers. 'He's still reeling with the knowledge of what Dad did, and he's not coping well with what he's found. In many ways, it's knowledge he wishes he didn't have.'

'Have you noticed he's still carrying around the grieving stone that Katherine Mosely gave him? Jem said he's taken to keeping it beside the bed at night.'

'Hmm. Who knows? Maybe you can teach an old dog new tricks. Anyway, once the money from the estate comes through, he'll breathe easier.' Evonne squeezed Kelly's fingers again. 'And you too, with the kids. I never understood why you wouldn't accept more help from Mum and Dad over the years.'

Kelly recalled the only time she had asked her parents for a loan – a measly thousand dollars, after Eden was born, to repair her clapped-out Suzuki hatchback that hadn't been on the road for several months. Her father had grimaced as he handed over a cheque. The amount was less than her mother spent on a typical shopping spree.

'I'm hesitant to lend it to you because I know you'll be worried if you have trouble paying it back,' he had said.

'If you hadn't been so … irresponsible,' her mother had intoned, 'you would still be working and wouldn't *need* to borrow money from us.'

Kelly had folded the cheque into a small square and it had sat in her wallet for weeks before she finally tore it up and flushed the pieces down the toilet. Her parents had never mentioned it again. They didn't ask why the cheque hadn't been cashed, or how Kelly had eventually afforded the repairs. And she never asked them for money again.

But she didn't want to rake all this up with her sister, so she changed the subject. 'What about you, Vonnie? How are you feeling about it all? It's probably been the hardest on you, out of all of us.'

Evonne grunted. 'Honestly? One moment I feel overwhelmed by all we've learnt about him. I think he's been brave and sincere. He's admitted his flaws and he's tried to make amends. And the next, I'm pissed off. I find myself swearing at him under my breath. I look at Libby and I feel this enormous sense of rage at his duplicity. It sucks the breath out of me. I feel like there are a whole lot of years just … lost, you know? Wasted years.'

Kelly embraced her. 'And you need some time and space to mourn those years.'

'Yeah, the years I could've been focusing on my relationship with Libby, the years we could've been concentrating on making a family. You know how long we spent on IVF, paying a small fortune and hoping for a miracle. The guts it took to ask friends to be sperm donors. The disappointment of being turned down. All the hopes we pinned on the laws changing around adoption, and surrogacy, and even fostering.'

'Knowing about Dad wouldn't have changed the laws, though, Von.'

'No, I know that. But we never fought harder for those other options because we were tiptoeing around Mum and Dad. We always thought they would've accepted a child born to us; we dared to hope they'd even welcome a pregnancy and just avoid thinking about how it happened. We kept praying one of us could fall pregnant through IVF without any fuss. God, Kel, the nights we wept. The years we suffered through, alone, all because our parents could only just cope with the fact we were a couple; the idea that we might be jumping up and down demanding a child horrified them. It seemed to come so easily to everyone else. I felt like such a failure. It was humiliating. And if we'd had more support ...' She trailed off.

'You would've felt like you deserved more,' said Kelly.

'Exactly. But I thought I wasn't worthy of those choices.' She sighed. 'I feel like I've thrown away a lifetime by putting myself last, by putting the opinions of my parents first. I felt relieved just to have Libby; I thought I was being greedy by wanting children too.' She smiled sadly. 'I've allowed the convictions of others to govern my life.'

Kelly gave her a gentle smile. 'It's true that your life's taken a different path from the one you'd hoped. But that's true for so many of us. And you have Libby. What you share with her is something most of us envy, Evonne. You have a life together.'

'You're right.' Evonne exhaled loudly. 'Libby will be home from work by now. She'll be padding around the house in her bare feet. With those ridiculous purple toenails.'

'She'll be watering her plants and making dinner. Probably dancing to that jazz station she likes.' Kelly got to her feet and shimmied her backside, making her sister laugh.

'She'll be drinking red wine,' said Evonne.

'And she'll have a glass waiting for you. She loves you, Vonnie, like no-one else does.'

'Yes,' agreed her sister. 'Like no-one else does.'

...

Kelly was hugging her sister tight when she noticed Richard standing awkwardly at the doorway. 'Come, come,' she said, motioning him over. They opened their arms and included him in their circle, rocking slowly to unheard music. Kelly felt her brother relax.

She knew they would look a little silly if John Hardcastle chose that moment to re-enter the room – the three of them, grown adults, swaying back and forth. And yet the repetition seemed to lull them all, even Richard, who was the quietest she'd seen him for some time.

Eventually Evonne broke the silence. 'How's the serenity?'

Kelly choked back a laugh, and she saw the corners of Richard's mouth curling upwards. 'So much serenity,' he whispered.

...

Later that afternoon, Kelly went to pick Eden up from kindy. He came belting across the grass, his backpack bouncing on his shoulders. He had twigs in his hair and green stains on his shorts. He uncurled the fingers of his right hand, one at a time, to reveal a ladybug balancing on wire-thin black legs, her wings opening.

'Look, Mummy, look. She wants to fly away home.' The bug crawled across his palm. He turned his hand as the bug traversed the back of his wrist.

Kelly brushed a leaf from his ear. She, too, wanted to fly away home, to a place that conjured up all the word implied: safety, security, comfort, belonging. When she was growing up, her notion of home was tied to her father's protectiveness. At the time, she had railed against his questions about where she was and who she was with and what she was doing. She had longed to escape his boundaries. His letter to Simon had brought all those feelings rushing back, the childish desire to please, the need to appease. But now she saw him through a different prism. She saw his protectiveness for what it was, and recognised it in her own parenting.

Unlike Richard, she felt closer now to their father than she ever did when he was alive. Despite everything, his last request had allowed her to reimagine her life; he had given her another chance.

She didn't yet know what would happen with Billy. His introduction to Eden had been gentle and gradual, the three of them spending time together, getting to know each other. Billy's interest was genuine, his motivations transparent. She trusted him. She was gratified to see Eden's delight at the appearance of his father in his life, and grateful to witness their fragile bond beginning to form.

The ladybug spread its wings, and she and Eden watched as it flew across the grass.

AND SO, LOOK AT THEM. Gathered once more around his grave. What was a simple mound of earth is now a slab of marbled granite. Flecks of colour sparkle from the headstone – gold, pink and pearly-white – and the effect is one of constant movement, as if the whole memorial might at any moment break free and float upwards, dissolving into the ether.

But of course, it does not. The grave remains rooted to the ground, his body encased in its final resting place.

Kelly kneels to pull out a few recalcitrant weeds from the edges of the stone. Richard stands beside her as if struggling under a great weight, serious and solemn. Evonne brushes leaves from the headstone. She lifts the corner of her shirt and scrubs at a smudge of green lichen that has crept across one corner, partly obscuring the R at the end of their family name. The moss comes away cleanly. It has not had time to take hold.

Daniel Whittaker
Out beyond ideas

of wrongdoing and rightdoing
there is a field.
I'll meet you there.

Richard had wanted something biblical. Evonne thought the epitaph should be simple and succinct. Kelly had suggested that Ryan be invited to participate in choosing the wording, to Richard's chagrin. But they finally decided on the quote from Rumi: Kara's suggestion. Somehow it encapsulates all they have been through over the past twelve months.

Ryan is here now, and Billy too, standing apart from the others, keeping a respectful distance from their new-found family, chatting to Jemima and Libby, and watching the children play.

The cemetery is a clash of old and new. Where they stand, in the modern section, the graves are evenly spaced and symmetrical. Obelisks and pieces of sculpture mark the graves, well tended and adorned with photographs and mementos. Further to the west is a jumble of crumbling concrete and brickwork. Stained-glass mausoleums sit side by side with locked crypts. Tombs, surrounded by wrought-iron barriers, tower over unmarked graves, some with huge trees growing directly out of the sunken pits, the soil collapsing under the weight of a hundred years. Impossibly long-ago dates are inscribed under old-fashioned names – if they can even still be read, the engravings faded from wind and rain.

But in both sections, scattered throughout the many sites, there is the occasional flash of colour, fresh flowers wilting in the heat, or plastic offerings standing stiff and upright in their vases.

Someone, at some time, has remembered.

Eden, Violetta and Victoria are following butterflies over the gravestones and chasing each other through the trees. Their shouts and laughter bring life to this place. The adults supervise from a distance safe enough to intervene in any bad behaviour, while allowing the children to feel they own the sweeping majesty of the shaded hills and the cobbled pathways; to imagine this a world they can inhabit fully.

'Kara did well,' says Evonne, pointing at the epitaph. 'I like it. Dad's life was full of wrongdoing and rightdoing, like us all.'

'Mistakes were made,' replies Kelly. She squeezes Evonne's fingers.

Ben and Kara emerge from behind an overgrown thicket of trees, waving as they approach. Eden rushes towards them, aiming at treetops with a stick.

'We found it!' calls out Kara. 'Great-Uncle Brian's grave! We followed the map and asked the guy in the office. He helped us pinpoint the exact location. There's a marker.'

'But not much more,' adds Ben. 'No headstone or anything, just a standard wooden plot number.'

'Well, we can certainly change that. You're the official epitaph girl, Kara, you can come up with something suitable.'

Richard scoffs. 'Am I the only one who's not surprised that Dad never ordered a proper headstone for his brother?'

'He was only a child himself when Brian died, Richard.'

'Yes, but then he grew up, didn't he? He became wealthy and had a family. He could easily have marked his brother's grave at some point over the years.'

Evonne shakes her head. 'You're still so quick to judge. Brian's death scarred our father. He had no emotional support, no counselling or whatever, to help him get over it. He just had to get on with things.'

'All the while being blamed for Brian's death. What a burden.' Kelly points towards Jemima and the others, who are walking

242

towards them. 'I do think you could be a bit more … compassionate, Richard. Especially considering how certain people have acted towards you lately.'

…

The group troops together to the site of Brian's grave. Evonne, Libby and Kelly walk arm in arm. A breeze shakes the leaves on the trees and curls about the headstones. In the distance, they can hear the voices of other visitors.

Eden is atop Ryan's shoulders, pulling on his ears – now left, now right – to direct him, like a horse. The child is laughing, his mouth open with delight. Jemima remonstrates with him gently, but nobody – least of all Eden – is listening.

Ben and Kara walk with their arms around each other's waists, content, both deep in conversation with Billy, who gestures expansively at the sky. The three stop and stare up at the billowing clouds rolling across the firmament, the sun settling into the blurred smudge of the horizon. Billy gestures again, and laughs, and Ben and Kara laugh too, the lovely echo of their voices sounding bold and joyous in the muted twilight.

Richard has hold of one twin with each hand, the girls skipping lopsidedly and scuffing leaves with their feet. Violetta pulls at her father's pocket and he reaches in and retrieves the grieving stone. The twins roll the black obsidian in their own small hands, pass it back and forth, hold it up to the light, and then replace it in their father's pocket, where it sits, warm and smooth against his thigh.

The evening breeze blows across the gravesites, unmooring keepsakes and fluttering flowers in their urns.

Night birds are beginning to call. The insect choir is tuning up.

The sunset paints the cemetery in fallen panels of gold and palest pink. Statues stand guard against the coming night. The last rays of the sun cast lengthening shadows from each headstone, covering the ground in an undulating pattern of light and dark. Curved and shifting shapes intersect with the lattice of lines that mark the earth. So many lives, resting now below. Too many loved ones gone too soon, too many people misunderstood.

Daniel Whittaker's family traverses the matrix of lives beneath their feet. They move as one; their fingers touch, their arms entwine. His family.

Acknowledgements

THANK YOU TO MY PUBLISHER, Madonna Duffy at the University of Queensland Press, for recognising the value of this story before it was fully formed, and for her encouragement and her perceptive questions. Thank you to my UQP editor, Ian See, who accompanied me on the journey of this story from beginning to end. Ian's editing skills are legendary and I am incredibly lucky to work with him. If this story resonates, it is because of his curiosity and his compassion, his keen insight, his ability to draw more from me than I knew I had, and his astute sifting of my words.

So often we do judge a book by its cover, and I have to thank the very talented Kirby Armstrong for the striking design and artwork on both my novels.

Thank you to the Women Who Do It All: Sally Piper, Sarah Ridout, Melissa Ashley and Kali Napier (aka the Coven), who provide daily inspiration and enthusiasm, and ensure my novels are face out in bookstores. All four are accomplished authors and you should buy their books. Thank you to Sheryl Gwyther,

Samantha Wheeler and Angela Sunde, a trio of talented children's authors, who provide valuable feedback and advice, and day-long lunches that feed my creative spirit. Heartfelt thanks to authors Karen Foxlee and Krissy Kneen, who patiently answered my many writing-related questions and who are never too busy to chat. Thanks to everyone at Queensland Writers Centre for ongoing professional support, and a gold star to the Queensland Literary Awards for recognising and celebrating Queensland literature.

Since my debut novel was published, I have found a new tribe, and many new friends, in the writing community – thank you to all the writers, booksellers and industry professionals who have welcomed me with open arms. Thanks to all those with whom I connect from afar via social media – your tweets and posts brighten my days, keep me laughing, and remind me that I am part of an interconnected community of like-minded souls. Thank you to all the dedicated readers who have bought or borrowed, recommended or gifted my books.

Special thanks to my family, especially my husband, Sean, who provides the emotional and financial support necessary for me to write, and to my children, who give me space and keep me grounded. And thank you to the family I have chosen for myself – my friends (you know who you are): these stories are for you.

Author's Note

THE CHARACTER OF MARGARET SONNET in *Parting Words* was inspired by Moshlo (Morrice Shaw), a passionate and talented musician who first introduced me to the doina. While we met only once and corresponded a mere handful of times before he sadly took his own life, Moshlo's influence is testament to the truth that from little things, big things grow. I hope that this story is a small tribute to his extraordinary life. You can listen to doina and find out more about Moshlo (31 December 1935 – 11 April 2015) here: <http://www.youtube.com/watch?v=ChH1zx8Bqkc> or here: *Last Portrait of Moshlo* <https://vimeo.com/131606113>. Thanks also to Carla Thackrah for generously sharing both her memories of Moshlo and her knowledge of doina.